The Osprey Flies Alone

Christie Peavyhouse

*This book is dedicated to my Matma, Kathleen.
Thank you for your love and support
throughout my entire life.
You are truly an inspiration for us all!*

CHAPTER 1

It's finally here! The last day of school and the last day of my middle school career! I cannot believe this school year has flown by so fast, but when I think back to last summer it seems like an eternity.

"What do you think?" I ask Maria as I spin around in my black satin dress that fits just right.

Maria is my best friend. She still lives at my house. She's been here since her sister, Ashley, passed away tragically last summer. No, Maria's not homeless. She has six siblings, well, five now since Ashley is gone and her house is complete chaos all the time. I think she really likes staying here with me. Since I don't have any siblings, Maria is the closest thing I have to a sister. We even call each other sisters, although we look nothing alike since Maria is Hispanic and I'm white.

"Oh, Kimmy! You look stunning!" Maria exclaims as she fluffs my hair. "What about me?" she asks.

I hesitate as tears start to fill my eyes. I know this is not a good time to cry, because I will ruin my makeup. I start to feel a tightness in my throat as I try to fight back the tears that are stinging my eyes.

"Sis, you are so beautiful! You are beginning to look more and more," I hesitate, "like Ashley every day."

Maria looks down then back up at me. "Come here, Kimmy. We can't do this today! Remember, we've cried enough over the past year to do us for the rest of our lives."

Maria wraps her arms around my shoulders and gently squeezes me. I lean back and look up at her as she is much taller than I am now and see a tear trickle down her cheek.

"I know, but it's getting to the point that every time I look at you, I see Ashley and it just makes me so sad." I walk over to my mirror as I fan my face with my hands. "Not ruined, thank goodness."

Tonight is a very special and exciting occasion for us. It is our eighth grade graduation ceremony. This will be the last time that we can call ourselves Bay Middle School students. Some people think eighth grade graduations are dumb. I think they are wonderful! They are kind of like a bridging ceremony in Girl Scouts. When I was in kindergarten, I was a Daisy Girl Scout. The summer after I finished kindergarten, I bridged up to being a Brownie Girl Scout. It was so cool! We even walked across this little white wooden bridge. I felt so much older and more mature when I got to the other side of the bridge. I know it was just a symbol of moving up in ranks, but it really meant a lot to me. People also give you graduation gifts, and we are having our last middle school dance tonight too. Our boyfriends are even allowed to come! I'm super excited!

"Are you nervous?" I ask Maria as she touches up her makeup.

"Why would I be nervous? It's not like I'm just giving the most important speech of my whole entire life or something."

Maria is our eighth grade valedictorian. She is so smart, unlike me. Maria told me she has a perfect 4.0 grade point average. That means she has made straight A's in all her classes since the beginning of sixth grade. She also has had perfect attendance all three years at Bay Middle. I, on the other hand, have been in special education classes since preschool. I have a really hard time getting my words out, and I process my thoughts much slower than others, but that has never stopped me from anything I've wanted to do. I'm even going to be in marching band at the high school next year with my boyfriend. He plays snare drum and I'm going to play saxophone. Nanny has already signed me up for private lessons this summer.

"So, this hat thing that we're supposed to wear, it keeps sliding off my head," I say to Maria as I adjust it for the fourteenth time.

"Here, Kimmy," Maria turns me toward her and adjusts my graduation cap so it is perfectly centered on my head. "You have to wear it on top of your head, not on the back, silly."

I really don't know what I would do without Maria. We've been through thick and thin together over this past year. From Ashley's death to first boyfriends, to first kisses, and to capturing a murderer you could say. I'm just ready to put last year behind us and move on to the next.

As we file into the gym, I look around to see where my family is sitting. There are so many people in here that I'm having a hard time finding them. I am looking over my right shoulder when all of a sudden, I run into the boy who is walking in front of me.

"OMG, I'm so sorry, Aiden!" I whisper to him as he gives me a dirty look. I'm so embarrassed right now, but not as embarrassed as Aiden was last year when he was running down the football field during P.E. to catch the ball, and as he jumped up his shorts fell down. And not just a little bit. They were all the way down to his ankles and everyone saw his tighty whitey underwear. I should remind him of that when we sit down, then maybe he would change his tone with me.

When all of us were seated in the fancy chairs on the gym floor, Mr. Lawrence, our principal, stepped up to the podium on the stage.

"We gather here today in the beautiful town of Bay St. Louis, Mississippi for the eighth grade promotion ceremony of the Bay Middle School class of 2011. I would first like to welcome you to Bay Middle..."

I look around the gym again and spot Maria's family, the Hernandezes. Mr. and Mrs. Hernandez each have a baby in their laps, and Alex, Maria's older brother, has a kid on each side of him. I cannot even imagine what an ordeal it was to get them all gathered up this evening just to get here to the graduation. When they want to go somewhere as a family, they have to take at least two cars. That's another reason why Maria likes staying at my house. We can jump in the car with my parents and just go without having to sort out who is going where.

I still don't see my family. Our gym is huge though. We have around a hundred kids in our eighth grade class and I'm pretty sure all their parents, grandparents, brothers, sisters, and cousins are in this gym at this very moment. Just when I think they all bailed on me, I spot Nanny and Chas with bright pink matching Hawaiian shirts on. Why on earth are they dressed like that? They look ridiculous! I look to their right and see my mom's father, Grandpa Eugene, sitting next to Nanny with Mom on his other side next to Dad. Down below Mom and Dad are my and Maria's boyfriends, Kylan and Peyton. Kylan Dean Wright is my boyfriend and Peyton, I don't know his middle name, Hancock is Maria's. Kylan is the most gorgeous guy I have ever seen in my life and Peyton claims that his great, great, great, great grandparents founded Hancock County, Mississippi, but I'm not so sure about that. I can now breathe a sigh of relief knowing that they are all here. I knew they would be. I have the most supportive family on this planet, but I am always second-guessing myself for some reason.

I was so wrapped up in my thoughts that I didn't realize Mr. Lawrence had finished talking. I look around the gym and notice Maria getting up from her chair and walking toward the stage. The gym is completely silent. Did I miss something? Why is no one clapping?

Maria gracefully steps up the four stairs to the stage. She insisted on wearing mile-high heels tonight. I tried to talk her out of it, but she said it makes her legs look so much sexier in her short dress. I guess she's right about that, but I'm afraid she will trip and fall on her face. That's what would happen to me if I were wearing them. I settled on flat sandals. I didn't want to take any chances.

Maria steps up to the podium and adjusts the microphone. She looks out to the crowd, and I can feel my heart beating in my chest. I'm so nervous for her. I'm pretty sure I'm more nervous than she is tonight. There's no way I would be able to do anything like what she is getting ready to do.

Maria clears her throat. "Hi friends and families! It is my honor and privilege to address you tonight as your 2011 Bay Middle School valedictorian." Maria pauses and then looks down at her speech which is written on tiny white note cards. We've gone through her speech at least fifty times in the last week perfecting it for this moment. I try my best to focus on her words, but all I can think about is when Ashley made a very similar speech last year at her high school graduation. I shake my head to try and get those thoughts out of my mind then I look over at the Hernandez family and see them all fixated on Maria. I bet they are so proud that Maria is following in Ashley's footsteps.

"As most of you know I lost my sister, Ashley, last summer to a senseless tragedy. Her death has forever changed the way I view life." Maria's voice starts to shake. "Life is hard...but it's a lot easier if you go through it with someone who is always there for you. Kimmy, will you stand up please?"

What? Did Maria just say my name? What is happening?

"Kimmy Favre, please stand up," Maria repeats as she looks in my direction and motions me to get up.

Yep, she just said my name. We didn't practice this nor did I know she was going to do this to me. I take a deep breath as my heart starts beating faster and faster. Just when I think things just couldn't get any worse, I try to stand up, but my rear end is glued to my seat. Not literally, but I can't make myself get up for some reason. My legs feel like spaghetti noodles, my palms are so sweaty I can't push myself up, and I can hear my heart beating in my ears.

I have what many people refer to as anxiety. Yeah, it can be pretty bad at times. I have learned how to deal with it over the years. My teachers have helped me with breathing strategies, but when it happens suddenly, I struggle to get a hold of myself unless somebody snaps me out of it.

"Hey, Kimmy, she said your name. You need to stand up."

I can hear my friend Abbey talking, but I can't get my body to move. I look up at Abbey as she is standing in front of me. I take a deep breath. I can do this. I am strong. Abbey gently takes my hand, and I reluctantly rise. My knees wobble as I feel like I am going to crumble to the ground. Then I glance up at the podium where Maria is standing. We make eye contact, and I take a couple of deep breaths. I nod to Abbey, and she sits back down. I hear giggling from the crowd.

"This here is my best friend, Kimmy." Maria puts her hands out like she is presenting me to the audience. "I would have never made it through eighth grade without her. We have shared all our ups and downs with each other this year. I want to thank you, Kimmy, for never losing hope in me and always trusting your instincts." I bow my head as I can feel the tears welling up in my eyes. "Don't cry, Sis. Don't do it. Remember, we've cried enough. Now it is time to celebrate! Here's to my best friend, Kimmy, and four more years of living life to its fullest!"

As Maria finishes her speech, the crowd erupts in applause and everyone in the gym gives her a standing ovation. After the crowd settled down, we received our diplomas and sang some silly song about climbing mountains before Mr. Lawrence bid farewell to all of us. He thanked everyone for coming to our ceremony and said a few more things about high school. Then, he did the stupidest thing a middle school principal could ever do. He invited the parents to attend our dance. Yeah, that's what I said. Old Mr. Lawrence told all the parents to come chaperone the dance. Can you believe that? Well, so much for having fun tonight, because we all know how boring our parents are.

CHAPTER 2

Even though Maria and my last names are close in the alphabet, she sat at the front of the gym since she was giving a speech. After we threw our hats in the air, all the parents ran down to the floor to take pictures. I just stood there feeling a little lost and a little confused. As if I couldn't find my family earlier, I really can't find them now in all this disorder. So I just keep standing here in the middle of the floor, alone. I can feel a slight rush of panic come over me. My eyes are darting all around the gym. I'm not really sure what I'm seeing and what I'm not. Then suddenly someone grabs my shoulders from behind and I quickly turn around.

"Kylan! I'm so glad you're here!" I say with a sigh of relief. I can feel my heartbeat already slowing down as Kylan embraces me in a hug. Out of the corner of my eye, I see two bright pink Hawaiian shirts walking my way.

"Nanny and Chas! What on earth are y'all wearing?"

Nanny laughs, "Kimmy, we wore these so you would be able to spot us in the crowd. Did it work?"

I roll my eyes. "Not only did it work, now I will be known around town as the girl with the crazy grandparents who wear matching Hawaiian shirts."

Nanny looks over at Chas and elbows him in the side, "Success old wise man! Our plan worked in more ways than one!"

Oh no, here comes Mom to take a zillion pictures.

"Ok, y'all, everybody gather around the graduation girl so I can snap some pictures!" Mom says with a ridiculous amount of excitement in her voice.

Snap! Snap! Snap! Snap!

Pretty sure I'm completely blind now from all the flashing of Mom's new camera. When I am finally able to see again, I stand on my tip toes trying to find Maria, but I don't see her. I want my mom to take some pictures of us together.

Still in a daze from the flashes, I hold my hand up for Mom to pause her camera.

"I gotta find Maria. Can you help?" I look over at Kylan.

"Let me call Peyton to see where they went," Kylan says as he puts his arm around my shoulder and kisses my cheek.

Have I told you yet that I have the absolute best boyfriend in the whole world? He really is! I'm mean, moody, and grumpy, but he still treats me like a princess. How did I get so lucky?

I can hear Kylan on the phone, but it's so loud in the gym I don't know what he is saying. Kylan takes the phone from his ear and says, "Peyton said they are outside with Maria's family. They are taking pictures by the angel trees over in the courtyard. I told him we were on our way out so don't go anywhere."

Our walk to the courtyard was bittersweet. I realized that this is probably the last time I will walk through these halls of Bay Middle. I will never have a reason to come back unless I have kids one day who go to school here, and by then they will probably have built a new school. I look around at the old rusty lockers. Some still have combination locks hanging from them, others are missing numbers, and a few have large dents in them from various fights and such. I'll never forget the very first middle school fight I witnessed in seventh grade. It was between two girls and hair was flying everywhere. When all was said and done, it looked like a beauty shop had exploded in the hallway, makeup, broken nail polish bottles, and all. There is still some of that nail polish splattered on the lockers that they never could get off.

I take in all the sights, smells, and sounds as we continue down the hallway. I wave to several friends along the way but feel a lump in my throat when I try to speak. I never imagined I would have an overwhelming desire to cry at my middle school graduation, but for some reason

I do. As we are almost to the courtyard, we walk by the bathroom that I used every day. The same exact bathroom I was in when Kylan was texting about the pictures he found on his phone that led to the capture of Ashley's murderer.

I stop in front of the bathroom door and turn toward my family. "Can I have just a minute?"

"Sure, Honey. I need to use the restroom too," Mom says. "Nanny, how about you?"

Mom and Nanny follow behind me into the bathroom. I go to the exact same stall I always use and close the door. I look around the tiny area at all the graffiti on the walls: Jules loves Mac, Call Shell for a good time and the one I wrote...K + K together forever. Yeah, I know I could get in a lot of trouble if someone figured out who wrote it, but at this point, I don't really care. I snap a picture with my phone, flush the toilet pretending like I used it, and open the stall door to see Mom and Nanny washing their hands.

"Are you ok, Sweet Pea?" Nanny asks as she gets some paper towels to dry her hands.

I look up at her and feel a wave of emotions sweep over me. "It's...It's...It's just I'm really sad to leave this place. I have so many memories here." The words come rushing out of my mouth like a river overflowing.

"Oh my sweet girl, you have so many more memories to make. This time next year you will have already forgotten these middle school days and you will be looking forward to your last few years in high school. Then after high school, you will be getting ready for lots more memories in college. Let me tell you a little secret about memories." Nanny pauses as she puts her arm around my shoulder to walk beside me. "You may not realize this, but you make them every second of every day. It's the ones you can always relate back to that make the most impact in our lives, good and bad. When you get my age, your memories start to fade. That's when you learn to live every day like it's your last and just hope you can remember a few things," Nanny says as she laughs. "It's natural to feel sad when you're closing a chapter in your book, but just think of all those chapters you have to look forward to in your future."

My Nanny always knows the right words to say. She is such an amazing woman!

"So you don't remember your middle school days, Nanny?"

"Nah, those were the days of my life that I'm glad I don't remember, Sweetie. I had buck teeth, poop brown hair, and I looked like a beanpole. I don't even remember if I had any friends back then. I'm sure I did, but I don't talk to any of them now."

We turn the corner to the courtyard. I can see Maria and her family laughing, joking, and playing with the kids. Peyton is on one side of her and Alex is on the other. Mrs. Hernandez is chasing Maria's little brother around the yard. If I didn't know any better, I would think this family had zero cares in the world. They all look so happy gathered around celebrating Maria. I stop briefly before I walk through the doors to go outside. I glance back at Kylan. The look on his face tells me he knows exactly what I am thinking.

"It's going to be ok, Babe. I promise. We have each other and always will," Kylan reassures me.

But what if there comes a time when he's not there for me and I'm all alone like the osprey? I think back to when I've been sitting on the beach watching my pelicans fly together with each other and then the lone osprey flies over. It looks so sad and lonely. I just can't bear to think about not having Maria or Kylan in my life. This last year has really taken a toll on me and it's starting to show. This should be a joyous time for me, but it's not. Why do I feel this way? How do I shake these thoughts away? I take a deep breath and try to push open the door, but it won't budge. My vision goes blurry. My head feels as though it is detached from my body and all of a sudden, everything is dark.

CHAPTER 3

S omebody call an ambulance! Quick! This girl needs help!"

I hear screaming and crying all around me, but I can only see darkness. I feel my body moving, but my eyes are glued shut. Am I floating?

"Kimmy, wake up! Open your eyes!"

Is that Kylan? What is happening?

"KIMMY! HELP! SOMEBODY PLEASE HELP!"

Maria? Why are you so upset?

Then everything goes completely silent.

Beep Beep...

Beep Beep...

Beep Beep...

Why is Maria's alarm clock going off? I think to myself. Why did she bring her alarm clock to graduation? I think Maria's lost her mind. I try to open my mouth to tell her to turn off her alarm, but I can't move. My body feels heavy. My chest hurts. I have a strange sensation in my legs like I've been running a marathon for days. I turn my head to look for my family, but all I can see is dark. I'm not panicked, though. I'm very relaxed as I drift off to sleep.

"Are you the parents?" I hear a deep unfamiliar voice ask.

"Yes, we are." Is that my mom?

"Sir, I think you're a little too young to be in here," the deep voice says again.

"It's ok, Doctor. He's with us. He's family."

Kylan! They must be talking about Kylan! I've got to open my eyes and see what is going on. Did my mom just say doctor? What in the world is wrong with me and why is a doctor talking to my parents?

"We are trying to figure out what is going on with your daughter. It is my understanding she collapsed right after her graduation ceremony. Correct? Is this something that happens often?" The deep voice seems very concerned about me, I think.

I can hear my dad clearing his throat like he's been crying. "We don't really know what exactly happened. The ceremony was over, and we were all heading outside to take a few more pictures with her best friend Maria's family. That's when it happened. And no, Kimmy's never done anything like this before. She did have a lot of issues when she was born, but that was because she was very premature. We thought she had outgrown everything."

The room is silent. I can feel pressure in my chest again. It's kind of like someone has placed a weighted blanket on me. Maria used to have one of them. She brought it over to my house when she first moved in after Ashley passed away, but Oscar chewed a hole in it and the plastic beads went all over the place. He's notorious for tearing up people's blankets. Mom said he was no longer allowed to sleep in our bedroom, but that only lasted a few days. He would sit outside the bedroom door and whine until Mom finally gave in and opened the door.

"We saw something we didn't like on her MRI. It's her heart. Has she ever had any issues with her heart?"

My heart? My heart is totally fine. Why is this strange deep voice talking about my heart? I'm in love and that's the only problem with my heart I have right now if you consider that a problem.

"We were afraid this might happen one day. They told us it would close on its own, so we never went back to the cardiologist. They told us she would be fine and live a long productive life. Kimmy has never had a problem. She's always been a poster child for her physical health."

"Mrs. Favre, I'm so sorry, but it doesn't appear to have healed as they expected. Let us conduct a few more tests before we make any final decisions on the operation. The tech will be in shortly to take her for an ultrasound of her heart. We should know more soon. Until then, please try to get some rest. We may have a long evening ahead of us."

Operation? OMG! I can't have an operation!

Then all of a sudden, I feel my voice reach the back of my throat. "Mmmm..." is all I can scratch out. My throat feels dry like the desert and raw like sandpaper. I try my hardest to swallow some spit down, but I have none.

"Oh Honey! I'm here." I hear my mom's voice and feel her fingertips touch my hands. Her hands are ice cold.

"Babe, I'm here too. Can you hear me?"

That's Kylan. I manage to nod my head yes but am unable to open my eyes. I feel his lips softly kiss my forehead as he places his hand on my cheek.

"I love you," Kylan says with pain in his voice. "I'm right here, and I'm not leaving your side, Kimmy."

I feel Kylan gently hug my shoulders and ease down beside me. My eyes want to open, and I feel much less tired. I turn my head in the direction I heard Kylan's voice.

"Oh Babe, you're gonna be ok now. They're gonna get you all fixed up and you'll be as good as new."

I open my eyes and all I can see are bright lights. "Kylan, where are you?" I say with my scratchy voice.

"I'm here."

I see Kylan's face come into view. My eyes start to burn with tears as I am still unsure what is going on with me.

Kylan moves my hair out of my face with his soft gentle touch. I can smell my favorite cologne as he leans over me. Home, he smells like home to me. I know I'm safe when he's nearby. Kylan and I have been through many obstacles this past year. There were times when I just knew he was going to break up with me, but he never did. He says he loves me, and I know I love him. Maybe someday we will get married...someday.

"What happened?" I ask as I'm pretty sure I'm in the hospital at this point, but I certainly don't know how I got here.

My mom leans down. "Sweetheart, you fell as we were walking out to the courtyard to take pictures with Maria's family. You hit your head pretty hard, too."

Ok, that explains why my head is throbbing. I manage to lift my hand up to my head. *Ouch!* Yeah, that hurts.

"The doctors think you might've passed out. They are checking on your heart. There's a slight possibility you might have to have surgery to mend a hole you've had in your heart since you were a baby. We thought it was healed, but apparently, it's not. Something triggered it last night after graduation. They also think this could be the reason why your anxiety has been so bad here lately."

I look around the room to process what my mom just said. I don't remember ever having any problems with my heart. I used to go to a lot of doctor's appointments when I was young, but I never thought my heart was the issue. Last night? Did my mom just say last night? Have I been asleep since yesterday? Oh no, I missed my last middle school dance. Now I really want to cry.

"Where's Maria?" I ask my mom.

"She's at her house with her parents. Your fall really scared her last night...well scared all of us for that matter. She and Peyton came to the hospital with us, but they wouldn't let them in since they are minors. So, Alex picked them up and took them over to Maria's. She texted me first thing this morning to check on you."

"But they let Kylan in?" I ask

"Yes, I told them Kylan was family, and they said he could stay with us."

I look over at Kylan and smile. He smiles back, kisses me on the forehead, and squeezes my hand.

"So y'all slept here last night?" I ask as I can feel my eyebrows form a V across my forehead.

"Of course, we did!" Dad says as he stands up and walks over to me. "We would never leave you alone in a strange place like this, would we Kylan?"

Kylan shakes his head. "You'll never be left alone again if it's up to me. Well, except to go to the bathroom you know," Kylan says with a giggle.

"Can I sit up? I am so thirsty!" I raise up and feel dizzy. "I think I'm dehydrated. I feel bad. Like I haven't had anything to drink in years."

"Oh, I'm so sorry, Honey. You can't have anything to drink right now. There is a possibility you might have to have surgery, and they don't want anything on your stomach. Let me call the nurse to see if you can have some ice chips," Mom says as she pushes a little button on the side of my bed.

"Am I dying or something? I don't understand. Why is this such an emergency? I was completely fine yesterday. I don't need any stupid surgery. There is nothing at all wrong with me!" I can feel my heart beating faster and the beeping next to my bed starts getting louder. "What is that, Mom? What is going on? Can somebody please explain all this to me?" Gosh I am really feeling quite confused right now to the point that I just want to kick my legs in the air and jump out of this bed.

"Babe, it's your heart. You need to try and relax. You're going to make your machines go off again. Here, roll over."

I take in a big deep breath and roll toward my mom as Kylan nudges me in that direction. I feel his rough hands start to massage up and down my bare back. Then I feel him make tiny little circles in the middle. He moves to my shoulders and gently squeezes until I can hear the beeping getting softer and slower.

"There, there, Kimmy. Put this wet rag on your forehead. You have to try to stay calm. The doctor said we can't risk the chance of you getting upset like that right now. It could cause you to have a stroke. I love you too much to watch you go through that or even worse, possibly losing you. So let's just try to not think about it right now."

I feel Kylan crawl up in my bed and wrap his arms around my waist. I look up at my mom for approval and she just nods her head. As she is walking back over to the couch to sit by Dad, she stops and turns back around.

"Kimmy, just do as Kylan says, please. You're all I have." Mom drops her head, and I can see a tear running down her face.

"What about Oscar, Mom? Who is taking care of him?"

"Don't worry about the Osc. Nanny and Chas are at our house with him. I'm sure he's in hog heaven right now being spoiled rotten. You know Nanny even brushes his teeth twice a day," Mom says as we all laugh.

Yeah that's right, my Nanny absolutely loves Oscar too. She brings him organic homemade pumpkin treats when she visits and always brushes his teeth before he goes to bed at night. He sure is a rotten little Boston Terrier.

I hear a knock on the door, and it slowly opens.

"Are you Kimberly Favre?" the woman in a white lab coat says to me.

"Unfortunately, yes that's me."

"Unfortunately? What do you mean by that? You're one of the most beautiful thirteen almost fourteen-year-olds I've ever seen in this hospital," the lady says as she winks at me. "I'm Kathleen and I'll be taking you to get a few tests done. Are you ready?"

"No, I'm not."

"Well, you're in luck. All you have to do is lie there while we push your bed down the hallway. Are you her brother?" Kathleen says as she looks at Kylan.

We all giggle. "No, ma'am, I'm her boyfriend."

"Oh goodness! I'm so sorry. So you're the lucky man the nurses have been talking about?"

"You're exactly right! The luckiest man in this world!"

"Well, I hope you're strong too, because I'm going to need your help getting this beautiful young lady rolled down the hall to the lab. Would you be willing to help?"

Kylan looks at me then at my parents. "Yes, most definitely!"

"I'll even let you hold her hand while they are running the tests," Kathleen says as she starts unhooking all the machines.

"I'd love that," Kylan says as he is gently tucking in the covers around me.

Kathleen unlocks the wheels, waves to my parents, and says with way more enthusiasm than I can handle right now, "Ok then, let's go have some fun!"

Chapter 4

"Surgery is imminent." Once I heard those three words leave the doctor's mouth, I didn't hear anything else he said. I felt that tightness in my chest return. The machines start beeping louder and louder. Kylan had gone down to the cafeteria with my dad to get some lunch. It was only me, Mom, and this doctor who is standing there insisting that something is wrong with me.

I suddenly remember what Kylan said about not getting overly anxious. I start pinching the skin underneath my arm. You know that really tender area opposite of your bicep? Yeah, I've learned over the last few months that pinching that area sends enough pain signals to my brain to get my mind off of whatever was giving me the anxiety. The only problem with that is all the little bruises I've created.

"MR. DOCTOR! I HAVE SO MANY QUESTIONS FOR YOU RIGHT NOW!" Wow! Where did that come from? I just yelled at my doctor.

The doctor snapped his head around to me and just stood there. Oh no! My words are gone!

"What do you need to ask me Miss?"

All I can do is stare at him. "Um...Um..."

"It's ok, Kimmy." I hear Kylan say as I see him out of the corner of my eye standing next to my bed.

"When did you get here?" I ask as I am starting to feel confused again.

"We just walked in. I guess you were focused on what the doctor was saying."

No, that wasn't it at all. I'm angry and when I get angry I get anxious and start pinching my skin, but I don't want Kylan to know that so I don't answer.

"Ok, Kimberly," says the doctor sternly. "I will be back shortly to review the procedure with you and your family. If you can remember your questions, that will be a great time to ask me."

As the door to my room closes, I already feel relief. For some reason, that doctor makes me really uncomfortable. He's nothing like the lab tech, Kathleen, who took me to have the tests done. She was kind and made me feel relaxed the whole entire time. This doctor of mine, he's rigid.

"Hey Babe, let's write down some questions for when the doctor comes back. That way, I can at least read them off if you are unable to."

"Gosh, Kylan, I have so many questions. I guess my biggest one is about going to band camp this summer. I have been looking forward to it all year! I would really be heartbroken if I didn't get to march with you in the fall."

Kylan leans over and whispers in my ear, "If you can't march, then I won't either."

I give him a puzzled look. "But no, that's not right. You're working on getting a scholarship to Mississippi State. Taking a year off from marching would ruin your chances."

Kylan glances out the window then turns back to me. "Your health is more important than a piddly ole scholarship. My parents are just happy I'm wanting to go to an in-state college. They're paying out the wazoo for Ken to go to school in Tennessee. By the way, Ken is planning a trip down here this summer. Which got me thinking about another question for the doctor. We need to ask him when you will be able to go swimming. Mom and Dad finally got the pool chemistry under control and are wanting to have a party for Ken when he gets here. I'm sure you would want to go swimming."

And then it hit me. "A scar! I'm going to have a huge scar on my chest. Aren't I? Kylan, I may never want to put on a bathing suit again! OMG! And I just started wearing bikinis last summer! This is devastating!"

I feel the tears start to well up in my eyes just thinking about how embarrassing it will be to have a bright red scar running down the middle of my chest. As the tears reach my lashes and fall to my cheeks, Kylan reaches over with a tissue and pats them dry.

"Why are you so worried about a scar? Scars fade. Who cares anyway? It will make you look tough. Like you went to battle for something and came out alive. If you want, I'll get a big scar tattooed down the middle of my chest to match yours. What do you think?"

I cannot even imagine Kylan getting a tattoo. His body is perfect to me! I don't want him to ruin it by getting a stupid tattoo of a scar just to make me feel better.

"Nah, that's ok. I don't want you to ruin your body for me," I say as I rub my eyes with the back of my hands trying to wipe away the tears.

"Well, Babe, that's just one more thing to ask the doctor. We need to find out what kind of incision you will have and how long it will take to heal."

"When do you think the grumpy ole doctor will come back in? I definitely want you to be in here with me when he comes back."

My mom gets up and slowly walks over to my bed. "Honey, Dad and I are going to get me a cup of coffee and a snack from the cafeteria. Unfortunately, I can't get you anything, but as soon as you come out of surgery, I will have Nanny go by Cuz's and get you a big bowl of shrimp and crab bisque. How's that sound?"

"Delicious. So, stop talking about it before I start eating these bed sheets!" I snap.

I watch Mom and Dad leave and close the door behind them. Kylan and I are finally alone, but I don't know what to say to him. I look like complete crap! My makeup is all smeared and I haven't had a bath since yesterday. Now that I think about it, Kylan hasn't bathed since yesterday either. I giggle under my breath just thinking about how stinky I bet we all are. Maybe that's why the doctor has been so grumpy with us.

"Can you help me wash my face?" I look up at Kylan as he is still standing beside my bed.

He raises his eyebrows. "Um, sure, but I've never helped anyone wash their face before. What do I do?"

"Well, I'm not helpless. I just need you to hand me a clean wet washcloth and put some soap on it from that soap dispenser over there by the sink. Here," I hand him the damp washcloth that was on my forehead. "Hang this one up and get a fresh one."

Kylan angles his hand to his head and salutes me. "Yes, master drill sergeant!"

I laugh. "Oh come on! I'm not that bossy am I?"

Kylan stops and turns around while wringing out the washcloth. "Well...I wouldn't say you're bossy. Maybe sassy...but oh so cute!"

Knock, Knock, Knock

Before we could say come in, my doctor pushes the door open and walks in the room. "Oh hello. Is there more to this story than what I know about?" The doctor points back and forth from me to Kylan.

"Ok, I confess. I'm not related to Kimmy. I'm her boyfriend."

"Um-hum. Just as I suspected, young man. You're in love with this little lady and you want to be by her side during this difficult time? Am I right?" Kylan and I look at each other as this conversation is becoming more awkward by the moment. "You don't have to tell me anything. I've heard it a thousand times," the doctor says to us as he pulls up a chair to sit by my bed. "Come over here son, let's have a talk."

Kylan cautiously walks over to me with the soapy washcloth. "Ok, we were getting ready to wash her face."

"That's fine. You can still do that while I'm talking to you two. Have a seat." The doctor pats the side of my bed and Kylan sits down. "So, I'm guessing you've been working on some questions for me?"

Kylan and I both nod our heads.

"Well, first things first while the parents are not in here. No...you know," the doctor clears his throat and looks away. "Um what do you kids call it these days? Fooling around? Doing it? I don't really know, I'm an old man."

OMG! I am petrified!

"Sir, Doctor, we don't do that. We are saving ourselves for marriage," Kylan says as his face starts to flush.

"Whew, thank goodness!" The doctor wipes his forehead with the back of his hand. "There aren't many of y'all out there anymore. You guys are smart. Don't ever let your hormones get in the way. Trust me, I've seen it all in my thirty-four years in practice."

I'm pretty sure I have scrubbed the skin completely off my face since the doctor has been sitting here.

"Ok, your turn. What questions do you have for me?"

Kylan proceeds to get his phone out of his pocket which reminded me that I have no idea where my phone is at. Oh well, I'll find it later. The only other person I want to talk to is Maria and I'm sure she's been texting with my mom.

"Doctor, we have so many questions," Kylan says as he starts scrolling through his phone.

About that time, Mom and Dad walked back in. I'm so glad they weren't in here for the humiliating "doing it" talk we just had with the doctor.

"Oh hi, Dr. Sheffield! We didn't expect you back so soon!" Mom says with surprise in her voice. Well, guess what mom, neither did we.

"I just wanted to start getting Kimberly prepped and ready for her surgery. Looks like it has been scheduled for three o'clock." Dr. Sheffield looks down at his watch. "That gives us about two hours to get everything ready. What questions do you all have for me?"

Kylan looks back at his phone and starts rattling off the questions we came up with. Dr. Sheffield gave short and sweet answers. No swimming for at least two weeks. No major scar down the center of my chest. They will make a few tiny incisions and repair my heart with a robot. That's interesting! The only scars I have to worry about will be about an inch long and probably covered by my bathing suit. As for marching band, Dr. Sheffield wants to reevaluate me in a month with a stress test to see if my heart will be ready to withstand the weight of carrying an instrument while playing. Hmm...I guess only time will tell.

CHAPTER 5

As I open my eyes, I feel extremely relaxed. The room is dark, but I know someone is in here with me. I feel their presence. I also know it's probably not Oscar because I don't hear snoring. Although, Kylan has been known to snore just as loud as Oscar at times.

I gently place my hand on my chest. I feel a slight soreness already creeping in. One, two, three...that's how many bandages I can count. I guess that's how many times they had to cut me open to repair my heart. Yep, it's over. I guess my so-called broken heart has been mended and I can now move on with my life. I think I'll rest my eyes for a little bit longer like Grandpa Eugene does.

"Hey, Sweet Pea." I hear Nanny say in a whisper. "Do you want to wake up and eat some bisque? Chas and I are here with your dinner."

Ah, shrimp and crab bisque from my most favorite restaurant in BSL, Cuz's. I haven't eaten in over 24 hours.

I'm starving, but I am so relaxed that I'm not sure I can sit up and respond right now.

"The doctor said she would probably be out for a while, Nanny." The smoothness of Kylan's voice lets me know that I am safe and sound.

"Well, Kylan, we can just leave this here with you. When she wakes up you can help her eat. Chas and I brought you a shrimp po boy and some fries. I guess we will join Nina and Jimmy down in the waiting room so Kimmy can sleep. Let us know when she wakes up."

"Sure thing, Nanny."

As I hear my door latch shut, I feel Kylan ever so tenderly kiss my cheek and snuggle up beside me in the bed. "I haven't left your side this entire time, Kimmy. Well, except for when they took you back to the operating room."

I take a deep breath but get a sharp pain in my chest. "Ow...I'm having some pain in my chest."

Kylan pushes my hair behind my ear and kisses the top of my head. "The doctor said you'll be a little sore for a few days. If the pain gets any worse, let me know so we can call the nurse. Are you hungry?"

"Oh, Kylan, I'm starving," I groggily say still unsure if I can raise up enough to eat. "Hang on for a few before you call my mom to tell her I'm awake. I want to spend a few minutes alone with you."

I try to push myself up in the bed, but my strength seems to have left me.

"Here, Babe. Let me help. See," Kylan says as he points to the side of my bed. "You have these handy dandy little buttons on the side of this rail that move your bed up and down."

Kylan raises the top of my bed, so my head is now elevated. "How about your feet too?" he asks.

"Sure, whatever you think will make me feel better."

Kylan pulls a chair up next to the side of my bed. "Did you want to talk to me about something, Kimmy?"

"No, nothing in particular. I just wanted to spend some time with you before everybody came in to visit with me. Have you talked to Maria or Peyton? I was hoping they would be allowed to come up to my room."

"I have been texting with both of them all afternoon. Actually, I didn't want to ruin your surprise, but they are down in the waiting room with your family. They all plan on coming in when I let them know you're awake."

I nod my head. "Can you help me with my bisque? Then we will call them."

"Of course, Babe!"

Kylan gets everything set up on my bedside table and then rolls it over to me. I reach for my spoon, but my hands are really shaky. After a couple of attempts, I grasp my spoon. Kylan is intently watching as I think he knows I can't do this myself.

"I know this will sound really cheesy, but can I feed you?" he giggles. "I just can't stand the thought of seafood bisque getting all over you. As if it's not stinky enough in here already, can you imagine what that would smell like later?"

I try to laugh back, but the pain is real right now. I take half a breath and let it out. "That's probably the most romantic thing you have ever said to me," I say as I wink at Kylan.

He crawls in my bed and gets as close to me as he possibly can. "Well, Kimmy, now I can officially say that I've spoon-fed a baby."

I raise my hand up to smack his shoulder only to see he's already loaded the spoon back up with bisque. "Just think of this as practice for when we have our first child."

Yeah, I know. Once again, I'm too young to be talking or even thinking like this, but I tell you I'm going to marry this man one day. Just you wait and see!

"I guess you can go ahead and text Mom to let her know I'm awake," I say as I would love for this moment alone with Kylan to last forever.

He looks at me and turns his head sideways. "Are you sure?" he pauses. "You know there are a ton of people in that waiting room. Are you sure you're ready for them all?"

I shrug my shoulders. "Might as well get it over with."

It's not two minutes after Kylan sends my mom a text that I see my door opening.

Maria comes in first with a huge bunch of balloons. "Oh, Sis! I've been so worried about you." She doesn't even acknowledge Kylan. She just hands him the balloons and runs over to my bed.

"Oh, easy please!" I put my hand out and say to Maria as she practically jumps up in my bed.

"I'm so sorry! Did I hurt you?" Maria asks with a look of concern on her face.

"Nah, just be careful. I'm a little sore."

Peyton is right behind her with a bouquet of beautiful fresh-cut flowers. I can see all the colors of the rainbow in one vase. He sets the vase of flowers on my bedside table.

"Peyton, thank you! Those have to be the prettiest flowers I've ever seen!"

Peyton nods. "I hope you're feeling better, Kimmy."

My mom and dad were behind Peyton, followed by Nanny and Chas. Then I see someone slowly scooting their feet through my doorway holding on to Kylan's mom.

"Grandpa Eugene!" I throw my hands up like I'm giving him an air hug. "I'm so glad to see you! And Mrs. Wright, I didn't expect to see you today either!"

"Kimmy," Kylan's mom says. "Please call me Allyson. Mrs. Wright was my mother-in-law," she says with a grin on her face. "I had to make sure my son was taking good care of you."

Suddenly, I feel a sense of peace. All my loved ones are here with me in one place.

"So which one of y'all is gonna bust me out of here? I need to go home and take a hot bubble bath."

The rest of the evening was spent hanging out with my family and friends. Well, if you could call it that. I pretty much just laid in the bed while everybody took turns sitting and talking to me. Mr. and Mrs. Hernandez came by and visited for a few minutes while Mom and Dad watched the little ones in the waiting room. I could tell by the look on Mom's face when she came back to my room that those littles gave her a run for her money.

Kylan's mom brought him a change of clothes and stuff to use in the shower. So that's what he is doing right now. Nanny and Chas went back to my house to take care of Oscar. They act like that silly little turd dog is a baby and shouldn't be left alone for any amount of time. Mom and Dad stepped out with Grandpa Eugene to run him back over to his home in Gulfport. Peyton went to get him and Maria some dinner. So now it's just me and Maria in this sterile hospital room.

"I'm sorry this had to happen," I say to Maria as I feel guilty for ruining our eighth grade graduation.

Maria grabs my hand with hers and pats the top of it. "Kimmy, I'm just glad you're going to be ok. You really gave us quite the fright! My entire life flashed in front of me, and I was scared you weren't going to be in it." Maria bows her head. "I started praying as soon as I got my senses about me. I knew at that point everything was in God's hands."

"Well, I guess we missed our last middle school dance. That's such a shame."

Maria straightens up her back and leans toward me. "Let me just tell you. We didn't want to be there anyway. I talked to Abbey this morning and she said it was hideous. There were parents everywhere and the teachers were walking around with rulers keeping the couples dancing twelve inches apart."

I put my hand over my mouth. "Are you being serious? Rulers? OMG! That's hilarious! If I weren't in so much pain I'd laugh right now."

"Yeah, but do you want to hear the best part?" I shake my head, yes. "Some kids from the high school showed up and spiked the punch. One of the parents took a big swig and spit it out all over the place," Maria laughs. "Then, they turned the lights on and made everyone leave."

"OMG! That really happened?" I say as I nearly fly up out of my hospital bed.

"Sure did!" Maria says as she nods and flips her ponytail over her shoulder.

"Gosh, Maria, I'm sure glad we didn't go then. That would have been such a bummer. Well, I guess this is a pretty big bummer too though." I place my hand over my heart and feel the steady beats. "I could've died!" I whisper under my breath.

"But thank goodness you didn't. It wasn't your time to go yet. You know, Kimmy, God has big plans for you!"

I look around the room trying not to cry. I hear the shower in the bathroom turning off. As Kylan opens the bathroom door, I smell a rush of his body wash and feel the steam from the hot water drift over my bed. I still can't believe that he is my boyfriend. I watch him walk across my hospital room and momentarily recall all the fun we had at the beach last summer. Just the thought makes me all warm and fuzzy inside. Then I think about how badly I have missed watching my pelicans the past few days. This is probably the longest I have ever gone without seeing them that I can remember. Since I've been in this room, I have felt more like the lone osprey. I had such big plans for this summer. Well, I wouldn't call them big, but I planned to spend as much time at the beach as possible. Now, I feel like everything is ruined!

"Ok, Babe! It's your turn!" Kylan says as he rakes my brush through his curly wet hair. "I see you over there feeling sorry for yourself. Come on and get up, you'll feel much better when you're clean."

Maria grabs my hand. "I'll go get your nurse and tell her you're ready to get cleaned up. I'll even help if you need me to."

My face flushes as I can feel the heat reach the tip of my nose. "Well, that's embarrassing," I say as I drop my head down and see the top of one of the incisions on my chest. I gently pull up my hospital gown so no one can see the dreaded spot. I look over at Kylan and smile.

"It will heal and fade away and you'll forget any of this ever happened, Babe," Kylan says as he walks over and kisses the top of my head. "And if not, I guess we'll be heading to the tattoo parlor in a few months," he laughs.

I really do have the best family a girl could ask for. Even though I'm not technically related to Kylan and Maria, they mean more to me than just about anyone else in this world right now.

CHAPTER 6

I now truly understand the meaning of how nice it is to finally sleep in your own bed. I got home yesterday, Sunday. Kylan went home to sleep in his own bed too. I could tell he was starting to get tired of sleeping on the couch in the hospital room. Kylan has never once been grumpy with me since we started dating almost a year ago, but last night his nerves were wearing thin. I actually thought it was kind of funny. One of the nurses came into the room to help me get dressed. She asked Kylan to step out of the room and his reply was, "I know, you don't have to keep telling me." That's when he stormed out of the room and down to the family waiting area. My mom came up and asked me what happened. When I told her the story, she said that explains why he is sound asleep downstairs. Poor Kylan.

My doctor gave me strict orders to just lounge around the house for the next few days. No chores, no lifting, no running and no going outside in the hot sun. He just wants me to relax. My next doctor's appointment is on Thursday. I am hoping he will clear me to go to the beach and start soaking up the sun. He said as soon as my incisions heal, I can get in the ocean, but until then only shower water should touch my body.

So, I totally forgot to tell you some very important information! Last week when we went out to eat at Cuz's, Nanny and Chas had a huge surprise for us. They have sold their home in New Orleans and are moving to BSL! Isn't that exciting! Well, I haven't even told you the best part. They have found a house right on the beach with a huge in-ground pool. Nanny said as soon as I feel up to it, she will drive me by it. They plan on closing on it in the next few weeks and moving in this summer!

I still can't believe they will be living just right up the street from me. But you know what? Something worries me just a little. I absolutely love Nanny and Chas. I couldn't have made it this far without them, but sometimes they're a little strict on me. I know they're just trying to protect me, but I'm afraid they might cramp my style. Nanny is known to just pop in without warning. What if Kylan and I are making out on the couch, and well, here comes Nanny! I guess that's probably something I shouldn't even worry about right now.

I raise up in my bed and look around my room. It's pretty dark in here, but my phone says eight o'clock, so I know it's daylight outside. Maria's bed is made. She must've slipped out pretty early to go babysit her younger siblings. Kylan is supposed to come over later this afternoon. He has some yard work to do at his neighbor's house. So, it's just me and Oscar until Nanny and Chas get here. Mom told me last night she would be going back to work at the casino this morning to work a double. Several of the cocktail waitresses started calling in sick yesterday. I suspect because today is Memorial Day, and they want to spend it with their families. Mom said she and Mel would be making extra tips today since they would be so shorthanded.

Speaking of Oscar, where is he? He's not in my bedroom because I would hear his snoring. Mom said Oscar probably shouldn't sleep in here while I'm healing. I'm sure he's in his true chocolate donut fashion curled up on the couch in his little bed.

I guess I should get up and eat breakfast. I raise up on my elbows and feel a tugging pain in my chest that I haven't felt before. I feel slightly panicked. I'm home alone right now and not sure what I would do if something were wrong. I could call my mom. She said she would have her ringer turned up loud on her phone in case I needed her. I can feel my heart starting to beat a little faster, but it feels differently than how it used to. I don't have the sensation that I'm going to throw up like I used to have. This is much different. I actually feel pretty calm. My head is clear. I don't feel the need to pinch my arm either. Hmm...I guess the doctor was right about the anxiety thing being caused by my heart this whole time.

I look down to see my nightgown stuck to my chest. Ugh, my bandage has come off and the sticky side has flipped inside out. No emergency! Thank goodness! So, what can I easily fix for breakfast?

Buzz, Buzz...Buzz, Buzz...

Who is calling me this early in the morning?

Buzz, Buzz...Buzz, Buzz...

I look over at my phone on my nightstand to see Kylan's name appear on my phone screen. Something must be wrong.

"Hello?" I answer unsure why he is calling so early.

"Good morning, Babe! How are you feeling? I've been worried sick about you! I don't think I slept at all last night." I can hear the concern in Kylan's voice. So much so that it sounds like he might have been crying.

"I'm good, I think. I slept like a rock last night. I didn't even hear Maria get up and leave this morning. I think this medication my doctor gave me for pain knocked me out. I'm actually still lying here in bed debating on getting up and eating breakfast."

"Oh no, don't do that!" Kylan says as he is nearly screaming at me. "I'm heading your way in about five minutes. Peyton is coming to pick me up and we are stopping by Buttercup to get some to-go orders. Mom called them in and paid over the phone. All I have to do is run in and grab it."

"Ok," is all I can say. Why is he acting like this? I thought he had to work for his neighbors this morning.

"So don't eat anything before I get there!" He hangs up the phone before I could even get a word in.

I take a deep breath in and slowly let it out. Since I took a hot bath last night and washed my hair, I guess I just need to get up and brush my teeth. No need for makeup. Kylan has seen me look my worst already.

As I ease to the edge of my bed, I can feel the soreness in my chest starting to fade away. I think about how much my life has changed over the course of a year, especially over the last few days. I look around and wonder what life would have been like if Ashley was still here with us. I miss her. I miss how her long silky black hair would sit on her shoulders when pulled high in a ponytail. I miss the way her perfume would linger in the air after she left a room. I miss how she always looked perfect even when she didn't think she did. I miss everything about her. I still think about her every day. Then, I think how different everything would be if we hadn't gone to Joni's party last summer.

I shake my head to try and clear my thoughts. I slide my feet into my Boston Terrier house shoes that Kylan's mom gave me for Christmas last year. They are so cute and look just like Oscar except for the dog on my shoes is black whereas Oscar is brown. Oh well, I still love them.

As I open my bedroom door, I notice the quietness of my house. No TV on, no adults talking in the kitchen, no silly yacht rock radio playing, and no Maria ranting about whatever Peyton has done. Just peace. This doesn't happen often. I am rarely home by myself since Maria moved in. I love Maria, I really do, but sometimes I need a moment like this to kind of reset and reflect on my life. This is nice.

I turn the corner to the living room. There's Oscar. Yep, I was right. Curled up just like a glazed chocolate donut in the middle of his bed. He's so cute and so sweet when he's asleep.

I grab a hold of the arm of the couch and lower myself beside Oscar. He doesn't move. I put my hand on his velvety ears, and he twitches. I giggle and ask, "Oscar, did I scare you?" If he could talk, I'm sure Oscar would have answered "yes" back to me. He's such a sweet puppy, except for when he's not!

Knock, Knock, Knock

"Kimmy, are you in there?"

Knock, Knock, Knock

I jerk my head up and look toward the door only to realize I must've fallen asleep on the couch next to Oscar. "Coming!" I yell back.

I put my hand on the inside of the door to open it and feel the heat from the sun. Gosh, I can't believe how hot it is outside already. As I open the door, I see Kylan standing on my front porch with the biggest smile I've ever seen on his face. He's holding a huge brown paper bag in one hand and a drink tray in his other.

"The sun is blinding!" I say as Kylan steps into my house. "I guess that's what happens when you don't go outside for a few days. Where's Peyton?"

"Oh, he just dropped me off. He went on down to Maria's house to take her some food," Kylan says as he rushes past me and heads on toward the kitchen. Well, nice to see you too, I think to myself.

"Don't come in here!" Kylan shouts across the house.

"What? Why? I'm starving."

"Just don't, please. Sit down with Oscar for a minute. I'll come get you when it's ready."

Ready? What is wrong with him? I get a strange feeling that something is going on with Kylan. He just hasn't been himself since all this happened to me.

I hear rustling in the kitchen, but at this point I'm too tired to care. I know I just woke up, but for some reason I'm already exhausted. The doctor said this was to be expected, but I didn't want to believe him.

Kylan walks slowly into my living room. "Ok, Babe. Are you ready to eat the most romantic breakfast you've ever had?"

I raise my eyebrows as I have no idea what to expect. "Sure, I guess."

Kylan grabs my hand and puts his other one behind my back to help me up. I can get up off the couch on my own, but this is kind of nice, so I don't say anything at all.

"Close your eyes, Kimmy." Kylan puts his arm around my shoulder and escorts me to the kitchen. Then, he stops me in what feels like the middle of the kitchen floor. "Ok, open your eyes! SURPRISE!"

I open my eyes to see the most beautiful tablescape anyone could ever imagine! My kitchen is decorated with "Class of 2011" balloons, confetti, party hats, and those cute little party horns that sound like a dying cow when you blow on them. There are even plastic champagne glasses filled to the top with orange juice. And the food...OMG the food! I'm pretty sure every breakfast food known to man is spread across my kitchen table.

I look over at Kylan as he can tell I'm about to cry. He turns me toward him and ever so gently embraces me in the most sensual hug. "I wish you wouldn't cry," Kylan says as he wraps me in his warmth. I can feel my body melting into his. I lean my head down on his chest and feel his heart beating on my cheek. It's like the rhythmic ticking of a clock. Comfort. That's how I have felt this past year every time he wrapped his arms around me like this.

"What do you think, Babe?" Kylan looks down at me and leans in for a kiss.

"Oh, wait! I haven't brushed my teeth this morning!" I say as I put my hand over my mouth.

"Really, Kimmy, really? Your stinky morning breath is the least of my concerns. I'm just happy you're alive and well and standing next to me in your kitchen right now. You scared the crap out of me the other day. I seriously haven't been right since. Then when I found out you were having surgery, all I could think about was you not waking up afterward. I have always feared that for some unknown reason whenever a family member has had surgery. I guess that's why I've been acting kind of weird and grumpy. I've been trying to process everything," he says looking around the room.

Kylan pauses and locks his eyes on mine. Although I don't want him smelling my breath, I consent anyway and allow him to kiss me. I will have to say that this kiss right now is probably the most incredible kiss we've shared. It is one of those foot-popping kisses. My body is starting to tingle as I can feel his hands moving around my back and up to the sides of my face. I know my breath stinks, but I don't want this kiss to end.

Just when I think this moment couldn't get any better, Kylan slowly pulls away from me and says, "I love you, Kimberly Ruth Favre. You are the absolute love of my life. I know we're young, but I feel it between us, and I know you do too." Then he leans back in and picks up where he left off.

CHAPTER 7

I t's been nearly three weeks since my heart surgery, and I am feeling great! You'd never even know anything had happened unless you saw the three tiny incisions on my chest. The doctor was pretty much right, my swimsuit covers them nicely. Well, the swimsuit I've been wearing this year. I started wearing bikinis last summer. Which was just about the coolest thing ever! But this year, in order to cover up my scars, Nanny bought me something called a tankini. It's kind of like a bikini but with a tank top. It's still two pieces, just not as revealing on the top. I'm hoping I can switch back to my regular bikinis by the end of the summer.

I finally got to enjoy a day on the beach last week. My doctor released me to enjoy life again, at least that's what I'm calling it. The first two weeks post-surgery were actually quite miserable. I felt totally fine, but my doctor didn't want me anywhere near the ocean water. You see, in the hot summer months the Mississippi Sound has been known to grow some type of weird bacteria. And guess what? Yeah, you guessed it, when they did their weekly water test they sure enough found that nasty bacteria. It didn't last long though. A few days after the positive test for bacteria, it was negative again. In the meantime, I was able to go over to Kylan's house and swim in his pool.

Speaking of pools, Nanny and Chas are moving into their new house here in BSL next week! Nanny took me over there the other day and it's a huge mansion sitting right on the beach. It's actually in a town called Waveland that's right next door to BSL. If you didn't know any better, you'd think that Waveland was BSL. The only difference in the two towns is that Waveland has these really cool murals painted on their concrete retaining walls at the entrances to each road coming off the beach. They are such bright colors! My favorite is the one that has a pelican perched up on his pelican pole overlooking the ocean. I call him Mr. Pelican.

Getting back to Nanny and Chas' pool at their fancy new beach house, it needs some work. It had gone without pool chemicals all winter long for some reason and was green with lots of frogs and other creatures swimming in it. So, my Chas is what we refer to as "the pool guy" around here. He even went to Pool School to learn the ins and outs of maintaining a pool. At their old house in New Orleans, Nanny and Chas had a really nice above-ground pool that Chas always kept spotless and crystal clear. I am fully confident that he will get this new pool up to par in no time flat!

"Kimmy! Look what came in the mail today!" Maria yells as she busts through my front door.

"Oh geez, Maria! You nearly gave me a heart attack! What's up?"

"Well look! It's my letter for band camp." Maria runs over to me as I am snuggled up on the couch with Oscar. It's raining outside today, so Osc and I are having a movie day.

She stands over me and proceeds to read what is written on the paper. "Dear Maria Hernandez. You are invited to attend the annual Bay High School Marching Band Camp the week of July 25-29, 2011." Maria pauses, looks up into the air and says, "Yeah, I'll be in town that week. What about you Kimmy?"

Laughing I say with sarcasm, "I don't know, let me check my calendar."

"Oh, come on! What've you got going on that week?"

I raise up off the couch and smooth Oscar's fur back. "Um, just a little thing called BAND CAMP!"

I jump up off the couch and grab Maria's hands as we laugh and twirl each other around in the center of my living room.

After our celebration dies down, I get a slightly sick feeling in my stomach. I stop and put my hand over my heart. "Maria, my doctor hasn't cleared me yet for marching band. What if I don't get to go?" I can feel my newly mended heart sink down in my chest as the thought of my boyfriend, my best friend and her boyfriend all getting to go to band camp and me being stuck home alone for a week.

Maria looks at me like I just told her my big toe fell off. "Why wouldn't he clear you?"

"Oh, I don't know. That's just me worrying. I feel totally fine. I just get tired really easily now."

"Do you want me to go check your mailbox since I'm already wet from the rain?" Maria asks as she wrings the water out of her hair.

"Nah, I'll get it later when the rain lets up. So what's on your agenda for today?"

"Just the same ole same ole. I've got to get back to those littles. Alex just came home for his lunch break. I told him not to leave until I got back. Now that mom and dad are both working the day shift, I'm pretty much on diaper duty during my waking hours. It sucks!" Maria says as she rolls her eyes and throws her hands in the air. "I don't know what they're going to do when we are at band camp for the week and I especially don't know what they're going to do when school starts back."

Maria's parents are really hard-working folks, but they refuse to put their kids in a daycare. I'm sure they make pretty good money since Mr. Hernandez got his promotion at the casino. They are paying Maria this summer to babysit, but that will end soon with camp and school. They've talked about the daycare at their church, but it is an English-speaking daycare and they want to make sure their children remain bilingual. I think they're afraid the babies will grow up not knowing Spanish even though they speak it in their home. I don't know. I think that's just an excuse to save money this summer and get cheap childcare. But clearly, it's none of my business.

So, my band camp letter came the same day as Maria's and it said the exact same thing as her's except it had my name at the top. Also in the envelope was a list of items you need to bring to camp with you. I was very puzzled by some of the things. Ten pairs of socks? Really? That seems excessive. Two cans of bug spray. Ok, I can understand that. The insects get pretty tough inland around July. A bathing suit, ugh, I'm still wearing my granny tankini. Maybe by July I can get my cute top back out. Five packets of presweetened Kool-Aid? Ok, now that's strange. A dress or semi-formal outfit for the dance. Dance? Kylan didn't tell me about a dance. Now that sounds interesting!

I've been reading this silly letter every single day since it came in the mail. I pretty much have it memorized now. I'm just going to put my letter aside for now until I get back from my doctor's appointment today. It might be going directly in the trash once I get home if I don't get a good report. I'm so nervous about going today that my palms and the soles of my feet have been super sweaty. This appointment will determine how the next year of my life will play out, literally. Mom is coming home shortly to pick me up and take me over to the hospital where my doctor's office is. Until then, I'm just going to sit here with Oscar and hope for the best. I've learned over the past month that there's no sense in getting all worked up over something I have no control over.

"Hmm..." Dr. Sheffield says as he looks over my paperwork. "So how are you really feeling, Kimberly?"

I look over at my mom as I can feel my heart starting to beat faster. I take a few deep breaths before I am able to talk.

"Fine, I'm just fine," I manage to say without looking away from my mom.

"Kimberly, I need you to look at me," Dr. Sheffield says with a stern tone to his voice.

I slowly turn my head in his direction. There is something about this man that just absolutely terrifies me! I know he saved my life and all, but geez, dude, lighten up a bit.

I breathe in so hard that it makes me cough. I am able to catch it and quickly cover my mouth but not before accidentally spitting on my doctor.

I gasp, "I'm so sorry. I'm just really, um, nervous. You know, the rest of my summer and next school year is weighing heavily on what you are about to tell me."

Dr. Sheffield stands up and walks over towards me. He squats down in front of me and grabs my hands like he's getting ready to pray with me. "My dear, Kimberly. It is my responsibility as your doctor to take care of your health care needs and oversee your plan." He stops and looks over at my mom. "Mrs. Favre, it is up to you to execute this plan I have laid out for your daughter." My mom nods.

Execute? Why would he use that word? I thought that's what is going to happen to R.L. when he gets convicted of Ashley's murder. Why would my doctor use that word with me. I turn my head to the side just like Oscar does when he tries to understand what I am saying.

"Kimberly, I don't think you're going to like what I'm getting ready to tell you."

Oh no! It's happening! I have been afraid of this since I woke up from surgery. I feel like I'm going to throw up. This is the first time I have felt like this in over a month. I lean back in my chair to receive the dreaded news.

Dr. Sheffield pats the top of my hand. "Kimberly, I cannot clear you for marching band for next school year. I'm so sorry." He puts his head down and shakes it. "I know how excited you and your friends have been about this big adventure, but it's just not safe for you next year. You're healing nicely, but I can't risk the chance of releasing you to participate in an extremely strenuous activity such as band. I know how hard it can be on the body. I played tuba in my high school's band."

My life is now officially over! I feel the tears streaming down my face before I can even do anything about it. Dr. Sheffield stands up, grabs a box of tissues, and hands it to me. I have a thousand thoughts flooding through my head right now. How am I going to tell Kylan? How will he react? I definitely don't want him dropping out of band for me. I just can't bear the thought of watching from the stands again this year like last. I especially can't sit back and watch Maria and Peyton all snuggled up during those cold football games while I'm sitting all alone with Kylan's mom.

"Although I cannot release you to march, I can try to make this situation a little better."

A little better? Nothing could make things any better right now except for letting me be in the band. But I look up and listen anyway.

"I never like to mix my personal life with my professional career, but I can maybe pull some strings for you if you're interested."

Ok, now he's speaking my language.

"Mr. Mayberry, the band director at Bay High, and I are good friends. We've known each other for many years. I can see about him maybe making you the band manager for next year. Have you heard of the football or basketball managers?" I stare intently at Dr. Sheffield. "Their job is to fill up the water bottles, make sure all the equipment is packed and ready for games and just pretty much anything the coaches or players need. I would release you to participate in all the activities such as band camp, but with restrictions. You will need to take frequent breaks in the air conditioning and limit your lifting capacity to no more than ten pounds. What do you think? This would still allow you to be in the band with your friends, but with some limitations."

I sit and process what my doctor just told me. This is so much to take in right now that I don't know how to respond. I am completely devastated that I can't play the saxophone and march out on the field, but maybe this whole band manager thing would suffice until I am completely healed.

I ever so slowly nod my head and look up at the doctor. I feel my face flushing as I'm pretty sure I'm furious, but I know I can't unleash on my doctor. "I'm really upset right now," is all I'm able to say.

"Dr. Sheffield, I really appreciate this offer you have made. Kimmy, what do you think?" Mom leans down and pushes my hair behind my ear.

I shrug my shoulders. "I guess it would be ok. But what if he says no?"

"Well there's no guarantee Mr. Mayberry will go for this, but it's not going to hurt to ask. And by the way, Mr. Mayberry owes me a favor, so I think you have a pretty good shot."

Mom puts her arm around my shoulder and squeezes me for a hug. "I think it sounds like a great idea, Kimmy."

"Ok, ladies. Here's what we'll do."

Dr. Sheffield proceeds to tell us the plan and how he will write orders for some very basic physical therapy which will help with my strength and endurance. He said over time I will notice the tiredness gradually disappearing.

Then he reassured us that I am on the mend but still need to take it easy. The last thing Dr. Sheffield said is that he will have Mr. Mayberry contact me about a decision on band. Now all I have to do is wait. I HATE WAITING!

"Yeah, you heard me right! Can you believe that?" I sit on the other end of the phone and wait for Kylan's response, but he doesn't say anything at all.

"Are you still there, Kylan?"

"Sorry, Babe. That just wasn't the news I was expecting to hear today." I can hear the sadness in his voice.

"Well, I don't think that was the news that any of us were expecting to hear today. I feel totally fine except for the tiredness."

A long silence filled the phone. "Did you hear about the alligator that was swimming in the sound yesterday?"

I giggle, "No, not again! Let me guess, the tourists freaked out and called 911?"

"Yup!"

I lie back on my bed and place my hand over my heart. The bandages are gone and all that's left are those three little spots where they did the repairs. My heartbeat is slow right now. I feel the same calmness as when I'm out in the middle of a sandbar watching my pelicans fly overhead. I can see their wings slowly flapping up and down soaring with the wind. That is a feeling like none other to me.

CHAPTER 8

D o you have everything packed?" Maria asks as she plops down on my bed.

"I guess. I have everything on the list and much more. EEK! I'm so excited! Can you believe we are getting away from our parents for an entire week?" I can feel the excitement pumping through my veins, but I'm not really sure what to expect from this whole band camp thing.

Yep, you heard me right! I'm heading off to band camp today! Mr. Mayberry agreed to let me be the band manager for the next school year. He actually called my mom that same afternoon after my doctor's appointment. He was very excited to hear that I was interested in that position because his previous manager graduated last year and he was in dire need of a replacement.

The past couple of weeks have been pretty blah. My birthday came and went. I'm fourteen now and Kylan will be sixteen soon. For my birthday, Kylan got me a set of real diamond earrings. They're tiny little diamonds but very sparkly. He said I can wear them all the time and not worry about taking them out. I love them!

Maria has been babysitting so much that I've hardly seen her. When she's not babysitting, she's hanging out with Peyton. I pretty much only see her when it's bedtime or she needs a "peace break" from her siblings.

Kylan has been keeping me good company. When he can track down Peyton, he bums a ride to my house and we just chill. I haven't spent as much time at the beach this summer as I had expected. Most of my time has been snuggled up on the couch with either Kylan or Oscar. My tan is not as dark as I wanted either, but that's ok. I'm sure I'll be out in the sun at band camp.

I look around as Maria and I walk into the band room at Bay High School for the first time. The parent meeting was held in the cafeteria, so we didn't get to see it then. There are so many unfamiliar faces. I'm so nervous that I don't really know what to do. Everybody looks so much older than us. I feel like a baby in here.

"Hi! Are you Kylan's girlfriend?" says a very attractive girl with long blonde wavy hair. She tosses it to one side and then the other. I'm pretty sure she's a supermodel.

"Um, yes I am," I say as I can feel my face blushing. I'm nowhere near as pretty as she is.

"Great! We've been expecting you. I'm Cassidy, but you can call me Cass. I'm the head majorette and also your Bunkhouse Big Sis. I'll show you all the ropes of being in band this year. I'm super excited to finally meet you. I've heard so much about you!"

I nod. That's strange because I haven't heard anything about this girl. I kind of remember seeing her on the field last year, but her enthusiasm for me is a bit odd.

"And you must be Maria." Cass turns to Maria and puts her hand out. "It is such a pleasure to meet you. Your speech at graduation was phenomenal!"

Maria looks over at me with a puzzled look then looks back to Cass. "Thanks."

"Well, ok, then. That was awkward. All right girls, this way." Cass motions toward a table where it looks like kids are signing in.

"Kimmy, that was so weird," Maria whispers to me as soon as we are out of ear shot of Cass.

"Nah, I think she was just trying to be nice. Do you see the guys anywhere?" I look all around the band room, but I don't see our boyfriends. I know they're here because Kylan texted me already that they were. Oh well, I guess they're loading up their percussion stuff. Kylan is running for section leader for percussion this year so he's trying to make a good impression on all the newbies, at least that's what he told me.

Once Maria and I got signed in, we headed outside to say goodbye to our parents. Maria's mom is crying and I'm pretty sure I just saw a tear fall down her dad's cheek. That's so sweet. I think my mom is ready to get rid of me for a week. I feel like all I've done all summer is bug her for Kylan to come over and ask for money for snacks.

Mom squeezes me tight and says, "Remember your manners and your morals. I may not be there, but God is always watching."

I pause and look up at my mom with a sour expression. "Why would you say something like that?"

She glances over at my dad and smiles then gives me another hug. "You're all we have, Honey, and we just don't want anything to happen to you."

After a long speech from Mr. Mayberry about how to behave on a bus and everything to not do like hang out the windows and yell at cars passing by, we finally boarded.

"How about we try to get the back seat?" I ask Kylan as I wrap my arms around his waist.

He turns around and gives me a half-smile. "You can try, but I promise you won't be successful," he laughs.

As we make our way toward the back of the bus, I see a head pop up in the back seat.

"Nope! Not here!" an older lady with bright red curly hair says to my friend Liz who will also be a freshman. Then another lady on the opposite side pops up and says the same thing.

"See, I told ya. They're pretty strict about that. So if you want to get freaky on the band bus, we probably should sit in the middle," Kylan says as he pulls me over to a middle seat on the right side of the bus.

"Hey, y'all sit over here," I say to Maria as I point to the seat across from us.

We get settled in and as the bus starts to pull out of the school, I can see all the parents on the sidewalk waving bye. Some look sad, others look glad and then there's one mom who is shouting "freedom" and throwing confetti in the air. I guess she is ready for a break from her kid.

Kylan puts his arm around me and I cuddle up next to him. "So Maria and I met this girl named Cass. She was very friendly but in a strange kind of way. She told me she is the Bunkhouse Big Sis, whatever that means."

"Oh Cass," Kylan sighs. "She's harmless. I learned that real quick last year. She wants to be friends with everybody. She's just trying to get the title of "Band Sweetheart" again this year. She's been it every year since she was a freshman. I think her parents have a lot of money or something."

"Kind of like yours?"

Kylan giggles. "What are you talking about? My parents aren't rich. Well, maybe they are a little rich."

"Yeah, your mom just drives a brand new Mercedes and you live in a mansion."

"Oh Kimmy, I wouldn't go that far, but yes, my parents have done well for themselves."

Kylan is such a humble person. When we've been shopping at the Gulfport mall with his mom, he never wants to buy anything. He always says, "I have plenty at home and don't need anymore," to whatever he is looking at. I, on the other hand, would love to buy everything I wanted if my parents offered.

"So are you excited about a week of hell?" Kylan says as he pulls me closer.

"What do you mean by that?"

"I never told you about band camp last year? Oh geez...it made me want to run home crying to my mommy." Kylan winks and softly kisses me on the forehead.

Then I hear a sharp voice shout, "I just saw that! No PDA on this bus!"

Kylan slides further down in the seat and whispers, "That's Mr. Mayberry's wife, Sheila. You'll get used to her. I just try to avoid her and not make eye contact. She's the one with red curly hair."

I raise up to look back to see her again, but Kylan pushes me down. "I wouldn't do that if I were you. We're already on thin ice with her now. Come here."

Kylan pulls my face up next to his. I can feel the heat from his breath. "I've been dying to kiss you since I saw you in the band room at the sign-in table." He cups my face in his hands. "Look up, can you see the bus driver's mirror?"

I look up but all I can see is the ceiling of the bus and the back of the brown vinyl seat. "No."

"Ok, then we're safe."

Kylan slowly leans in and softly kisses the side of my neck. Chills run through my entire body. I can feel his mouth move up to my chin and then to my lips. He eases me even farther down in the seat as I feel like I am almost lying down. My body starts to tingle as his kisses get more intense. Suddenly I am snapped back into reality with a tap on my shoulder.

"Hey, you better stop that!" whispers Maria. "She's standing up now looking in your direction."

I slowly raise up and look over at Maria and Peyton who are sitting at least a foot apart. "Pish," I wave my hand in Maria's direction like I'm shooing a fly away. "Live a little. Remember, that's what you always say to me. What's the worst that she could do?"

"Um...what's the worst I could do you ask? You must be a new freshman. I'll tell you what I could do?"

I look up to see the woman with curly red hair standing over me with both hands on her hips. My eyes are as big as saucers and I'm sure my face is blood red.

"You must be the Favre kid? Am I correct?"

I freeze. I'm not sure who I am right now. The Favre kid? Nobody has ever said that to me. I make eye contact with Maria as she has her hand over her mouth like she's about to explode. Then I see Peyton with his hand up to his forehead covering his eyes and shaking his head. Who am I again?

"This is Kimmy, Mrs. Sheila." I hear Kylan say. "This funny thing happens where she loses her words when she gets nervous."

"Well, I don't think it's very funny, Kylan, and you shouldn't either. Let this be your warning for the year. The next time I see PDA between you two, I will separate you for the rest of the season!" Mrs. Sheila pauses to fluff her frizzy hair. "And Kimmy, maybe this manager thing was not the best idea for you. I have to have someone who is responsible and follows all the rules. Understand?"

I shake my head up and down so she knows I'm serious. As she walks away she stops and turns back around. "One more thing, I'm keeping a close eye on you two," she says as she points two fingers at us.

I slide down in the seat and look over at Maria who is busting out laughing. I mouth to her, "shut up." She just rolls her eyes at me and keeps laughing.

"I'm not a bad person, am I?" I ask Kylan.

"Babe, you're the most amazing person I know, but we have to be careful around Mrs. Sheila. She's a real stickler for the rules. Mr. Mayberry isn't nearly as bad as her. I heard that she's so grumpy when she's around the band because she's used to drinking wine all the time and she can't do that when she's at a school function."

"So I know what to get her for Christmas this year!" I say with a giggle.

CHAPTER 9

Ok ladies! Bunkhouse two, over there behind bunkhouse one, is for freshmen and sophomores. Oh, and me of course. In case you didn't already know, I'm your Bunkhouse Big Sis! I will be staying in the captain's quarters this year in bunkhouse two," says an overly enthusiastic Cass as she points to the right. "Unfortunately, it's a pretty good ways from the bathhouse, but you'll make do. I, however, have my own private bathroom so I won't have to worry."

I elbow Maria to get her attention.

"What?" Maria whispers.

"What the crap is this? Is she like our boss or something?"

"I don't know, Kimmy, just go with it."

Cass prances around to the front of the group of girls. "Upperclassmen, you know the drill. You're in bunkhouse one. You may go ahead and unpack and get your beds made. Follow me freshmen and sophomores." Cass waves at us over her shoulders to follow her.

We all follow Cass on the long walk to our bunkhouse. "Maria, what are we going to do if we have to pee in the middle of the night?"

"Wake me up and I'll go with you, and you do the same for me. I think we're pretty safe here, but we have to be wary of wildlife. I still laugh at Kylan's alligator story from last year."

As we walk into the bunkhouse, the smell of an old musty basement smacks me in the face. And it's HOT! I swear it's two hundred degrees in here! Geez...how am I ever going to get any rest in this sauna? I'm used to our thermostat being set at sixty-eight degrees at night in the summertime.

"Remember ladies, sophomores on the top bunks and freshmen on the bottom. No exceptions!"

I look over at Maria and roll my eyes. "This is ridiculous."

My friend Abbey from middle school raises her hand. "Miss Cass, how do we turn on the air conditioner?"

Cass lets out the loudest belly laugh I have ever heard. "Oh yes, didn't they tell you? Bunkhouse two doesn't have AC. Only the captain's quarters and the boy's bunkhouses do. Apparently, whoever built these things thought that girls don't get hot. You all do know that this place has been around for at least fifty years now."

I shake my head in disapproval. "Maria, I'm ready to go home. We're going to die from heat exhaustion in here."

"Oh, come on Kimmy. Don't be such a wussy. They don't call it camp for no reason."

"Well, it's not just that. My doctor gave me strict orders to take breaks in the air conditioning throughout the day. Should I say something?"

Maria gives me a concerned look. "Oh, I'm so sorry. I forgot all about your heart surgery. Maybe you should talk to Mr. Mayberry about it. I'm sure the cafeteria has AC."

"But I can't sleep in the cafeteria." I slap Maria on the shoulder.

"Let's just get set up and then we can figure things out."

Maria and I set up our beds on the far-left side of the bunkhouse. There were four bunkbeds on each side. Our friends Abbey and Liz took the other two bottom bunks on our side. Some sophomore girls took the top bunks. They seem pretty nice so hopefully they won't be jumping up and down on their beds all night long.

Cass showed us how to open all the windows around our room. She even helped us open the windows at the top. There is this neat little handle on the wall that you crank, and it opens up all the top windows. Oh, and there are ceiling fans! Once we had all the fans going and the windows open, it started to cool off nicely in there. Maybe I panicked for nothing.

The rest of the afternoon was pretty boring. Once everyone got their beds made and their bags unpacked, we had a whole group meeting in the main lodge. They also called it the dining hall. It is the place where we eat our meals, have meetings, and practice the instruments when it's raining outside.

Mr. Mayberry and his wife, Mrs. Sheila, spoke to the group about staying in our bunkhouses all night and not sneaking out to another one. They're acting like we're dumb kids or something. They talked about how dangerous the alligators in the lake are and the incident with the alligator on the practice field last year. Mrs. Sheila made sure she told us how the chaperones take turns staying up all night long and will catch you if you even attempt to leave your bunkhouse. And if you get caught, you get sent home immediately AND get kicked out of the marching band. No warnings or anything!

Mrs. Sheila also talked about PDA, you know Public Display of Affection. I'm pretty sure I rolled my eyes so hard they almost got stuck in the back of my head. What is with her and this childish PDA rule? Doesn't she know we're teenagers and we just like to kiss our boyfriends? She's such a mean old hag!

"Dinner tonight folks is your favorite, pizza! We decided to treat y'all since we know you'll be suffering and probably not be hungry come this time tomorrow," announced Mr. Mayberry.

I look over at Maria who is intently watching Mr. Mayberry speak. "What in the world is he talking about, Sis?" I whisper in Maria's ear.

She turns to me with a look of fear on her face and shrugs her shoulders. I lean forward and look past Maria to see Peyton's reaction. He's got one earbud in and skipping songs on his phone. Did he not hear any part of Mr. Mayberry's spill? Geez.

I nudge Kylan and he jerks in my direction. I nearly melt when he looks at me. All I can see are his dark black eyes. Looking at him is like gazing into the night sky when you're out on the boat in the middle of the Mississippi Sound. He reaches over to put his hand on my thigh, but I quickly shove it off. "Let's not take any more chances. Ok?" I pause, as now I'm sure I have hurt his feelings. But dang, Kylan, you should know better than to put your hand on your girlfriend's thigh after the long speech from Mrs. Sheila earlier.

He leans over in my ear and whispers, "Sorry, Babe. I can't keep my hands off of you here lately for some reason." I can feel the heat from his breath on my neck. It makes me want to stand up and walk right out of here and be done with all this mess just so I can kiss my boyfriend. How am I ever going to go all week without kissing Kylan? I'm feeling kind of like him. I just don't know if I'm going to be able to control myself. Maybe I should go ahead and give my mom a heads up that she might be driving up to Hattiesburg to pick me up in the near future.

"Dude! This is the best pizza I have ever eaten!" yells Peyton across the table.

Kylan nods his head as he is chewing, "Yeah, I guess it's pretty good. It tastes kind of like Tony's Pizza from over in the Pass. What do you think, Babe?"

I sit and savor my bite of pepperoni pizza as I think back to the last time I went to Tony's, but I'm having a hard time remembering. Oh yeah, it was shortly before Ashley left us. We took Grandpa Eugene over there one Sunday afternoon before school was out for the summer. My life now is broken down into two parts: before Ashley left us and after Ashley left us. That's the only way I can mentally organize everything. When you go through a tragic event like we've gone through, you have no other choice but to remember a before and after.

"Hey Babe! You ok?" Kylan says as he shakes my shoulder.

"Um, yeah. I must've zoned out for a minute. What were you saying?"

"I was asking you about pizza. Are you ok, Kimmy?"

I sit and look around the large room. I spot an old rock fireplace that has a few burned logs left in it. I can almost smell the stale smoke coming off those logs. Above the fireplace is a picture of a large black bear standing next to an alligator holding a fishing pole with a fish on it. The fish looks sad and so does the alligator. You know, alligators always look like they're smiling, but not this one. This one looks like it just lost its best friend.

"Yeah, the pizza is good," I say as I come back to reality.

Peyton stands up to get more pizza as Maria follows closely behind him. I've noticed she has been very clingy to him since we've been here.

Kylan turns my shoulders toward him and grabs my hand. "What's going on with you? Did something happen earlier with you girls while y'all were unpacking?"

I think back to a few hours ago to when Mrs. Sheila reamed me out on the bus for kissing my boyfriend, although I know for a fact that she didn't really see us doing anything that my parents wouldn't approve of. Then my mind went to when we first stepped foot in our bunkhouse. The smell. The heat. The sweat that was running down the crook of my back while I was making my bed. The thought that I'm not sure what I've gotten myself into. If it weren't for Kylan, I definitely wouldn't be here. Was this whole band thing all a big mistake? Do I only want to do this so I can spend more time with Kylan?

"Well...I'm just not so sure I'm cut out to be a band manager let alone a marcher in the band. I'm already feeling homesick, and we haven't even spent one night here yet. I miss Oscar terribly and for some strange reason, I'm missing my mom and dad. What's wrong with me?"

Kylan's grip tightens on my hand as he looks me directly in the eyes. A warming sensation starts to fill my entire body. I feel a mild sense of peace just gazing into his eyes. Kylan briefly looks away then back at me and whispers, "You will be fine, Kimmy. I am not going anywhere, and neither are you. It's time to be strong and start enjoying life for a change. You've been through a tremendous amount of trauma from everything that happened with Ashley and just when life was starting to get back to normal your heart decided it needed to be mended. And I've been by your side through every second of it. Now it's time for you to do something for me. I want you to be in the band with me and enjoy this marching season. Just listen to me," Kylan grabs both sides of my face and squishes my cheeks together, "you will not regret this decision."

CHAPTER 10

As darkness sets in, the feeling of loneliness is overtaking my soul. I had the hardest time separating from Kylan after supper. I wanted so badly to hold on to him and never let go. I wasn't even able to hug him. I hate these rules here and I hate being outdoors. I'm really dreading the next five days of what I'm pretty sure will be hell.

Suddenly, a loud squeal comes over the intercom, "Attention Bay High School Marching Band. At this time, everyone needs to report to the outdoor amphitheater!"

We all freeze in our steps. I can feel my eyes darting around the room as no one is speaking. Then I hear loud footsteps walking toward our side of the bunkhouse. The door flies open.

"Girls! Y'all heard him! SCOOT!" Cass yells at us from the doorway. Gosh, she just about gave me a heart attack.

"What's going on, Cass?" Liz asks.

Cass grins and says, "Oh...I'm sure it's nothing. Mr. Mayberry just likes to give us a good talking to before we go to bed to make sure we all sleep well at night." Cass turns to walk away but stops and turns back around. "Y'all might want to bring a big stick with you. I hear the alligators can get pretty rambunctious after dark around here," Cass says as she snorts and walks away.

"A stick? There's no way a stick would beat an alligator off of somebody. Has she lost her mind?" I ask Maria.

Maria grins, "I think she was kidding, Kimmy."

I look over at Liz and Abbey who are staring at us. "Do you think Cass was kidding?" I ask them.

Liz giggles and shrugs her shoulders, "I don't know, I guess we're about to find out."

"Dang, it's dark out here and creepy," I whisper over to Maria. I can hear the leaves on the trees blowing in the wind. The leaves here are not like the palm leaves. They sound much different than the palms, kind of like a shushing sound. It's like these trees are telling us to be quiet. "Do you think the guys heard the announcement?"

Maria is trying her best to walk and text at the same time. Whenever she is looking at her phone, it is like she is lost in space or something. You could ask her to borrow a million dollars, and she would probably just nod her head yes not really knowing what you asked her. Then she'd be out of a million dollars.

Maria looks up from her phone. There's a weird shadow on her face from the light of her phone screen.

She looks like she is holding a flashlight under her chin like we used to do when we were little kids. Her eyes appear as hollowed out frying pans and her nose is as red as Rudolph's.

"What?" Maria asks with her eyebrows almost crossed.

"Did you not hear me?"

"No, I heard you whisper something, but I couldn't hear you," she says with her head still down looking at her phone.

"Turn your screen off, you're scaring me."

"Geez, Kimmy. Why are you freaking out like this?"

"I'm not FREAKING OUT!"

I can feel my heart starting to beat faster as we walk along the nearly black sidewalks to the amphitheater. I reach down to grab a stick just in case we run into an alligator.

"AAAAAHHHHHHHH!! THAT'S NOT A STICK!" I jump up and down and scream at the top of my lungs. "I'M GOING TO DIE!"

"OMG, Kimmy calm down!" Maria says as she grabs me by my shoulders and starts shaking me until I feel like my head is about to fall off.

"A SNAKE! IT'S A SNAKE!" yells Abbey. "EVERYBODY RUN!"

As all the girls are shrieking, I start spinning in circles shaking my hands vigorously like they are on fire. Then, I feel familiar hands grab me from behind and squeeze me with all their might.

"Babe! What happened?"

My breathing instantly slows, and I can feel my heart rate returning to normal as Kylan embraces me in a warm tight hug. His arms are wrapped around me as my body starts to sync with his.

"Deep breaths, Babe. Take five deep breaths." Kylan moves his hands up and down my back as he is gently caressing every vertebrae in my spine. My head falls into his chest like a lifeless rag doll. I can feel his lips on the side of my face. His warm breath goes in and out of my ear. "Did you get bit, Kimmy?"

I hold my hand up to the night sky hoping the moon can shine some light on it. Kylan thoroughly examines every inch of it. Then he lowers my hand to his lips and ever so softly kisses it.

"I don't see any fang marks. Are you having any pain?"

I bury my head back into his chest and inhale the scent of his cologne. "No," I say as I wrap my arms around his waist.

"Are you ok, Sis?" Maria says as I can feel her gently touch my back.

I raise my head off Kylan's chest and turn it toward Maria. "I'm fine, I think." I look around and notice we're the only ones around. "Where is everybody?"

"Well, all us girls ran for our lives when Abbey announced it was a snake. That's when Kylan ran over here and scooped you up into his arms. I knew you would be safe with him, so I just joined suit and ran."

"Oh my gosh, I'm so embarrassed. Why did I think picking up a stick was a good idea. I'm the one who said a stick couldn't beat down an alligator. What is wrong with me? And the snake, where did it go?"

I release my tight grip on Kylan's waist and take a step back. I'm afraid to try and look around due to the fear of seeing that snake. I know it's near, because I just touched it.

"Babe, let's not worry about the snake. I'm sure it's far, far away from here now with all the screeching those girls were doing. Come here. Let's get one last hug in before we have to go join the others."

Kylan brushes the hair out of my eyes and tucks it behind my ears. I look up at him as we can barely see each other in the dark of the night. It kind of reminds me of the time when he was stuck inside my closet last summer. He nudges my head onto his chest and squeezes me tight. Then, just like two synchronized swimmers, our movements mirror the other. Our heads both raise at the same time, and our lips are pulled together like they are being controlled by magnets. A huge sigh of relief exits my mouth as our lips are now the last part of our body to sync. I wish this kiss would last forever. I feel Kylan slowly pulling away, but I grab the back of his head with my hand and push him back in. No, we're not done so don't stop.

"Ok, y'all, that's enough," Maria says as I can hear the annoyance in her voice. "We better get on over there to the amphitheater before we all get caught and sent home."

I look back up at Kylan and whisper, "Thank you for always being there for me. I love you."

"Babe, I love you more, forever and always."

As we got closer to the amphitheater, we could hear Mr. Mayberry addressing the band. Kylan, Maria, and I were able to slide into the back row without being seen. Unfortunately, that put me sitting right next to Cass. She just looked over at me and smiled. No words, no nothing.

I look around Kylan over to Maria and make big eyes at her. Maria rolls her eyes and never even looks in my direction.

"So, with that being said, please remember to stay on the paths and don't wander around the campgrounds tonight or any night this week for that matter. I heard we already had our first snake sighting a few minutes ago. Thank goodness no one was hurt. Mrs. Sheila, do you have anything you want to say?"

Oh no! Mrs. Sheila walks up the four steps to the stage and steps up to the microphone like she is getting ready to introduce herself at one of those frilly beauty pageants. I just shake my head.

"Ok, campers!" she says pointing to us with a sharp tone in her voice. "Remember this is still a school function and all school rules apply when you're here. No PDA, no hugging, no kissing, no necking, or any of the such. If you're afraid you will get in trouble, then just don't do it," states Mrs. Sheila. "As for sneaking out, that's a first-class ticket back to Bay St. Louis. So, I'd advise you to stay tucked in your snuggly little sleeping bags and get some rest tonight, because tomorrow will be a long day. Any questions?"

Mrs. Sheila looks around the audience hoping someone will ask a question. *Crickets!*

Mr. Mayberry steps back up to the microphone. "Well, then, I hope you all have a restful night, and we will meet back here at seven o'clock in the morning. Adios amigos!"

CHAPTER 11

Our first full day of band camp was...HOT! That's about the only word I can use to describe my day. In case you didn't know, summers in Mississippi are miserable. Apparently, it's even worse inland. I'm used to our cool ocean breeze in the evenings. Here in Hattiesburg, there's no breeze, no ocean, and no relief from the sun except for in the shade of the big oak trees. However, I do have to say that everything here is a beautiful color of green. The abundance of rain here this summer has really made all the living plants just pop!

My job has been pretty easy so far. All I really did today was help clean up after breakfast, wash and fill the water coolers, and hang out on the practice field watching the band learn their drill. Then before lunch, I got to go back to the lodge early and help make up the sandwiches. Surprisingly, those sandwiches were the best I've ever tasted! Maybe because I was starving. You see, I'm used to snacking all day on chips, candy, and other stuff like that. Whenever I'm hungry, I just eat. I always have food in my backpack at school for when I need it. My mom doesn't understand how I'm always eating but never gain any weight.

I'm just really glad that Mr. Mayberry has given all of us the afternoon off for a little rest and relaxation. He said we put our time in this morning and deserve a much needed two-hour break. Then everybody will head back to the field for the evening rehearsal before supper. It should be much cooler by then.

Smack!

"Ugh, these bugs are driving me crazy!" Maria says as she slaps another one on her arm. "I don't think this stupid stuff my mom gave me is even working. I just feel like an oily mess."

Oh yeah, and the bugs here are horrendous! I guess that's why they recommended we bring all that bug spray.

"I can't believe how well I slept last night. Being in such a strange place and all," I say as I look over at Maria who is fiercely scratching the bug bites on her leg.

So, you know, I was really worried about sleeping at this place last night. It was hot and I'm pretty sure I sweat through my clothes because when I woke up this morning, I was completely outside of my sleeping bag and soaked and wet. I should've brought sheets to put on my bunkbed here. I guess I'll know next time. I mean, who would've thought our bunkhouse wouldn't have AC in it? Don't they know we're in southern Mississippi?

"Oh, Kimmy, I am miserable with all these bites on me. I want to go home."

"You should have Alex bring you some ointment or something for those bites." I look over at Maria who is nearly crying with pain.

Maria looks up from scratching and waves her hand at me. "Pish, Alex is too busy working at the fire station and hanging out with Joni to bring me anything. You know, he and I got into a big fight right before we left for camp because I wanted to borrow some of his camping stuff, and he told me NO. I told him he was being a selfish brat. He said I was too immature, and he didn't trust me with his things. Can you believe that? After all we've been through."

We really thought Alex was turning over a new leaf with his attitude when he was hanging out with Kylan's brother, Ken, all the time. Now that Ken has gone off to college, I guess Alex has reverted back to his old butthole ways.

Maria and I are sitting on the rock wall waiting for the guys when Cass walks up. "Hey girlies! How's everything going?"

I look over at Maria not really sure what to say. Maria pipes up, "Good for the most part. I'm just really itchy with bug bites."

Cass bends down to look at Maria's legs, but she doesn't just do a regular ole squat. She bends over from her waist like she is trying to make her shorts come up on her rear so any guys around can see her exposed cheeks. Yuck!

"Oh, my sweet girl, you're eat up! I've got this cream in my room you can use. I sure don't want you to be uncomfortable all week. You've got a lot to learn," Cass says with a twang in her voice. She looks up and winks at Maria.

"Ah thanks, Cass, but I'll be fine."

Cass raises her eyebrows as if she doesn't believe Maria. "Well, if you change your mind let me know."

As Cass swiftly turns to walk off, she nearly slams directly into Peyton and Kylan. "OOF! Oh my goodness!" Cass slings her long blonde hair over her shoulder and is nose to nose with Peyton. "I'm so sorry. I was just leaving." Cass stands there looking at the two guys as if she wants to say something but doesn't because of me and Maria.

"So...you must be Kylan's friend?" Cass says in a subtle and sexy tone.

Peyton looks over at Kylan and just nods his head. Kylan puts his arm around Peyton. "Cass, this is my friend Peyton. He's new here, but he's going to be a sophomore. We're best friends and so are our girlfriends," Kylan says as he puts his hand out pointing toward us.

"Oh, I see. Kylan, I know you're with Kimmy because that's ALL you ever talk about," Cass says as she rolls her eyes. "So, that means this new beast of a man is with Maria?"

OMG! What did she just say? Beast of a man? Bahahahaha! As if things weren't awkward enough already, they sure are now.

Maria stands up, walks over to Peyton, and puts her arms around his waist. "Yes, right Babe?" Maria says nuzzling up to Peyton. "We've been together for over a year now. And what a wonderful year it has been with this beastly man!" Maria puts her hand around his neck and pulls him in for a kiss.

I look over at Kylan and totally lose it! I am covering my mouth with both of my hands as I am trying to hide my hysteria, but it slips out through my fingers and sounds like a big old fart which makes me start laughing even harder. Kylan is looking down at the ground with his hands behind his back like nothing is even going on, but I know he heard me.

"Well, I'm just going to give you a heads up," Cass pauses and puts her hands on her hips. "You better not let Mrs. Sheila see you doing that crap! She'll send you home so fast your head will be spinning." She turns around and walks off.

When Cass is finally out of ear shot, Kylan busts out laughing. "I have to say, that was just about the funniest thing I have seen in a long time. Beast of a man? Who the hell is she talking about?"

"I'll tell you this," Maria says as I can hear the fire in her voice. "If that blonde haired bitch comes any closer to my man, her head will be spinning, because I'm going to knock her into next year!"

"Maria! Calm down! She was just trying to flirt with him. I'm sure she does that to all the guys. Right Kylan? Didn't you tell me she tried that with you last year, but you made it clear you were taken?"

Kylan nods, "Um hum, she sure did. Peyton, you're going to have to let her know or she'll keep on with you. And I do have to agree with Maria. She is kind of a bitch. After I made it clear to her that I wasn't interested, she's left me alone since."

Peyton pries Maria's arms off of his waist and takes her hands in his. "You know I'm in it for the long haul, Maria. You're too good to let go now. And plus..." Peyton leans down and whispers something in Maria's ear and she giggles. Then he kisses her on the forehead.

"So, love birds. What are we going to do for the next hour?" Kylan asks.

Peyton obnoxiously raises his hand like he's asking a question in class. "Yes, Peyton?" Kylan calls on him.

"Um I can think of something that me and Maria can go do for the next hour, but it doesn't involve you and Kimmy." Maria smacks Peyton's shoulder as her face turns ten shades of red.

I look over at Kylan whose face is quite red as well. "Ok, Peyton, we don't want to hear about y'all's sex life," Kylan replies.

"We're not having sex! Why would you imply that? We're waiting until marriage like you and Kimmy!" Maria blurts out.

"We are?" Peyton asks with his head tilted to the side.

Maria smacks Peyton again but much harder this time.

"Oh yes, I remember now, we are," Peyton says bashfully knowing he's in trouble.

Several seconds went by without any words being said. This really got my mind to wondering. Have Maria and Peyton done it, and she just hasn't told me? That would be like betrayal. We agreed to save ourselves for marriage. Especially after finding out about Ashley being pregnant when she passed away last year. Surely to goodness she wouldn't do that with him. Peyton is cute, but he's not very mature. I definitely wouldn't want him as my baby's father. As for me and Kylan, we are perfectly content with keeping everything as it is right now. Yeah, I'm sure he'd like to take things a little further with me, but I'm clearly not ready and I make that known to him. Kylan is truly the most understanding human being on this earth.

We ended up spending the next hour with all of us sitting on the rock wall trying to figure out why Cass doesn't have a boyfriend. Kylan said he was pretty sure she was dating some guy last year that went to the community college over in Gulfport. This dude would come to the ballgames all decked out in Bay High School gear. Kylan thought he was maybe a thug. He would wear his BHS hat backward and sag his pants nearly down to his knees.

Peyton says that most boys think Cass is "easy" and just hang out with her to get pleasure. Peyton further explains that when girls are "easy" boys don't want a relationship because they can't be trusted to be loyal. And who wants to have a girlfriend with that type of reputation? Ok, that makes sense. Peyton finally said something intelligent for a change.

Maria's opinion about Cass was much more sharp! She said, and I quote, "Cass is just a whore trying to steal my boyfriend. That's something she will never get away with!"

At this point, I'm not really sure what to think except for this afternoon's encounter with Cass will be permanently etched into my memory.

CHAPTER 12

"Wake up, Maria! Wake up!" I loudly whisper and shake Maria as hard as I can. She just lies there motionless. Then I see she has earplugs in, so I reach over and pull one out of her ear. And there's earwax on it. Eww, gross!

"What's wrong with you Kimmy?" Maria says groggily.

"I'm not trying to panic or scare you, but I'm pretty sure I just saw a human head floating past the window!"

Maria rolls over and shoos me away. "Kimmy, you're dreaming. Go back to sleep."

I look at my phone. It's one thirty-five in the morning. Maybe I was just dreaming. I lie in bed looking up at the springs from the girl's bed on the top bunk. I think her name is Dani. Yeah, that's it, short for Dannica. She's really nice but kind of quiet. I wonder if she would notice if I kicked her mattress from underneath her bed. She probably would. I better not do that.

I roll over on my side and gaze out the window. I have fully convinced myself that I was sound asleep a few minutes ago and dreaming. There's no way I saw anything out the window.

I close my eyes and try to go back to sleep. No luck. I check my phone again, one forty-seven. Maybe I need to go to the bathroom. Maria is definitely not going to get up right now to go to the bathhouse with me. I could just pee in a cup. Um, no, that's disgusting. All these thoughts are going through my mind, and I can't turn them off!

Just when I think I have almost drifted off back to sleep, I hear an eerie scratching sound on the glass doors. I nudge Maria again. "Wake up! For real this time!" My voice is much louder than a whisper now.

She slings her body over and almost smacks me with her arm. "Geez, Kimmy. What is it now?"

"Maria, I'm not hallucinating! I saw a head floating outside the window and I just now heard a scratching sound coming from around the glass doors! I'm too scared to go over and move the blinds to see what's out there!" I can feel my heart beating nearly out of my chest. The darkness of the night is hanging over our bunkhouse. The moon is not shining, streetlights don't exist here at the camp, and no one brought a nightlight. So, to say it's dark in here is an understatement. The only light I can see right now looks like it is coming from a cellphone on the other side of the glass doors.

"Ok, Kimmy. Let's go peek through the blinds together and see what's out there."

Scratch, Scratch, Scratch

"OMG! Did you hear that, Maria?" I look over at her feeling as if my eyes might bulge out of my head. I grab Maria's hand, and she stops in her tracks.

"Kimmy, what was that?" Maria says as she squeezes my hand tighter.

We tiptoe over to the outside wall where the sliding glass doors are. Long white vertical blinds are hanging straight down from the top over the doors all the way down to the floor. The blinds are swaying back and forth with the air from the ceiling fans. I start to hear a low swishing sound coming from them.

Scratch, Scratch, Scratch

I grab Maria around her shoulders. "I can't do this! I think I might pass out!" I loudly whisper to Maria and step back away from the doors.

"Ok, let's wake up Abbey and Liz," Maria whispers back.

"I think we're both awake already," Liz says as Maria and I are about to jump out of our skin. "I heard the scratching too, but I just figured it was a mouse outside from the field."

Abbey rolls out of bed and her bare feet hit the concrete floor like someone just got smacked across the face.

"Shh," Liz says with her finger to her mouth. "Let's try not to wake up the other girls unless we absolutely have to. I overheard them talking about us freshmen earlier and how it wasn't fair they were made to be in a bunkhouse with us this year." Maybe they're not as nice as I thought they were.

We all lock arms and slowly walk over to the doors. As Liz leans forward, we hear the scratching sound again. We jump back and huddle closer together.

"Ok, on the count of three, let's each open a section of the blinds and see what's out there," Liz suggests. "Ok?"

I can feel us all nodding our heads. "Ok," I agree. "I'll count. One...two...three..."

We lunge forward and each of us grabs a section of the blinds and yanks it open. The four of us stand there in awe at the sight we see.

"Um...what do we do now?" I quietly say looking around to the other girls.

Abbey pipes up, "Well hell, Kimmy, let them in!"

"Oh no! We can't let boys in our bunkhouse," protests Liz. "But we can open the door and go outside with them." None of us speak as we are looking at each other's faces in the dark.

"Who all is out there? I can see my hunny bunny Peyton, but who else?" Maria says with romance in her voice as she puts her face to the glass cupping her hands around her eyes to block out any inside light.

"Just open the door, Maria. It's OUR guys," Abbey insists.

Maria puts her body against the handle and eases the door open. It makes a slight squeak as the door starts to slide to the side. We all stop and look up at the girls on the top bunks to make sure they're still asleep.

Maria fans her face as I can tell she is getting hot. "This is too much y'all," she mouths to us. "Somebody take over, please."

Abbey marches up to the door and slings it open with a bit of rage. "There!" Abbey states. "Have at 'em!"

Maria is the first to run out the doors and jumps into Peyton's arms like they haven't seen each other in weeks. Liz carefully steps out the door, looks around, then comes back in the room.

"Well, I guess James was too chicken to come. I'm out then. I'm going back to sleep," Liz says as she crawls in her bed.

Abbey trots out the door, spots her boyfriend, and takes off. They grab hands and run off into the dark.

I poke my head out the door and look around at the remaining guys. "Where's Kylan?" I ask the group.

"Oh, Kimmy, I'm so sorry. Kylan was sound asleep, and I just didn't have the heart to wake him up," says Brad a senior trumpet player. "I know he wanted to come with us, but he passed out as soon as the lights turned off."

I take a deep breath in and let out a discouraged sigh. "Bummer. I guess I'm going back to bed too." As I start to slide the door back closed, I see a hand come forward and stop the door. Then I see his face, "Kylan?" I snarl up my nose trying to figure out if it's really him.

"Yeah Babe! Did you think I would miss out on getting some alone time with you tonight?"

"EEK! I can't believe you snuck out to see me! If we get caught, we're going to be...dead!"

Kylan takes me by the hand and leads me out the door. "We're not going to get caught, Babe. I know a secret place where we can go."

A secret place? Oh my goodness! I already feel my body starting to get hot and tingly. I ease the door shut behind me. Then, Kylan and I start our trek into the woods. We only make it about fifty feet from the bunkhouse when he stops and drops to one knee.

"Are you proposing?" I ask in amazement.

"Um, kind of," he pauses and grabs my left hand. "Kimmy, I have so much I want to tell you right now, but no words could ever express how I feel about you."

As Kylan continues to talk, all I can think about is how nervous I am. I can feel my knees shaking and my teeth chattering and it's not even cold out here. Actually, it's probably about eighty degrees still. What is he getting ready to say to me?

"Over the past year, we have grown so close that I feel like we can finish each other's sentences. Kimmy, I truly think you're my soulmate, the love of my life. God brought us together for a reason. We may never know what that reason is, but I feel so fortunate we found each other at such an early age."

My heart is pounding out of my chest. I feel it beating up in my throat. I'm not scared, even though I should be. I could have a rattlesnake slithering across my foot right now and I would probably never know it.

Kylan goes on. "I know this is probably not the most romantic place to do this, but I feel like we can never get a second of privacy here lately. Plus, I really didn't want anyone to see me doing this. I had planned to do this at the beach last week, but there were so many people around I just wanted to share the occasion with you."

Kylan reaches into his pocket and pulls something out. "I've been carrying this around since before your heart surgery just waiting for the perfect moment, and this is it!"

He feels each of my fingers one by one. He finally settles on my ring finger. "Kimberly Ruth Favre, please wear this ring as a symbol of my love for you. It's not quite an engagement ring, that one will come later with a very expensive diamond. But this, my love, is a promise ring. I promise to be loyal and love you no matter what. All I ask is that you do the same to me."

I cannot speak. All the words I thought were in my head have now left. I never thought in a million years that Kylan would give me a ring. I'm only fourteen. My mom was in her twenties before my dad ever did anything like this for her. Actually, come to think about it, Dad never even gave Mom an engagement ring. They just bought wedding bands and went to the courthouse. Neither of them even wears their rings now. Dad says his is uncomfortable and Mom swears it messes with her tips at the casino. I don't know.

"Kimmy, are you in there?" I hear Kylan talking, but I just can't seem to snap out of it. That's when he puts his hands on each side of my face and pulls me in for the most romantic kiss I've ever had. My foot definitely pops in the air!

"So do you accept my gift?" Kylan hesitantly asks.

I look up at Kylan and all I see is the darkness of the night. "Are you kidding me? Of course I do! I could not be happier! I'm just dying to see what this ring looks like."

Kylan grabs my hand and leads me on through the woods. Where on earth is he taking me?

After we walk for what seems like miles, we finally stop. "Well, here it is!" Kylan points to a shadow of a rickety old shack.

"What is this?" I ask in dismay.

"Babe, it's the Love Shack!" Kylan laughs and proceeds to open the door.

"I'm pretty sure this is not a Love Shack. It looks more like somewhere we would go to get murdered by a masked madman, Kylan. I'm a little worried right now."

As we walk through the doorway of the shack, Kylan flicks open a lighter. The brightness of the flame nearly blinds me. I wonder where that lighter came from. He doesn't smoke nor does he carry a lighter around with him.

"It's safe, Babe, I promise. Please trust me." Kylan does his absolute best to reassure me.

"Oh, I trust you or I wouldn't be out here in the middle of nowhere just waiting for a madman to show up. And what's that smell? It's like a family of rats gathered in here for a wild party and died from having so much fun."

Kylan laughs. "So, last year at band camp, everyone was getting pissed off with our percussion section because our drums are so loud. Which is not always a bad thing, but when others are trying to practice, I understand how annoying that would be. So we just took off through the woods one day trying to get as far away from the rest of the band as possible. That's when we came upon this little building. We think it must've been an old ranger station for the state park. It's really cool! Look!" Kylan points over to a sitting area with a couch, table, and two chairs. "I'm sure we weren't the first ones to find this place as someone left candles and this lighter behind. We suspect it's been used as a makeshift Love Shack in the past from former band members."

I giggle, "So, what are we going to do here?"

"We're going to celebrate, Babe!"

"What are we celebrating?" I ask puzzled.

Kylan pauses. "The ring!"

"Oh yeah, duh! Hold that flame over here so I can get a good look at it." As the flame from the lighter gets closer to my hand, I start to see the sparkling of all the tiny little diamonds. "Kylan! It's beautiful! Thank you! I love you so much!"

I wrap my arms around his neck and pull him into me. My boobs are pressed so hard against his chest that they almost hurt but in a good way. I can feel his hands working up and down my back. I slowly start walking backwards until I feel the back of my legs hit the couch. We ease down to the couch together without breaking our lips. His hands start massaging the back of my head as the tingling sensation returns.

"How does that feel, Babe?" Kylan whispers in my ear.

I have no words to describe the feeling I'm having right now, but I manage to say, "It's wonderful. You have no idea."

"Oh, yes I do, Babe, because I'm feeling the same way."

Our breathing is getting faster as our bodies become one. I could lay like this for the rest of my life. Hours could pass and we would still be in this same position.

Kylan slowly raises up. "Babe, I'm ready whenever you are?"

I raise my eyebrows, then they cross. "Ready for what? To go?" I ask.

"You know, what we were about to do in your daydream you were having that day when we were looking out over the harbor." He leans down and starts kissing the side of my neck.

I think back to what Kylan is talking about. Oh yes, I remember now. We were getting ready to do it. "Um, Kylan," I pause not really knowing what to say to him. Did he think we were going to have sex out here? He knows I'm waiting for marriage. "I'm content with just doing this right here," I reply hoping he understands my feelings.

Kylan doesn't speak. He just picks back up where he left off like we never even stopped.

CHAPTER 13

---

*B*ang, Bang, Bang

Muffled voices are screaming through the door! Kylan jumps up and runs over to the door of the shack. As he opens it, two dark shadows come running in.

"OMG! Shut the door!" one screams in a familiar voice.

"Maria, is that you?" I ask.

"Yes, Kimmy! It's me and Peyton!" Maria shrieks as she struggles to catch her breath.

"Pretty sure we all just got busted, man!" Peyton announces as he starts pacing around the room.

"You mean, you and Maria are busted? Because Kimmy and I have been in this here little cabin for the past hour now," Kylan makes clear.

Maria plops down on the couch beside me as she is still struggling to breathe. I calmly ask her, "How do you know you're busted?"

She takes in a deep breath and lets it out. "We were in a hammock someone put up back behind the boys' bunkhouse and..." Maria stops. "Well, let's just say we were making the trees sway." We all laugh, and Maria continues. "Then, out of nowhere, we see all these flashlights from the main lodge coming in our direction. So, we jumped down out of the hammock, got ourselves put back together, and took off running through the woods."

"That's when I remembered about this little place y'all found last year. Kylan showed me the path to it yesterday saying it would be a great little Love Shack for someone looking to get lucky," Peyton chimes in.

I look over to Kylan and smack his shoulder. "Really?" I mouth to him.

"Anyway, you better put out that flame on your lighter unless you want us to all get caught out here. Maria and I stopped to see if they were following us, and fortunately, we didn't see any flashlights."

Kylan extinguishes the flame on the lighter. We sit in the dark silence for several minutes. Then a thought pops into my head, "Who has their phone with them?"

"Geez...Kimmy, I left mine on my bed. I guess I was so excited to see Peyton outside our bunkhouse that I totally forgot all about my phone," Maria sighs. "What about you?"

"Same here. It's sitting on my bed in the bunkhouse. Peyton?" I look in his direction even though it's pitch black.

"Nah, man, the upperclassmen told us not to bring our phones because they can be tracked."

"So, you're all telling me that out of us four teenagers, none of us have a phone?" What are the odds? I think to myself.

Silence

"Wake up! Everybody WAKE UP!" I gasp. "It's daylight outside, and I have no idea what time it is without my phone. Kylan, do you have your watch with you?"

I wait impatiently for his response as I am pretty sure he's still sound asleep along with Maria and Peyton. I guess we all fell asleep when we were trying to hide from whoever was running toward them.

"Yeah," Kylan raises up from lying down on the floor. "Gosh, my back sure is stiff." Kylan yawns and looks down at his watch. "CRAP! It's six thirty! We have to be at morning warm-ups in thirty minutes!"

"Oh my God! Oh my God! We're dead! How are we going to get back to the bunkhouses?" I yell as I can feel my heart nearly beating out of my chest. I put both hands to my heart. "I need to lie down! I think I'm having a heart attack!"

Kylan grabs me and squeezes me tightly. "It's not a good time for this, Babe. You're going to have to snap out of it and help us come up with a plan."

I can feel my body tensing up even more. I ball my hands into fists and bite my bottom lip. I close my eyes and try to imagine my happy place. "It's not working," I mutter.

"STOP IT, KIMMY! THIS IS ENOUGH!" Peyton shouts.

Kylan says something back to Peyton, but I can't hear him. Then he squeezes me harder to the point that I feel like my eyeballs are about to pop right out of my skull. I inhale deeply.

"Ok, I'm coming back. Just give me a minute." Kylan walks me over to the couch to sit down. "I feel like I just left this world for a few minutes." I drop my head into my hands.

"You did, Babe. It's ok, but I thought your heart surgery fixed all that?"

Shaking my head, "I thought so too, but apparently not. We can't worry about it now, though."

Maria chimes in, "I have a plan." We all lean in her direction. "Let's leave this cabin one by one so we won't be a big group walking through the woods together. That way if one of us gets caught the rest can be safe.

Typically, Maria has the best of plans, but I'm not so sure about this one. Here lately, I've noticed that Maria just hasn't seemed herself, especially when she is around Peyton. It's kind of like Peyton has some kind of spell over her, a love spell. It's so bad that I'm starting to wonder if I'm getting smarter than her. Maybe he's sucking her brain power out of her body. Maybe Peyton is really a vampire! Haha, that's a funny thought!

"How about let's just go. We need to get back to camp before anyone notices we're gone. Follow me," Kylan says as he motions us out the door.

Maria goes first, then Peyton. As Kylan is holding the door waiting for me, I stop to get one last look at this place. Since it's daylight, the entire cabin is illuminated. There are beautiful, colorized maps of the entire Paul B. Johnson State Park hanging on the walls. Each is a little cut out of a section of the park. This place is really clean, nearly spotless! As I spin around the room, I can tell Kylan is getting rather impatient. Then I notice one last thing, a suitcase in the corner that looks new.

"Hey," I point to the suitcase, "did you see that? It looks new. Like someone recently put it here."

Kylan walks over to the suitcase and looks it over. "Yeah, maybe, but we don't have time to fool with it right now. That will have to wait for another day. Come on, Babe. Let's get out of here."

As Kylan ushers me out the door, he grabs me around the waist and pulls me in for a kiss.

"Just one more," he whispers in my ear, "before we have to go back to band camp hell."

While walking through the woods, we decided to bypass our bunkhouses and go straight to the main lodge for morning warm-ups. That way, no questions would be asked, and we would all just show up on time. Well, most of us.

We get to the main lodge with about five minutes to spare. We are all still dressed in our pajamas, but that's how everybody shows up to warm-ups anyway. So, we fit in perfectly.

I go straight to packing the Tiger Tote. Mr. Mayberry said it is my job to make sure we have everything in there we could possibly need. It has new reeds for the woodwind instruments, bandages in case of accidents, this weird alcohol spray for when Mr. Mayberry needs to play one of the brass instruments, these very potent smelling salts that you break underneath someone's nose when they pass out, and lots of other junk that we will probably never need. Mr. Mayberry says, "It's better to have it and not need it than to need it and not have it." Whatever. I just do my job and make sure it's all in there.

"OMG, Kimmy, come here quick!" Maria calls for me across the room. I stand up so fast that I am slightly lightheaded. I look over at Maria and see stars floating all around. I guess I'm worn out from staying up all night last night. I manage to slowly walk over to her.

"What's up?"

Maria leans over so close to me that I can feel her breath on my cheek. "Word is that they caught Abbey and her boyfriend last night."

My eyebrows raise as I feel instantly panicked. "Really?"

"Yeah. That's what Liz just told me. She said Mrs. Sheila brought Abbey back to the bunkhouse around six o'clock this morning to get all her stuff packed up to go home. While Abbey was packing, Mrs. Sheila asked Liz about me and you."

"OMG! What did she say?"

Maria looks around to make sure no one is listening. "She told her we were in the bathhouse getting ready. Mrs. Sheila thought it was strange that we left our phones out in the middle of our beds. So, Liz got them for us. Here." Maria hands me my phone.

I look down at it only to realize the battery is nearly dead. "Well, this won't last long. Mine's on four percent. What about yours?"

"Mine too. Three percent actually," Maria sighs.

"So, I guess that's it for Abbey? No band for the rest of the year for her?"

Maria shakes her head. "Kimmy, do you realize how lucky we were to make it up here this morning without getting caught?"

"Yeah, I'm never doing that again. I had fun, but it wasn't worth risking the chance of getting kicked out of band. I'm really bummed about Abbey. I'm going to miss her, and I know Liz will miss her even more."

Maria and I stand there in the middle of the main lodge watching everyone gather in for warm-ups. Several of the sophomore girls from our bunkhouse walk in and look over at us like we stink or something. I'm starting to think they must hate us. Behind them is none other than Cass. When she spots us, she makes a B-line over to me and Maria.

"So, girls, hope y'all had fun last night!" Cass roars sarcastically. "Because that will never happen again on my watch! I can't believe y'all didn't get caught! If I weren't such a nice person, I'd turn both y'all's sorry asses in to Mrs. Sheila. You two disgust me! The nerve to sneak out of the bunkhouse. I'm keeping my eyes on you, both of you, so you better watch your backs from here on out!"

You know in the cartoons when someone yells at another and their hair blows back off their head? Well, I'm pretty sure that's what just happened to me and Maria. I even put my hand up on my head to make sure it was all there.

Just when we think Cass is out of earshot, she turns back around. "Oh, Maria!" We both look up. "I'm REALLY keeping an eye on you!" Cass points her middle finger at Maria. "I know what you and Peyton did in my hammock last night!" Maria and I look over at each other like we just saw a ghost. "And I can promise you, there will be hell to pay!"

As soon as Cass turns around, Maria and I bust out laughing. "That's just about the funniest thing I have seen in years!" I snort.

Maria bends over and grabs her side from laughing so hard. "I cannot believe that was her hammock! If I would've only known! Nah, who am I kidding? If I would've known it was Cass' hammock, I would've done much more!"

"Maria, did you and Peyton do it in her hammock?"

"Pish," Maria smacks me on the shoulder. "Sis, I'd love to have been doing that with Peyton, but it's my time of the month. Plus, I'm seriously saving myself for marriage no matter how hard it will be. It's not worth risking my entire life for just a little bit of pleasure."

I contemplate telling Maria about what Kylan asked me last night. "Maria, can I tell you something?"

"Sure, Sis!" Maria answered. "Does it have anything to do with that gorgeous ring Kylan gave you last night?"

"Um, maybe," I respond sheepishly. "So we were on the couch in that cabin heavily making out. I could feel Kylan's, you know, man parts on me."

Maria raises her eyebrows. "Go on."

"So I guess you could say we were in the moment. Then, Kylan said he was ready whenever I was."

Maria stands there and just stares at me. "So?"

"No, no, Maria, we didn't do anything. I wanted to and so did he, but I told him I wanted to wait. He seemed totally fine with that. But how long will he be fine with it?"

Maria puts her arm around my shoulder. "Sis, Kylan is madly in love with you. He will wait until you're ready. And if not, then he's not the one for you. That's when you have to make the decision to be done and move on with your life."

I ponder on what Maria just said. "So, what if Peyton wants to and you don't?"

Maria shakes her head and runs her hand across her neck like she's cutting her throat. "Well, that's when he gets axed. I'm not going to be dating a guy who doesn't respect my opinion, and neither should you."

"Ok. I'm really glad you and Peyton busted in on us last night, or I might've lost all my self-control. Things were getting pretty intense," I giggle. "Not to change the subject or anything, but did you see that suitcase over in the corner of the cabin this morning when we were leaving?"

"You know, come to think about it, I do remember seeing something suspicious that resembled a suitcase. I think I was so worried about getting out of there that I couldn't really focus on anything else."

I look over Maria's shoulder and see Kylan and Peyton coming our way. "Well, speak of the devil."

Maria turns around and we both smile our biggest smiles knowing that what we are getting ready to tell the guys about our encounter with Cass will absolutely make their day.

"The suitcase," I say to Maria as I lie in bed unable to get my mind to stop racing. It's pitch black in here right now and I'm just trying to wrap my head around what has occurred over the past twenty-four hours. I saw some floating heads. We heard mysterious noises that turned out to be our boyfriends. That was funny. Kylan gave me this gorgeous and probably very expensive ring. We made out for a really long time in the little cabin. Maria and Peyton almost got caught sneaking out. We managed to make it back to the main lodge on time for warm-ups. How on earth we managed that I will never know. Then, the suitcase I saw. I just can't get that stupid thing off my mind. "I'm dying to go back to that cabin and check it out!"

"Shh, Kimmy. Lower your voice! We'll get in trouble if they hear us." Maria points to the top bunks over us. "I'm sure it's probably nothing. There's no telling how long it's been there. It probably belongs to some homeless person. We're just lucky we didn't run into them last night."

I ponder the possibilities. Maybe Maria is right. Maybe it's nothing and it has been there for a while, but I just have this weird feeling about it. Kind of like somebody stashed it there secretly for some reason. I close my eyes and try to sleep, but it never comes to me.

I poke Maria in the side. "I can't sleep!" I whisper. Maria doesn't respond so I just lie here in silence.

I open my eyes as wide as I can then tightly shut them. I do that several more times hoping it makes me tired, but nothing. Then I notice a little red dot on the wall. What is that? Oh, it must be a smoke detector. Geez...why can't I go to sleep? I really miss home. I guess you could say I'm homesick for real now. I know I have Maria with me, but I miss Oscar. My snuggly little puppy dog. I wonder if he misses me too?

Then my mind starts to wander to this time last year. The last day we were with Ashley. I remember exactly how the sun felt on my skin that day. That was also the day I almost lost Oscar to the ocean. Gosh, so much has happened in a year.

CHAPTER 14

Good morning, Sweetheart! (5:34 AM)

Hi, Mom! (5:55 AM)

I was asleep still. It's been a long week. I miss home. (5:57 AM)

Oh, Honey, we all miss you too, especially Oscar. (5:58 AM)

How's everything going at camp? (5:59 AM)

It's fine. (6:01 AM)

Ok, stay safe. I can't wait to see you tomorrow afternoon! I love you! (6:02 AM)

Love you too. (6:04 AM)

Yep that's right! I have almost survived an entire week of band camp! Tonight we have our final dress rehearsal before we perform for the parents tomorrow afternoon. Well, the band will be performing, and I'll just be watching. Also, tonight is the dance. EEK! I'm super excited! I brought a cute little strappy dress to wear and some little kitten heels to match. The dress has yellow, pink, purple, and teal sunflowers all over it. Nanny bought it for me a while back when we went on a little shopping trip to Gulfport. Kylan hasn't seen me wear it yet, so it's going to be a surprise for him.

My crew has been laying low after our little sneak out the other night. We didn't want to take any more chances and risk getting sent home like Abbey and her boyfriend. I'm really sad that Abbey won't get to be in band with us this year. I bet her parents killed her when she got home. I haven't heard a word from her and usually she texts me several times a day.

All I can think about is the ring on my finger that Kylan gave me. Each time I look down at it, my heart flutters and I get a funny feeling in my stomach. Maria says it's butterflies in there, but I'm not nervous so I don't really know. But what I do know is that I am ready to be back home with the Osc! I'm really missing my pelicans too. We are already planning a beach day for next week. Well, me and Kylan are. Maria says her mom has been texting her about babysitting all week next week. Blah!

"I would ask you who you're taking to the dance tonight, but I'm pretty sure I already know," snickered Liz.

"Yeah, you know, Kylan would probably get mad if I didn't ask him to go," I joke. "What about you? Since you broke up with James, do you have any prospects?"

"Nah, not really. I'm just planning on going stag tonight."

Then I feel someone come up behind me and wrap their arms around my waist.

"Did I just hear my name?"

"Kylan!" I smack his hands down. "Stop that! You don't want us to get kicked out on our last day, do you?"

"I know, I know. I just can't get you out of my mind. What have you done to me?" Kylan says as he winks at Liz.

With tears in her eyes, Liz sighs, "Y'all make me sick! Why can't I find a good one like you, Kylan?"

Kylan puts his hand to his chin like he's thinking. "You know, Liz, my friend Brad is single. What do you think?"

Liz hesitates and looks around the lodge trying to see who all is in there. "But he's a senior. Don't you think he's too old for me?"

"Um, maybe, but who cares. If you want James back, then you're going to have to make him jealous," I suggest.

"Well, here's the thing, Kimmy. I'm not so sure that I want James back. He's nice and all, but sometimes a girl wants a challenge. You know, like a bad boy."

I gasp, "Oh, Liz! I didn't know you were like that."

"Neither did I, but sometimes when the mood strikes, you want to act on it," Liz says with a slight smirk on her face.

"Oh no, here comes Cass. Let's act like we don't see her," I casually say.

Cass waves to us. "Hey there lovies! How's your day going?" she asks with a bit of sarcasm in her voice.

Kylan takes a step toward Cass and puts his hand on her shoulder. "We're all fine, Cass. No need to worry about us."

Cass looks down her nose at Kylan's hand on her shoulder and knocks it off. "I'm not worried about y'all. Where's that Maria and Peyton? In case you didn't know, they can't be trusted."

I wrinkle my forehead. "What are you talking about? Maria is my best friend, and Peyton is Kylan's best friend. They are two of the most trustworthy people I know," I say with a hiss in my voice.

"You obviously don't know them very well, Kimmy. But really, where are they? I need to have a little talk with them about expectations at the dance tonight."

I roll my eyes and look over at Kylan. "We don't know where they are. Usually after we all each lunch, they go outside and sit on the rock wall. If you can't find them on the wall, then they're probably hanging out in your hammock making the trees sway," I giggle.

"AHHHHHHH! If I weren't a good Christian girl, I would slap you across the face right now and Kylan wouldn't be able to stop me!" Cass balls up her fists like she's about to hit me. "Kimmy Favre, just because you and your whore of a friend, Maria, solved a murder last year doesn't mean that you're untouchable."

As Cass pivots around to walk away, Liz calls her the B word. I'm pretty sure Cass' head spun 180 degrees. I don't think I even saw her body turn. It was like a flash of lightning struck and she was instantly possessed by a demon with fire in her eyes and all.

"Elizabeth Justice, what did you just say?" Cass snapped.

Elizabeth? Nobody calls Liz by her full first name. Liz just turns her head in the other direction and sticks her nose in the air.

"Effin' freshmen!" Cass spits.

"Um, Cass, who you calling a freshman? I'm a sophomore," Kylan grins.

"I hate all y'all!" Cass spins back around. As she walks away, she puts her hand behind her back and sticks up her middle finger so we can all see it. Yeah, she's such a flake.

I begin to uncontrollably laugh to the point that I can't breathe and then I start coughing. When I finally get my composure back, it hits me. "Why does she want to talk to Maria and Peyton? Do you think she's going to do something mean to them?"

Kylan nods. "No, she's too much of a wussy to do anything. She might give them a good tongue lashing and that is all. Cass really does try to keep everybody in line, but she just doesn't quite have the presence of authority to get the job done. I'm sure she's going to be one of those girls who goes to law school and even passes her bar exam but ends up being a stay-at-home mom because she can't hack it in the real world. I mean, there's nothing wrong with being a stay-at-home. My mom did it for ten years, but that's only because my parents couldn't afford to pay for daycare. Cass, on the other hand, comes from money. The day that somebody puts her in her place will be the day her world changes forever."

"Well, I'll tell you this right now, I'm not far from it! Nobody talks about my friends like that. Especially some stupid rich bitch like Cass!"

Kylan puts his hand over my mouth. "Kimmy, please don't talk like that. It's not very ladylike. Plus, when someone has to cuss because they can't think of any other words to say, it shows their stupidity."

I put my hands on my hips. "Who do you think you're talking to, mister?"

Kylan's eyes get big. "Babe, I didn't mean it that way. No, no!" He shakes his head back and forth. "I'm so sorry, that's not what I meant."

Liz butts in, "Ok, guys, that's enough. Come on, kiss and make up."

Kylan puts his hands around my face and squishes my cheeks together. "I'm truly sorry. I didn't think about what I was saying before I said it. As soon as the words came out of my mouth, I knew I had made a mistake. Please forgive me. It will never happen again."

I take a deep breath and drop my hands down to my side. "I know, maybe I overreacted a little bit too."

Kylan kisses me on the forehead with his hands still on the sides of my face. "You know I would never intentionally do anything to hurt you, Babe. You're my world, my everything. I love you."

"I'm still standing here, guys. I can hear you," Liz says. "Although very sweet, you're making me sick and also making me want to go talk to James about getting back together."

"Sorry, Liz," I bashfully say as I turn my head in her direction. "I think that would be a great idea for you to go talk to him. He's been pitiful since you two split. I'm pretty sure you broke his heart."

Liz nods, "Yeah, I think I will. I'll let you know what happens." Liz turns to walks away.

"In the meantime, Babe, let's go find Maria and Peyton. I'm dying to hear what Cass said to them"

CHAPTER 15

No way! I can't believe she said that to you! What was she thinking?"

"Oh, Kimmy, I was mortified! I'm just glad no one else heard her saying all that to us. I actually think she made sure no one overheard our conversation. Cass kept looking behind her to check. She seemed really nervous too. It was just so strange!" Maria explained. "But do you want to know what I said back to her?"

I nod my head. "Uh, yeah!"

"Well, I told her it was none of her damn business what Peyton and I do or where we do it at. And as far as she is concerned," Maria pointed her finger at my chest, "she can go piss off!"

I put my hand over my mouth. "Oh no you didn't?"

"Oh yes I did! But I didn't say piss...I used the "F" word!"

I am in complete shock right now! Maria never talks like that, but since she has been dating Peyton, her language has gotten atrocious! I remember when I first met Maria, she wouldn't even say the word butt because her mom said it was a bad word. She called it your bottom! Haha! I finally got her to say butt several years later.

"Well then!" I raise my eyebrows. "Do you think that's the last of Cass?"

Maria shrugs her shoulders. "I don't know, but I've decided to start lifting weights with Peyton over at his house just in case."

Puzzled I ask, "Why would you want to lift weights?"

"To build up my muscles, silly!" Maria laughs. "In case I ever needed to defend myself against Cass and her posse."

"I don't think you have anything to worry about. She's just trying to be a bossy senior and tell us what to do. It's like she's on some kind of power trip or something. I'm sure she'll get over it."

"So what else is going on?" Maria asks as if she is trying to change the subject.

"I don't know. I just can't stop thinking about the stupid suitcase in that little cabin."

"Kimmy, why are you so hung up on it? I told you it probably belongs to some homeless person. You need to stop thinking about that and start planning our trip to Gulfport with your Nanny next week to do school shopping. My mom told me she would give me some extra spending money to buy whatever I wanted. I can't stop thinking about all the stores I want to go to. I want to make a fashion statement when we go back to school. You know, kind of like how Ashley was always dressed to the nines? I want to be like that next school year."

Maria is certainly right. Ashley was always dressed to impress. Even if she just had on an old pair of pajamas, Ashley always looked beautiful. I think about her often. I try not to, because Maria said it was time to move on with our lives, but I just can't help it. She was such a kind soul to everyone. I can't believe that someone would ever try to hurt her let alone murder her. I hate R.L. more than anything on this earth. I HATE, HATE, HATE him! He took away so much from this world. Ashley was destined to do great things in her life and just like that, her life was tragically ended.

"OMG, you're wearing that?" I screeched to Maria. "Peyton is going to die!" As Maria spins around in her crushed red velvet strapless dress, I realize how much she really does look like Ashley.

"What do you think?" Maria says as she prances up to the only mirror in the entire bunkhouse.

"Gorgeous, just gorgeous, Sis! But can I make a suggestion?" I ask.

"Sure."

"You probably don't want to be spinning around like that tonight at the dance unless you want everybody to see your polka dotted panties," I giggle.

"Oopsie! I forgot I had them on. How about these?" Maria bends down and digs around in her bag. She holds up something black, lacy, and very delicate looking. I'm pretty sure I even see a sparkling rhinestone or two.

"What is that? It looks expensive whatever it is."

"Oh, these little things?" Maria spins the garment around on her finger. "These are some panties that I'm pretty sure Jason bought Ashley before she died. I found them when I was cleaning out her drawers. They still had the tags on them, so I know she never wore them. I took them and hid them in my stuff so my mom wouldn't find them. She would have been embarrassed that her daughter had something so scandalous in her underwear drawer and thrown them away. I've been waiting for the right moment to wear them for Peyton. I think tonight's the night. We have some plans for after the dance."

I stand there and stare at Maria. "Sis, no, please don't."

"Nah, we're not going to have sex. Don't worry. I just want to tease him a little."

I take a deep breath. "Maria, please don't press your luck. You know Cass is going to be watching your every move tonight. I don't want you to get in trouble. It's not worth it. Peyton can wait until we get back home. I know y'all have been sneaking around all summer. Heck, even Nanny knows you've been lying to your mom about being at my house but really you've been going out with Peyton."

"How on earth would your Nanny know?" Maria scoffs.

"She and Chas have seen you in his car riding through town. I made Nanny promise me she wouldn't tell my mom, or she would probably make you move back to your parents' house."

Maria rolls her eyes and puts her hand on her forehead. "Geez, a girl can't do anything in this small town without getting told on. I wish we lived in New Orleans. That place is so big I get lost just thinking about it. Nobody would know my business or care what I was doing. When we grow up, you want to move to NOLA?"

"Um, I don't know what I want to do when I grow up, Maria. New Orleans is not very safe for young women, or anybody for that matter. Don't you watch the news? Every morning when I'm getting ready for school I hear about a murder down there."

"It's not that bad, Kimmy. My parents were going to let Ashley go to Loyola. You know how strict they are."

Why did she have to say her name? Every time I think about her, my heart sinks and I start playing back all the events that have happened over the past year.

"Well, she didn't go, Maria! Maybe there's a reason why she died. Maybe something even worse was going to happen to her in New Orleans. You always tell me that God works in mysterious ways."

Maria immediately stops brushing her eyelashes with her mascara wand, shoves the wand in the tube, and stomps over to me.

"I cannot believe you just said that! Sometimes I just want to hit you, Kimmy! And right now is one of those times! I can't deal with you! Go on! Get out of my face!" Maria swats at me like I'm an annoying fly.

What just happened? I feel my eyes burning as the tears start streaming down my cheeks. Why is my best friend treating me like I'm dumb. I just worry so much. I'm afraid of losing her too.

I take a couple of steps backward and ease down on the edge of my bed. I drop my head into my hands and let it all out. The sobs are now uncontrollable. I want to scream but I know better. I don't want my friends or the other girls to hear me. My feelings are hurt, and Maria doesn't care. Maybe the real reason the osprey flies alone is because all the other birds are mean to it and it's tired of getting its feelings hurt all the time.

As Maria storms out of the room, I look up to see Liz standing over me. The tears have blurred my vision.

"You ok, Kimmy?" Liz says as she hands me a tissue. "Here, friend, let's get straightened up and ready for the dance."

I shake my head. "I'm not really in the mood for dancing anymore."

"What just happened? I could tell Maria was really mad."

I drop my head back into my hands and mumble out, "I don't even know anymore, Liz. She has changed so much here lately. I feel like I don't even know her."

"What do you mean by that?" Liz asks as she is gently patting my back.

I think hard about what I'm going to say. Liz is my friend, but she's not my best friend like Maria. I don't want to say anything ugly about Maria, but in the same instance, I am so tired of Maria deliberately hurting my feelings.

"I don't really know how to say this nicely." I look up at Liz and feel my bottom lip quivering. "Maria has changed since she's been dating Peyton. I don't think he's good for her. I know he's Kylan's best friend, but I think he's trying to pressure her into doing things she doesn't want to do. In turn, she's taking a lot of her frustration out on me because I'm not as smart or as pretty as her."

As I drop my head back down, Liz squats in front of me and lifts my chin with her hand. "Kimmy, you and Maria have gone through a lot this past year. I don't even know half of it or probably even a fourth of it, but I've seen changes in both of you. Some good and some bad. I know how close y'all are as friends, but sometimes, friends need some space between them. This might be one of those times. And let me tell you, that is totally fine!"

Liz and I sit in silence as I try to process what just happened. "I just don't want her to get hurt. I feel I'm always trying to protect her and keep her out of harm's way, but somehow, she always finds it. Just like this whole thing with Cass."

"Can I tell you something?" I shake my head yes. "You know my mom died when I was a baby. I never got to know her."

"I know, Liz, I'm so sorry."

Liz shakes her head. "No, Kimmy, don't be sorry. You didn't do anything wrong."

"Ok, yes, you're right, I didn't," I say.

"And just like you, I'm an only child. My dad and grandma have raised me, and it has not been easy on any of us." Liz sits down beside me on the bed. "Abbey and I met when we were in kindergarten and have been best friends ever since. I'm not really sure I would have made it this far in life without her by my side." Liz pauses and swallows hard. "Dad pretty much let's Grandma handle all the girly things. My grandma is very wise and open with me about life. I know I probably shouldn't, but I tell my grandma everything. I even told her about what Abbey and her boyfriend are doing. Just recently, my grandma gave me some advice when I wasn't sure how to handle something with Abbey." Liz takes a deep breath. "I cannot control what Abbey does or says. I can only control how I treat her and react to her situations. Grandma told me that I don't have to agree or support her way of life, but I do have to be a good friend and support her. I think this probably rings true to you and Maria as well. She might want to do things with Peyton that you don't approve of, but let me just tell you, there's not a dadgum thing you can do about it."

Liz's words sting. "I just worry so much about Maria."

"And that's ok, Kimmy. But it's not ok to say hurtful things to your best friend just because you don't want them doing something you can't control. Believe me, I've done it too. But what I always do next is apologize. Life is too short to be walking around mad all the time. And I can guarantee you that Maria is feeling the same way right now."

I decide it's time to put on my positive pants. "You know what? I'm going to do better with that. You're right, life is short." Liz leans over and embraces me in a hug. "Thank you, Liz. I'm so lucky to have such wonderful friends like you."

"All right, girl, you good?"

"Never been better!" I say with a little spunk in my voice.

"Come on now. Let's get ready. We have a dance to get to!"

CHAPTER 16

Why do old people always try and dance like the young people at these things?" Liz yells over the music as we all sit back and watch Mr. Mayberry and Mrs. Sheila dance to some weird '80s song. I just shrug my shoulders as I don't even feel like being here right now.

I apologized to Maria as soon as I saw her at the dance, but she just gave me the cold shoulder. I don't know what is going on with her. Maybe when this whole band camp thing is over, Maria needs to move back home. I can't handle all this drama!

I stare off into the distance not really looking at anything. Kylan grabs my hand and kisses it.

"Let's go dance, Babe."

I shake my head. "I'm not really in the mood. I think I might be depressed."

"Babe, you're not depressed. If you're still upset about that whole Maria thing from earlier, you need to move on. Seriously, look at her!" Kylan points to the dance floor where Maria and Peyton are slow dancing. They're so close I don't think you could even slide a piece of paper between them. "You're the last thing she is thinking about right now. Come on. Let's at least try and enjoy our last night at this hell hole."

I giggle. "Ok, I guess you're right. I need to stop dwelling on what Maria does. That's what Liz told me too."

I reluctantly follow Kylan out to the dance floor. A slow song from a '90s boy band plays over the sound system. Wow! The harmonies in this song are amazing! I don't think I've ever heard it before. As Kylan and I begin swaying to the music, my feet begin to feel lighter. It's kind of like I'm floating. Then I realize, I am floating! Kylan has completely lifted me off the ground with only his hands on my waist.

"Hey Babe," Kylan says as he has raised me to be completely eye level with him. "Have I told you how much I love you today?"

"Um, I don't know, have you?"

"Well, I love you more than anything in this world." Kylan presses his forehead to mine and I can feel his breath on my lips. "I'm not going to kiss you right now because I'm pretty sure Mrs. Sheila is staring a hole through me and is waiting to pounce as soon as I make a move. But, in just a few minutes, I'm going to slip out the door behind me for some fresh air. You stay seated with Liz. Give me a little time. Maybe check your phone and such. Then, when you're pretty sure no one is looking, I want you to slip out the door opposite over there. Ok?"

"Sure, I guess. Aren't you afraid we might get in trouble?"

"Not really. The adults don't do bunk checks on Thursday night. We learned that last year. I think they go have their own little party in the bedrooms off the main lodge if you know what I mean." I nod my head.

So, when the song ended and people were dispersing from the dance floor, Kylan made a beeline for the outside door, and I sat down with Liz. I told her our plan. I reassured her that everything was fine, and that she would need to join another group of people when I left so no one would notice she was sitting alone. She played along just fine.

I really like Liz. We've known each other since middle school but never really hung out. We were in homeroom together in seventh grade. Liz is very quiet and keeps to herself. She likes for people to think she's outgoing, but she's really not. Liz, however, was in the middle school band. That's where she learned to play the clarinet. She's really good at it too! She tried out for some kind of all-state thing last year in eighth grade and made alternate. Everybody said that was completely unheard of for a middle school kid to make all-state. And guess what? She ended up getting to go. She replaced some girl who had to have her wisdom teeth removed and couldn't participate. Liz said she plans on trying out for a scholarship to LSU in a couple of years. I'm sure she'll get one.

So, I studied the time on my phone. Kylan's been gone for a total of seven minutes. I figured that was enough time for me to make my move. I nudged Liz and we both stood up from the table. Since a lot of people had gotten back up to dance, we could easily maneuver through the crowd to carry out our plan. I watch Liz out of the corner of my eye as she goes over to a round table where her ex-boyfriend, James, is sitting. Maybe she's having second thoughts about him. Ok, my turn. I start to zig zag through all the sweaty bodies on the dance floor. The scent of body spray and musky armpits fills my nostrils. The smell is so strong I can barely refrain from plugging my nose with my fingers.

I turn the doorknob to leave the lodge and immediately realize the door is locked! What do I do now? Panic hits me like a ton of bricks. I feel my chest begin to tighten. I look around trying not to bring any attention to myself. I spot another door about twenty feet from where I'm standing. Should I try for it? Or just go sit back down and text Kylan? Just then, I feel my phone vibrate in my hand. I casually lean against the wall and bring my phone up to view.

Wrong door, Babe. Sorry, I forgot that one is broken. (9:30 PM)

So, what am I supposed to do now? (9:30 PM)

Brad is out here. He wants to see Liz. New plan... (9:32 PM)

What do you mean Brad wants to see Liz? She doesn't even know him and besides, she's over there talking to James right now. (9:33 PM)

I look like an idiot standing over here all alone right now. Come up with a new plan or I'm going to sit back down! (9:34 PM)

Ok, I'm sorry, I really am. Here's the new plan. Send Liz a text about Brad and tell her to go out the door I went out of. Ok? (9:36 PM)

Ok, that's fine and dandy, but what about me? I'm stuck against this brick wall over here. (9:36 PM)

See those ping pong tables over there? Go to that door behind them. It should work. I'll be waiting outside on the other side of it. (9:38 PM)

So about the same time I start walking toward the door behind the ping pong tables, the music stops and everybody goes to sit down. Great! Just great! I am standing here like a fool and now everyone will see me go out the door. So, I decide to change my plans and just go sit down next to Liz for a few.

"What's up, girlie? I thought you were sneaking out?" Liz says as I sit down beside her.

I roll my eyes. "Well, I was, but the stupid door was locked or broken or something. It was pretty much an epic fail." I drop my head into my hands. "Kylan is outside waiting for me and I'm so dumb I can't figure out how to get to him. Where's James?"

Liz lets out a long sigh. "He said he has already moved on. I guess I need to as well."

"I'm so glad you said that, because Kylan's friend Brad is outside waiting for you too! I think he's a pretty nice guy or Kylan wouldn't be friends with him."

"What? Why is he waiting for me? That's kind of weird, don't you think?"

"Liz, I don't really know what to think here lately. No, it's not weird, well, maybe a little," I say with uncertainty in my voice.

Liz and I determine that the safest time to escape through the outside doors is during a fast song when everybody is up on the dance floor whooping and hollering. And that's just what we do. As soon as the next song comes on, sure enough, it's a fast techno dance song.

I stand up, look around ever so unsuspiciously, and make my move. I shimmy through the same door Kylan went out and Liz is right behind me.

"Hey Babe! It's about time you made it." Kylan snatches me up and embraces me in a long overdue kiss.

"Dude, enough of that! Let's get out of this lame-ass place!" Brad says as he shoves Kylan off of me. "Aren't you going to introduce us?"

Kylan looks over at Liz. "Oh, of course. Brad this is Liz. Liz this is my dear friend Brad." Kylan winks. "He's a good one!" Kylan pats Brad on the back a couple of times with the last pat being more like a slap. I wonder what that was all about. Kylan grabs my hand and I follow him.

As soon as we are out of view from the main lodge, I begin to see all these amazing lightning bugs flicker before my eyes. We have lightning bugs in BSL, but not like they do here. I guess they live in all these big bushy trees. We mostly have palm trees and giant oaks back home.

"Are y'all seeing what I'm seeing?" I ask the group.

"The fireflies?" Liz asks.

"Yep, but I call them lightning bugs!" I grin at Liz as I know what her next words will be. We had this whole firefly versus lightning bug debate in middle school. Neither of us won the debate, we just agreed to disagree.

Liz pipes up, "Well, the proper terminology for those little glowing things is fireflies if you're from up North." Liz looks over at Brad. "In case you didn't know, I was born in upstate New York. We moved down here when I was little to be closer to my dad's best friend, Jack, who lives over in Long Beach."

"Yeah, well if you're from the south, they're called lightning bugs," I remind Liz. "But whatever you want to call them, they sure are beautiful! It looks like they are in harmony with each other. I've never seen them do that before." I gaze out in the distance through the thick forest and am completely mesmerized. It looks exactly like those rich people's houses at Christmas time when they have their Christmas lights synchronized to music.

"Where are we going?" I ask Kylan. I can tell he doesn't want me to know quite yet by the way he hesitates.

"Shh...I don't want to say it out loud in case someone is listening," Kylan whispers.

I give him a strange look, but he can't see me due to the darkness of the night and the forest canopy shading us from the moon.

"No one is listening to us. That's silly. We are out in the middle of nowhere," I snicker.

Kylan squeezes my hand tighter. "Just follow me, Babe. I want you to see something."

CHAPTER 17

We finally arrive at our destination, and I am thrilled to be standing in front of the old little Love Shack.

"Kylan, this is so sweet of you to bring me back here, but we have company with us."

I can feel Kylan shaking his head back and forth.

"No, Babe. That's not why I brought you here, unfortunately. Although, if that's what you had in mind..."

I give Kylan a love smack on his shoulder as he rings me in for another kiss.

He whispers in my ear, "I can't wait to get some alone time with you, Kimmy." I can feel his breath on my neck as he kisses behind my ear down to my shoulder. "Ok, I better stop before I get all riled up."

I push my hair back behind my ears and look over at Liz and Brad, who are just standing there staring at us. A moon shadow is cast across Liz's face and all I can see are her crystal blue eyes. I wish Brad could see her eyes like this. They're gorgeous! I'm certain if he saw them right now, he would fall madly in love with her. If that's what Liz wants, of course.

"The percussion section came out here this morning to do one last deafening rehearsal before the real deal tomorrow. We were all standing around in our drum circle just like we always do when I noticed the door to the cabin was propped open. I thought to myself, oh crap, we must've accidentally left it open the other morning when we fled from here. So, like the responsible human being I am, I went over to close it and was unable to." Kylan pauses. "That's when I looked down and saw this rock that had been placed here to deliberately prop it open. I'm not sure why someone would prop it open because you can't lock the door unless you're inside." Kylan leans down, picks up a rock about the size of a baseball, and shows it to us.

"Ok, and?" I question.

"So, I decided to go in and make sure everything was in order. That's when I saw the strangest thing." Kylan opens the door to the cabin, grabs the lighter off the table, and flicks it on. "Look!" Kylan points to the corner where the suitcase was. "It's gone!"

I gasp, "OMG! What happened to it?

Kylan physically moves my body to face the opposite corner of the cabin.

"There!" he points. And to my unbelieving eyes, there stood the suitcase.

I take a deep breath. "Someone has been in here."

"Ding, ding, ding...you're correct!" Kylan acts like he's ringing a bell.

"But who? And why would they be messing with that old suitcase?" I hesitantly walk over to the suitcase. "Should I?"

"Here, let's do it together." Kylan grabs my hand and moves me away from it. "Let's lay it down on the floor and open it. That way, if something falls out it won't tumble down on us."

Kylan maneuvers the suitcase onto its back. This thing is a lot bigger than I thought. He squats down on the floor. I decide to stand just in case a snake or spiders come running out I can quickly get away. As Kylan reaches for the zipper, I feel chills go down my spine. I shiver.

Kylan stops and looks up at me. "You ok, Babe?" I nod and look back at Liz and Brad who are snuggled up next to each other on the couch. Well that was quick. When Kylan gets the zipper completely undone, he stops. "You ready for this? I don't feel any movement, so I don't think whatever's in here is alive."

Kylan steadily raises the suitcase lid and flops it back to where it is resting against the wall. He moves the lighter closer to the contents to reveal nothing but clothes, women's clothes.

"Do you smell that?" Kylan asks. "Come down here."

I lean down and hunker next to Kylan. That's when the most familiar scent hit me smack in the face.

"Kylan, I know that perfume! But I'm not sure whose it is. I have smelled it a thousand times, though. Liz, come here! Smell this and tell me how I know it."

Liz walks over with Brad closely behind holding hands. She bends down and takes several big sniffs. Then she leans back on her heels and tilts her head sideways. "That's the same perfume of my dad's ex-girlfriend. It's very expensive! My dad bought it for her for Christmas one year and she practically bathed it in when she came to my house."

I look over at Liz even more confused than before. "But, I never met your dad's ex-girlfriend. So, I wouldn't have smelled it on her."

"True," Liz replies. "She and Dad broke up a couple of years ago and I haven't seen her since. Actually, Dad hasn't seen her either. Could this be her suitcase?"

"The odds are not in your favor, Liz. It's highly unlikely this suitcase belongs to anyone we know. I mean, how many people do you know come up here to this exact location and just randomly leave their suitcase in an abandoned cabin?" We look at each other and Kylan shrugs his shoulders. "Not many, right?"

"None, actually," I say. "Should we look through the clothes?"

"Um," Kylan hesitates. "Sure, but let's be super careful not to mess them up. Obviously, this case is here for a reason, and we don't want anyone to know it's been snooped through."

All four of us are now gathered around the large black suitcase. Our eyes are focused on Kylan gently removing each garment and placing them one by one on the floor being careful not to unfold anything. He held up each article of clothing to see if we recognized it. We would shake our heads, and he would move on to the next.

"That stuff looks like something my big sister would wear. You know she's in college now and dancing at those nightclubs to make money to pay her rent," Brad comments.

"What do you mean by that?" Kylan asks.

Bashfully, Brad responds, "You know, Kylan. I don't want to say it in front of these two young ladies, but those places men go to watch pretty girls dance up on a stage with very little clothes on."

"Gotcha, man. I had no idea Bec was doing that," Kylan laughs. "Well, I'm sure she makes good money. I always thought she was pretty but way too old for me. How old is she now?"

"Twenty-four, I think," Brad says.

"Anyway, let's take some pictures of this stuff before we put it back in?" I suggest.

"That's a great idea, Babe!" Kylan winks. "I knew I brought you along for a reason."

When we finally get to the bottom of the case, we think we have gone through everything when we see a folded-up piece of paper in the very bottom. "What's that?" I point to the paper.

"Um, I don't know. Let's see." Kylan grabs the paper and starts to open it. As he unfolds it, the smell of perfume starts getting stronger like it has been sprayed on the paper.

"It's a map...of this place. Why would someone need a map of here?"

"Why would anyone want a map of here?" I question.

Brad suddenly stands up and declares, "Man, I don't have a good feeling about this. Let's take some pictures and get the hell out of here!" I can sense fear in his voice.

So, we packed everything back in after we took several pictures with my phone. Kylan zipped it back up and placed it in the exact location where we found it.

"Ok, y'all ready?" Kylan asks.

As we ease out of the cabin, I take one last glance around to make sure nothing looks disturbed. Kylan places the lighter where he found it, and we head back to camp.

We sneak into the main lodge where the dance is still going on. It's nearly eleven o'clock! I can't believe Mr. Mayberry and Mrs. Sheila are still up!

We decide to go outside and sit on the rock wall to plot our next move. I attempt to jump up on the wall, but I fail. "Guess I'm tired," I tell Kylan.

"Here Babe, let me give you a boost!"

I jump up again and this time I feel Kylan's hand on my rear lifting me up. I want to smack him, but I know he was just trying to help. I am so fortunate to have Kylan in my life. I would be completely lost without him.

"So, what's on the agenda for the rest of the evening?" Brad asks as he grabs Liz up to sit on his lap. Whew, wee!

So much for the getting to know you phase. I guess she's totally over James now!

We come to the consensus that doing what we're doing at this moment is just fine for all of us. We made a pact to tell no one about the suitcase and what was in it. I am still trying to process the whole thing. And what makes my processing even harder is that I still cannot figure out how I know that perfume smell that came bursting out of it. When I get home, I'm going through all of my scents to see if I can pin it down. Until then, I'll just have to rack my brain.

Liz elbows me in the ribs. "Hey isn't that Maria and Cass coming out of the lodge together?"

I have a hard time making out the shadowy figures in the night, but sure enough, I recognize their voices. They are both laughing and carrying on like two long lost best friends.

"Yeah, that's them all right, and they're coming this way," I reply.

For some bizarre reason, my heart starts beating faster and faster the closer they get to us. I'm afraid Maria is going to tell me she hates me and doesn't want to be friends anymore. That would be devastating! But it would get her out of my house. No, that's not what I want to happen. I just have to remember my conversation with Liz. Maria is her own person, and I cannot control what she does or how she acts. This is one of those times I wish I had a TV remote, and I could push pause on everything for a few seconds to consider all the possibilities.

"Hey guys! How's it going?" Maria says as she bounces over and puts both her hands on my knees. "Cass and I got to talking at the dance and realized we have a lot in common! Isn't that cool? She wants to hang with us for a while."

Nobody speaks, but I'm pretty sure I know what we're all thinking. So I change the subject as I see who I think is Peyton slinking out of the lodge. He's got his hand up to his forehead like he's shielding the sun from his face, but it's nighttime.

"How was the dance? Is it over yet?" I ask Maria. Before I let her answer I point to the lodge. "Is that Peyton over there? What's he doing?"

"He's probably looking for us," Maria responds. "He's kind of getting on my nerves tonight. All he wanted to do was dance to the slow songs and try to slip his tongue down my throat. Blak! Sometimes he grosses me out! Right Sis?" Maria looks over at Cass.

Sis? She's calling Cass Sis now? What the hell is going on here? My eyes are nearly bulging out of my head. How dare she refer to Cass as her Sis! That's what we call each other. I turn to look at Kylan and his mouth is wide open like he's trying to say something but no words are coming out.

Maria and Cass begin to giggle about something, and I push Kylan's jaw back up to his face as I'm afraid it might fall off. About that time, Peyton finally makes his way over to us.

"Hey there beautiful ladies!" Peyton greets us as he pretends to put crowns on each of the girls' heads, even mine and Liz's.

Cass does a curtsy to Peyton and says, "Well there's my bestie's sexy boyfriend! Where've you been all my life?" Peyton drops his head in embarrassment. "So, how about we all go hang out in my apartment for a while? We can listen to some halfway decent music, turn the lights down low, and play spin the bottle. As long as you're with me, you won't get in trouble.'"

Peyton quickly responds, "Sounds fantastic! Let's go y'all!"

"Yeah, that sounds like fun, Sis! I'm in!" cheers Maria.

I look over at Liz and Brad. I don't think they heard a word that was said. Brad is kissing Liz on the neck and whispering something into her ear. One part of me wants to go just to see what happens. The other part of me says no way! I don't want to get caught up in that mess. I'm content to spend the rest of my night right here beside MY sexy boyfriend. By the way, Kylan is still way hotter than Peyton!

CHAPTER 18

O h Kimmy! We had the most fun last night! I'm dying to tell you all about it!" Maria exclaims with excitement in her voice.

I roll over and check the time on my phone: five forty-five in the AM. "Come on, Maria. Give me fifteen more minutes, please. I didn't get much sleep last night. You want to know why, Maria? Then I'll tell you why. Because I was waiting up for you all night hoping you were safe."

"Well, neither did I!" Maria huffs as she rolls back over.

I know I won't be going back to sleep, but I'm going to lie as still as I can. The longer it takes for me to "wake up" the less time Maria will have to gush about her night. I tossed and turned all night just trying to figure out why on earth she would call Cass Sis. Just earlier in the day, Maria hated her and now they're besties. I just don't understand!

Buzz, Buzz...Buzz, Buzz...

I hear my phone vibrating, but I cannot open my eyes to look at it. I'm so tired. "Just five more minutes, please," I say to whoever is calling me.

Buzz, Buzz...Buzz, Buzz...

I grab my phone off the charger and see it's Kylan calling. "Hello?"

"Babe, are you up?"

I rub my eyes and yawn. "Well, I am now. What's up?"

Kylan hesitates, "Peyton never came back to the bunkhouse last night. Did Maria?"

"Yeah, she's here right now, but I don't know what time she got here," I reply trying to remember if I woke up when she got back. No, I don't think I did.

Kylan let's out a long sigh. "Kimmy, what did they do last night?"

"I have no idea. Maria woke me up a few minutes ago trying to tell me about all the fun they had last night, but I refused to listen and went back to sleep until just now when you called me."

"Well, get ready and meet me at the main lodge. See what you can get out of Maria while you're getting ready. I'll see you in a few. Love you." Kylan hastily hangs up the phone.

I look down at my phone and see a blank screen. "Well, I love you too," I say puzzled.

I figure I might as well get up and get myself ready so I can help Kylan figure out where Peyton is. I look over at Maria who has fallen back asleep. I decide to let her sleep a little bit longer while I wash my face and brush my teeth. I guess I'll shower later since I took one before bed last night.

As I'm getting my bathroom bag out of my suitcase, I notice Maria's phone is plugged into the charger and sitting on the floor next to her bed. I am tempted to take a peek at it and see if Peyton has called or texted her. I kneel down and crawl on my hands and knees across the cool damp floor. I see her hand twitching, but I'm pretty sure she's asleep. I raise up to see her eyes still closed. As I crouch back down to the floor, I put my hand out to grab her phone. I touch the screen and see that she has no missed calls or texts.

"What are you doing, Kimmy!"

"AH!" I scream! "You just scared the crap out of me!" OMG my heart is pounding in my throat. My eyes are darting all around the room.

"What are you doing with my phone?" Maria snaps.

"Um, um, um..." Oh no I've totally screwed up now. How do I get myself out of this one. Maria and I made a pact when she got her new smartphone to never go through each other's devices no matter what. I have officially broken our pact. But then, it comes to me. "I was just checking the time on your phone to see if I need to wake you up."

Maria yawns and stretches her arms up in the air. She grabs a hold of the springs from the top bunk above her and pulls herself up.

"Oh, ok. Where's your phone?" she asks.

Without hesitation I say, "It's on my bed. I was just over here getting ready and didn't want to walk all the way around just to check the time."

"You're fine, Sis. I am just so tired. I guess I should get ready too."

She bought it! She totally bought my lie. Ok, now I have to think how to ask her about last night without being suspicious.

Maria puts her feet on the floor then grabs her head. "Ow, it's killing me!" she moans.

"What is killing you?" I ask.

Maria lets out a loud groan. "My head. I think I had too much fun last night."

Ok, here's my chance to ask. "Oh yeah, about last night. I'm ready to hear all about it!"

Maria stands up and holds her hands over her eyes. "I'm tired now. I was trying to tell you about it earlier, but you didn't want to hear what I had to say," Maria huffs. "Can you turn off these lights? It's dark outside and these lights are blinding me."

I do as she asks trying to figure out why she doesn't want to talk about her night now. Just twenty minutes ago, she was gung-ho on divulging all the details. And now, nothing. Plus, what's with this massive headache all of a sudden?

"Are you ok?" I ask.

Maria mumbles something as she shakes her hair out of the ponytail. Just then, I saw a glimpse of Ashley. Her long, black, silky locks flying through the air almost as smooth as a jet. Just as Maria is shaking out her hair, I catch a whiff of what smells like cigarette smoke.

"Maria, what's that smell?"

She shrugs her shoulders. "What smell are you talking about?"

I stand still and look around the room thinking maybe it was just my imagination. I begin to walk towards her, and she starts stepping backward.

"Why are you acting strange, Kimmy? There are no smells in here except for your minty toothpaste."

That's when I realize, it's Maria who smells like cigarettes, but Maria doesn't smoke!

"Why do you smell like cigarettes?" I question Maria.

Maria quickly starts putting her hair back into a ponytail. "I don't smell like cigarettes!" she snarls at me. "Maybe that's you, Kimmy! Maybe you've been hanging out with Liz too much. You know her dad smokes like a freight train, and I'm sure Liz does too."

What is she talking about? Liz doesn't smoke and if she does, she wouldn't dare do it around me! I am sensing some jealously right now or Maria trying to cover something up. So, I decide to drop the subject and just go about my business, but I'm ninety-nine percent certain that Maria smells like smoke. I'll just leave it at that.

As we walk up to the main lodge, I get the feeling that something is going on. You know, just that eerie sense that something is wrong, but I don't know what.

I go ahead of Maria into the lodge. She's right behind me though. I spot Kylan talking to Brad and a few other guys. He sees me at the exact same time and starts walking in my direction. Maria strays off to talk to some girls from her clarinet section.

As Kylan gets closer, I can see the look on his face. It's not good. He leans in and gives me a peck on my forehead.

"Good morning, Babe. I'm so glad to see you." Kylan takes my hand and leads me toward the outside door. "Let's take a walk."

We get to the rock wall and Kylan stops. "Ok, don't act like anything is up. I'm going to tell you something, but I don't want you to react. Ok?"

"Ok," I meekly reply. I look up at Kylan with uncertainty about what he is about to say. I know he's not breaking up with me. We're in love and we both know it.

"Peyton never showed up. I have called and texted him a thousand times but can't get a response. His phone goes directly to his stupid voicemail with a goat making a screeching baa and Peyton screaming for it to get off his back. It's so strange. I don't know why he would want something like that on his voicemail." Kylan looks down at me. "Anyway, I have no idea where he is or if I should even be looking for him."

I remember what Kylan just told me about not reacting. So, I take a deep breath in order to keep my face straight. "Maria smelled like cigarettes this morning, but she denied it. Oh! And I checked her phone, nothing from Peyton on there. Then, when I tried to ask her about last night, she pretty much said she wasn't in the mood to talk about it and claimed she had a headache."

Kylan looks away and pinches the bridge of his nose with his thumb and forefinger. "We need to figure out what they all did last night and why Peyton never showed up. The cigarette smell is very suspicious. Why would Maria smell that way and lie to you about it?"

With a straight face I say, "Maria and I are not on the same page about things anymore. We have drifted apart this summer. She's spent so much time with Peyton and babysitting her siblings that we rarely even hang out. I was actually going to talk to my mom when we get back from camp and see about Maria moving back to her house. She's just not the same person she used to be."

Kylan puts his arm around my shoulder and gives me a side hug. "It's ok, Babe. I promise. Maria will come around. She is just trying to live like a teenager and figure things out for herself. You've got me and I'm not going anywhere."

I remember what Liz told me last night and nod my head. "I know. It just hurts sometimes."

Kylan squeezes me a little tighter and kisses the top of my head. "But for now, we have to figure out where the hell Peyton is and why he's not up here."

As we walk back toward the main lodge, Kylan and I don't speak. Then, out of the corner of my eye, I see someone walking toward us. They are coming from the path that leads to the little cabin or the Love Shack as Kylan calls it. At this point, I'm afraid to look in that direction as I don't know if I want to see who it is. So, I nudge Kylan with my elbow.

"Who is that coming from the cabin?" I ask Kylan without even turning in that direction.

Kylan jerks his head around and immediately stops. "WTF? It's Peyton!"

We both stand there motionless and in complete awe waiting for Peyton to reach us. As he is walking up to us on the sidewalk, I instantly smell cigarette smoke. Now I know why Maria smelled that way. I've always been a little suspicious about Peyton. He's just not the same type of person that Kylan is. Peyton is what my Nanny would call a sneaky snake.

"Dude! WTF?" Kylan says to Peyton as he puts his hand out for their weird bro handshake. "Man, you reek of cigarette smoke. Where've you been all night?"

Peyton drops his head and stares down at his feet shaking his head. "You don't want to know. I'm going to be in big trouble."

Just then, I spot Cass walking down the path that Peyton just came from. Well, I wouldn't say she's walking. Actually, she's sprinting toward our bunkhouse only wearing a long white t-shirt, no shoes, and definitely no bra if you know what I mean.

Kylan looks up and sees what I'm seeing. "Oh, I understand now. Peyton, I wouldn't say you're in trouble." Peyton looks up at Kylan then turns his head just in time to see Cass round the corner and disappear behind the bunkhouse. "I'd say you're dead!"

"It's not what it looks like, guys." Peyton tries to convince us. "Well, maybe it is." Peyton pauses as his face turns ten shades of red. "Kimmy, please don't tell Maria. Let me do that myself," he pleads.

My heart sinks just thinking about how Maria is going to react to Peyton's news. This will be devastating for her. She has spent so much of her past year with him. How will she survive without him in her life? Well, I guess it's not really my business, but what the hell was Peyton thinking, though? Cass? Of all the girls here at band camp, he had to choose her to cheat on Maria with.

"Can y'all walk in front of me? I just don't think I can face Maria right now," Peyton says as he pushes us ahead of him.

Kylan and I walk through the doorway to the main lodge hand in hand. Maria spots us as soon as we enter the room. Peyton is slinking slowly behind us. Here comes Maria. Geez...this should be interesting.

CHAPTER 19

*S*MACK!

Yep, that's the sound I heard when I saw Maria's hand fly through the air and come across Peyton's face. I'm pretty sure everything happened in slow motion. At least that's how I saw it. No words were said, just one huge slap. Then, Maria took off running out the lodge.

I'm not really sure what Peyton said to Maria for her to haul off and hit him like that, because Kylan and I were talking to Liz and Brad about what we saw coming out of the woods this morning. Whatever it was, it obviously pissed Maria off.

Peyton lacks what I call tact. He tends to speak without thinking and just says whatever comes out of his mouth. I have often wondered if he has some kind of disability like mine, except for Peyton just doesn't care. I still can't believe what he did with Cass last night. If Maria hadn't been so rude to me yesterday, I would feel a little more sorry for her. Nanny always says, "You get what you deserve." I'm not so sure Maria deserved this happening to her, but maybe this will be a wake up call to her, and she'll see who her true friends are.

Like the true friend I am, I went running after Maria. She took off so fast toward the bunkhouse, I couldn't keep up with her.

"Hey! Slow down! Let's talk!" I yell as I can feel my heartbeat speeding up.

Maria looks back at me and just keeps running. I stop briefly when she is out of my sight. I lean down and put my hands on my knees to catch my breath. I look up at the sky as my chest quickly rises and falls. This would be a wonderful time to see my pelicans, but all I can see is trees and a little bit of the blue sky. Then, suddenly, I see a huge bird overhead circling the campground. It's not a pelican, but as I look closer, I can see a fish in its talons. That's interesting. I guess it just went fishing in the lake.

"Babe, you ok?" Kylan asks as he puts his hand on my back.

I point to the sky. "Look! Check out the beautiful bird!" I exclaim. "It has a fish!"

Kylan looks up and spots the bird immediately. "Yeah, Babe, that's an osprey. I'm sure it has a nest around here. They like to live near bodies of water. That's why we see so many in BSL. They catch fish in the ocean and rivers then take it back to their babies."

Of course, it's an osprey. The lone osprey. I think to myself.

"Did you talk to her?" Kylan asks.

"No, I lost her. I yelled, she turned around and looked but kept on going."

"Give her a few minutes," Kylan suggests. "I'm sure she's down in the bunkhouse crying her eyes out plotting revenge on Peyton."

I grab Kylan's hand. "Please don't ever do that to me. You know, what Peyton did to Maria. If you ever decide you don't want to be my boyfriend anymore, please tell me before you go and do something stupid and hurtful. Ok?"

"You have nothing to worry about here." Kylan puts his hands on my waist and turns me toward him. "Ok?" I nod my head, and he gives me a gentle kiss on the lips. "Now, go see how your girl is doing. I'm afraid this is going to be quite ugly."

As I walk past the first bunkhouse, I can feel the dread in my stomach start to build. You know the feeling you get when the dentist walks into the room to explain what he found on your x-rays? Yeah, I know that feeling all too well as I have had several cavities in my life and that is the sensation I'm having right now.

I get closer to our bunkhouse, and I can hear the wailing from outside. I grab a hold of the doorknob but stop to gather my thoughts. I take a few deep breaths and try to think about how I would feel if Kylan did this to me. I'm having a hard time processing how Maria must feel right now. I'm not sure if it's because my mind works a little differently or because deep down inside, I'm still mad at how she treated me yesterday.

As I open the door, I smell something strange. It kind of smells like a wet dog. No, wait, a wet duck? How would I even know what a wet duck smells like? Whatever it is, it stinks!

As I turn the corner to where our beds are, at first glance, I see what appears to be snow. But I know it's not snowing in our bunkhouse. It's stifling in here and it's mid-July. I squat down to the floor and pick up the white confetti looking stuff. I closely examine it. Blak! It stinks and it is definitely not snow! I think it might be stuffing from a plush animal.

I can hear Maria sobbing, but her cry sounds muffled. I tip-toe around to where our beds are to see the mass destruction. Feathers are flying through the air like a million tiny moths just emerging from their cocoons in the early days of spring. Piles of stuffing are scattered everywhere around the room. Poor little teddy bear has been ripped to shreds.

Then I spot Maria. "Are you ok?" I ask.

She raises up and slowly turns her head to face me. "ARE YOU KIDDING ME, KIMMY? ARE YOU REALLY ASKING IF I AM OK?" she yells with all her might.

I stand there in awe and disbelief. I just cannot wrap my head around what is going on right now. My best friend has treated me like dirt and now she is yelling at me for checking on her.

I can't do this anymore! I shouldn't have to do this anymore either. I turn to leave and hear Maria mumble something, but I can't make out what she is saying. So, I pause for a moment.

"Why, Kimmy? Why has he done this to me?" Maria utters as she continues to uncontrollably sob.

I stand there and just stare at her contemplating my next move. I feel like I have come to a crossroad in my life. I could stay and comfort her in her time of need, or I could leave and be done with her altogether. I think about the sleepless night I had last night worrying about what she was doing and if she was safe. Then I think about how rude and selfish she has been this whole entire summer.

Suddenly, it hits me! I have no control over anything Maria does or says. I can only control myself. At this very moment, I decide to take control over my own body and lead myself out the door. I am not wanted or needed here.

I make it halfway around the corner of the room when I feel someone grab me from behind and squeeze me so tight I feel like I might pop.

"I'M SO SORRY! I AM COMPLETELY HUMILIATED! I CAN'T GO ON WITH MY LIFE ANYMORE!" Maria sniffles and grabs me even tighter. "DON'T LEAVE, PLEASE, KIMMY, DON'T LEAVE!"

I take in a deep breath barely even able to let it out. I pry Maria's hands off me and turn to face her.

"Look at me! Look at me, Maria!" I insist. "Get a hold of yourself!"

Maria drops her shoulders and looks up at me the same way Oscar does when he knows he's done something really bad like eaten cat poop.

"I've been a terrible friend to you, and I know it," Maria softly says. "I just don't know what's been going on with me. I am so in love with Peyton and now look at what he's done! How will I ever get over this?"

"Come on, let's sit down." I put my arm around Maria's shoulders and walk her over to her bed. We ease down on the side of the bed together and sit in silence.

This is another one of those times when words cannot express what either of us are thinking or feeling. So we don't.

After a few minutes pass, I get Maria a clean washcloth to wipe off her face. Her streaks of mascara have stained her cheeks like a permanent marker.

"I'm not going to ask you what you did last night, because clearly it's none of my business. But I am going to ask you one thing," I pause. "Why have you been so hurtful to me here lately? Have I done something wrong to deserve this?"

Maria shakes her head. "I don't know, Kimmy. You and Kylan are so perfect for each other. I guess you could say I'm jealous about your relationship. Peyton and I never had what you guys do. He is always pressuring me to have sex with him and I keep telling him I'm waiting until marriage. One night, a few weeks ago, we were all alone at his house. He took off all his clothes and started taking mine off of me. We were both sitting there completely naked. We start kissing and all." Maria stops and begins crying again. "We were so into the moment. One thing led to another and right as it was getting ready to happen, Ashley popped into my head. She was yelling at me telling me that I was about to make the biggest mistake of my entire life. So, I abruptly halted what I was doing with Peyton, got dressed, and asked him to take me home. I was so disappointed with myself." Maria looks up to the ceiling. "But that wasn't the worst part, Kimmy." She takes a deep breath. "The worst part came when Peyton dropped me off at home and when I told him that I loved him, he never responded. He just put his car in drive and took off down the street with the passenger's door still open."

I put my hand over my mouth not knowing what to say. I just have so many thoughts running through my head right now. I've heard my mom say before that everything can look great from the outside, but you never know what goes on behind closed doors. I am in complete shock that Peyton would act like that.

"Why didn't you tell me this? I thought we didn't keep secrets?" I shyly ask.

Maria turns and looks me directly in the eye. "I was too embarrassed. I was afraid of what you would think about me. We made a pact and all," Maria lets out a huge sigh. "And I almost broke it."

"But you didn't break it, Maria. You overcame your intense desires and stood up for your beliefs. I'm just completely disgusted that he treated you like that, and you didn't break up with him."

Maria shook her head. "I was afraid to break up with Peyton."

"Why? After he did that to you?"

"I was afraid of being alone. You know, you have Kylan and y'all are happy with each other. I just was scared that if I did break up with him, I wouldn't have anybody." A tear falls from Maria's face.

"You know I'm always here for you no matter what." I turn and give Maria a hug. I can feel the heat coming off her face from where she's been crying so much penetrate through my shirt. "Come on, let's get this mess cleaned up and head out for the final rehearsal. We will be home soon."

"But I will have to see him and her."

"Just ignore them. That's what I'm going to do. I won't leave your side unless you want me to." Then a thought popped into my head. "Let's use a code word for when you're feeling anxious."

"Ok, but what?"

"How about Oscar? Because he makes everybody's day better!" I giggle.

Maria smiles. "You're funny, Kimmy. Let's go with it!"

CHAPTER 20

The final rehearsal was pretty uneventful. Maria kept her distance from Peyton, and Cass stayed miles away from all of us, thank goodness! I have so much anger towards both Peyton and Cass right now. It really hurts my heart to think how Maria must be feeling. If Kylan ever did something like that to me, I'm pretty sure I would just go ahead and kill him. Well, I probably wouldn't kill him literally, but I would make him wish he was dead.

My mom and dad along with both of Maria's parents came to the final rehearsal. The band was amazing! Everyone could tell that the students had worked really hard this week. I was even recognized at the end for being so helpful to Mrs. Sheila and the staff. Can you believe that? I really didn't do much, but Mrs. Sheila told me several times that I was doing a good job. Maybe she's not so bad after all.

So, Mom and Dad gave me the option to ride the bus home or ride home with them. All my friends were taking the bus, so I did the same. The ride back to our school was the quietest bus ride I've ever been on. Most everyone had their pillows propped up on the windows sound asleep, including me.

While I was sleeping, I had the strangest dream, though. It was about that stupid suitcase in the little "Love Shack." I dreamed that it belonged to R.L. and it was some kind of weird setup he had going on before he got arrested for killing Ashley. I just don't know. I got really bad vibes from that thing when we opened it. Kind of like it had some voodoo tied to it. I woke up in a slight panic but quickly realized it was only a dream, or was it?

Anyway, when we pulled into the school all the parents were yelling and screaming from the sidewalk like a bus of celebrities just pulled up. I groggily rubbed my eyes and nudged Kylan. He was completely out of it!

I looked across the aisle at Maria who was sitting by herself. She looked so sad and lonely. The black circles under her eyes have aged her at least ten years. When she saw me, she gave me a small wave and put her head back down.

"Come on, Sis. Let's get home. It's been a long week," I say to Maria as she doesn't even look up at me. I slide into her seat and put my arm around her shoulders. "You've got this! It's time to be strong and move on with life. Peyton was no good for you anyway."

Maria shakes her head. "I know you keep telling me that, but I love him. I really do, Kimmy. I just don't know what to do with myself. My whole world revolved around Peyton. I would sit for hours at a time and just wait for him to call." Maria looks up at me. Her eyes are as red as an overcooked hotdog. "I can't do this. I can't get off this bus and face my parents. I haven't told them yet. They're going to be just as devastated as I am. Then, it will be a big scene right here in front of everybody."

I grab Maria's clammy hand and squeeze it tightly. I can feel her negative energy flow into my body. I squint my eyes and look at her with sympathy and understanding knowing how Peyton has destroyed her heart. I'm worried about Maria. And what I mean by that is, I'm worried that she might go all crazy Latino on Peyton and Cass before this is all over with, especially if she has to see them every day in band class. Maria can get a temper. Trust me, I've seen it many times before.

"Don't tell your parents quite yet. Let's get our stuff unloaded from the bus and just act like nothing has happened," I say with a slight feeling of hopelessness.

"But look at me! My parents will know something is up just by the way my face looks right now," Maria exclaims.

"Just tell them you were asleep. They'll never know the difference."

"Ok, I guess that might work," Maria pauses and looks around the bus to make sure Peyton is nowhere near. "I'm going to hang out with my family for a while this evening, then I'll be over later. I have a lot to talk to them about."

I never thought I'd be so happy to see my house as I am now! I got chills just pulling into the driveway. As I walk up to my house, it hits me that my summer is almost over. In a way, I'm glad we only have a few days of summer break left before we go back to school. After the week we just had, I'm ready for a change of scenery. But on the flipside, I'm so mentally and physically exhausted I will probably just be sleeping this next week away.

Mom cracks open the front door, and I see a tiny, wet, black nose trying it's hardest to break free. "OSCAR! I've missed you so much!" Oscar bounds out of the door and leaps into my arms. A thousand slobbery Oscar kisses later, I finally am able to get into my living room. As I put Oscar down on the floor, he is still running circles around me and bouncing up on my legs trying to get me to pick him back up.

"Oscar, remember, I shouldn't even be picking you up! You're going to get me in trouble!"

Mom pats me on the shoulder. "He's missed his favorite girl." Mom turns me toward her and wraps me in a big bear hug. "I've missed you too, Sweet Pea. It just wasn't the same around here without you."

As I get older, I'm starting to realize how much I really do mean to my parents. Only four more years until I'm eighteen and on my own. What on earth will they do when I move out and go to college? College, it seems so far away, yet I have so much to do to get prepared for it, if I can even get into a college.

I open the door to my bedroom and finally feel at peace. I calmly look at my familiar surroundings. Then I notice something different. Maria's bed is not in here anymore! I throw my bag on the floor and sprint out of my bedroom.

"MOM!" I yell with all my might.

"What's wrong Honey? Did something happen?" Mom says breathlessly as she comes running down the hallway.

"Where's Maria's bed? It's gone!" I say in a panic.

Mom looks at me like I'm crazy. "Kimmy, don't you remember texting me last night?"

I tilt my head to the side and try to focus on what she's saying. "No, I don't."

"Oh Honey, you must be tired. Maybe you need to go lie down and get some rest." Mom pulls me in for a hug, but I don't have the strength to hug her back, so she grabs me by the shoulders and eases me out of the hug. "Are you all right?" she asks.

"I thought I was. Where's her bed? And why isn't it in my room anymore?" I ask once again trying my best to rack my brain about some text message I sent last night.

"Here, come sit down and let's look at your phone."

I hesitate as mom grabs my arm and leads me to the living room. I sit down on the couch beside Oscar and open my phone. I scroll to my last text message to my mom. When I see it, I put my hand to my mouth in utter shock!

"Mom, I don't remember sending you this!"

Mom raises her eyebrows at me. "Well, Sweet Pea, I can understand why, because you sent it at three forty-eight in the morning."

I read through the text to my mom and am ashamed about what I wrote:

Mom, I'm so upset right now. Maria has run off with Peyton and one of the girls here at camp. She's still not back to the bunkhouse and I'm so mad. I don't want to be friends with her anymore and I especially don't want her staying at our house. Please talk to her parents about her moving back in with them.

I sit in awe as I read it over several more times. "Mom, I truly don't remember sending you this. Do you think I was sleep texting? Is there such a thing? I know I was up all night, but I'm pretty sure I would remember sending you this."

Mom looks at me with concern. "It's ok, I'm sure you were just exhausted. I called Mr. Hernandez early this morning and told him about your text message. He was a little perturbed that Maria was sneaking around at camp. So, he told me she would be staying over there for a while until he can get this all worked out with her."

"Oh Mom, I don't want to get Maria in trouble! She's going to hate me forever!

Mom and I sat in silence for several minutes before I decided to come clean with her about everything that happened at band camp. And when I say everything, I mean EVERYTHING!

I told her about us sneaking out. Kylan and I almost doing something we shouldn't. I told her about Cass spying on Peyton and Maria when they were in her hammock. And then I finally told her about the outcome of Maria and Peyton hanging out with Cass.

"You've got to be kidding me, Kimmy!" Mom says stunned with her eyes as big as saucers.

"Mom, I am so embarrassed. I knew it was wrong to sneak out. But Kylan was out there, and I know I'm always safe when he's by my side." Mom drops her head in her hands. "And this whole thing with Maria and Peyton. We never saw this coming! They were like two love birds the entire week of camp. Peyton would sneak kisses from Maria every chance he got. Then this morning happened and, poof, it's all over with between them."

Mom was speechless. I don't blame her. She sent me off to this camp thinking I was being watched by adults at all times. She's never going to let me leave the house ever again!

"I just don't know what to say about all this. I was able to live with the fact that Maria was not following the camp rules, but you, Kimmy? I can't believe you would do something like this! I thought you learned your lesson last year when you went to that party." Mom shakes her head.

"I'm in disbelief!" She throws her arms in the air, then looks at me with her eyes as sharp as knives. "Did you drink alcohol at band camp?"

I shake my head back and forth with all the strength in my body. "No, Mom! Absolutely not! I did learn my lesson about that. I'll never do that ever again for the rest of my life!" Mom lets out a sigh of relief. "But I'm pretty sure Maria was smoking cigarettes with that Cass girl and Peyton last night. She reeked of cigarette smoke this morning. She slung her hair around to put it up and the smell smacked me in the face."

"Ok, that's all I need to know. Why don't you go lie down and get a little rest while I decide what I'm going to do with you. In the meantime, I'm calling Nanny to come over so I can head on to work. Dad took off for the shipyard and I don't trust you right now to be home alone."

Great! This is just great! I had to send some incriminating text message in my sleep about Maria and now I'm being punished for telling my mom the truth. Geez...sometimes life just sucks!

CHAPTER 21

W ell, now I'm grounded!" I say to Kylan as I try to hold it all together.

"What do you mean you're grounded?"

I took a deep breath and upon the release of it all the feelings that I've been keeping inside for the past few days just suddenly spilled out all over the place.

"I...can't...talk...right...now..." I croak out as my body and soul are filled with all sorts of mixed emotions. I close my eyes and try to forget everything that has happened. I keep seeing images of Maria and Peyton holding hands so happily in love. I think about all the fun times the four of us have had over the last year and how those times are over and will never happen again. Then I think about Maria and how much she must hate me right now. My thoughts swiftly move on to thinking about being grounded when school starts next week. OMG! I'm going to scream!

Why am I doing this to myself? Couples break up. That's normal. Friends have arguments then make up. That's normal too. I take some slow deep breaths to try and calm myself down. It actually works! I look down at my phone and see that Kylan is still on there. I know he has been listening to me cry like a baby on the other end for the last five minutes.

"Babe, are you still there?" he asks in a somber tone.

I breathe in so tight that it hurt my chest. "Yes," I quietly reply. "I'm here."

"What's going on? Did something happen?" I can hear the worry in his voice as he patiently awaits my answer.

"When I got home from camp, I went in my bedroom only to find Maria's bed had been taken out."

"What?"

"Yeah," I say. "Apparently I sent some kind of text in my sleep about how Maria had been acting at camp and how I wanted her to go back to her own house."

"Well, that's interesting. In your sleep, Babe?" Kylan asks.

"I don't know. I guess last night when Maria was out with Peyton and Cass, I got so tore up about it I texted my mom. Then, one thing led to another. My mom called her dad and made arrangements for Maria to go back to her house. I'm just really confused right now."

"Um...me too, Babe," Kylan hesitantly says. "Have you talked to Maria?"

I look up at my ceiling trying to think about the last time I spoke to Maria. "No, I haven't talked to her since we left the school parking lot. She rode home with her parents and said she'd be over later. Do you think I should call her and see what's going on?"

Kylan hesitates. "Probably so. I'm sure she's still upset about the whole Peyton/Cass break up thing. Give her a call and call me back."

Kylan always has such good advice and he's always so calm when I have drama. How does he do it? I'll probably never know. So, I decide to take his advice and give Maria a call, but she didn't answer. I bet she's probably talking to her mom and dad about stuff. I text Kylan to tell him she didn't answer, then curl up underneath my sheets for a quick nap before dinner.

Scratch, Scratch, Scratch

I rub my eyes and look around my room. It's pitch black in here! What is that scratching sound? Then I hear a faint whine and more scratching coming from my door. Oscar. It must be Oscar wanting in. I throw my covers off me only to realize I'm wet with sweat. How long was I asleep for? I check my phone and see it's eleven fifty-one at night. OMG! What the crap? Who let me sleep past dinner?

As I put my feet on the floor, I have a strange feeling that something is not right, but I don't know what it is. It could be the fact that Maria's bed is no longer in my bedroom, and it feels empty and lonely. Or it could be that I haven't eaten dinner and I'm starving to death. Either way, I don't like this feeling.

I open my bedroom door and Oscar bolts into my room and starts doing zoomies all over the place. I just stand there and watch until he's finished. Then he comes running up to me and nearly knocks me down. "Oscar! What's the matter with you?" He just stares up at me and tilts his head to the side like he's trying to figure out what I just said. Oh well, maybe he missed me.

I tiptoe out to the hallway. The living room lights are on, but no one seems to be home. The aroma of spaghetti and garlic bread linger in the air. Nanny must've fixed dinner. I still don't know how I slept so long.

I stand in the middle of my living room debating whether to heat up some dinner or just go back to bed. Instead of doing either, I decide to peek into the spare bedroom and see if Nanny is in there. I gently turn the doorknob to open the door. It creaks slightly so I stop. It's really dark. Usually, Nanny plugs in a night light, but no night light in here.

"Nanny," I whisper. "Are you in here?"

Nothing.

"Nanny?" I say a little louder.

Still nothing.

Hmm. That's strange. Nanny is a really light sleeper. She would definitely hear me if she were in here. So, I walk over to the bed to realize that it's still made and there's no Nanny sleeping in here.

Ok. So, if Nanny isn't here, then who is? I look out the window of my living room to see what cars are in the driveway. None. Ok, I'm so totally confused right now. Mom said Nanny was coming over and obviously someone was here and made dinner, but who? Does this mean I'm home alone?

I don't mind being home alone during the day, but at night I get a little creeped out. You see, my house is really old. I'm not sure exactly when it was built, but my mom was raised in it and she's old. Remember me telling you about how my grandmother Ruth passed away? She used to live here with Grandpa Eugene. Even though she didn't technically die in this house, she passed away in the flood waters from Hurricane Camille when she was trying to rescue that stupid cat of hers. Sometimes I feel like maybe Grandma Ruth is still in this house watching over me. I never met her, and my mom doesn't remember her at all, but I just have this strange feeling like she's with me.

Anyway, back to me being home alone. I'm scared! Yes, I said it.

"Oscar, come here!" I yell hopefully to scare any haints away. "Oscar, where are you?" I look around only to realize that he is sitting right at my feet. "Oh, I'm so silly, Oscar. I thought you had run away or something."

Oscar looks up at me with his sad puppy dog eyes. He's probably thinking, "That girl has done gone and lost her mind."

I head back down the hallway to my bedroom. I usher Oscar in the door and shut it tightly. *Click.* Now it's securely locked. Shew, maybe my nerves will calm down a little bit. Oh no! I forgot to make sure the front and back doors were both locked. I sprint out of my bedroom so fast that Oscar doesn't even budge. Quickly checked both doors and like a streak of lightning I'm back in my bedroom safe and sound.

Hey, you up? (12:16 AM)

I am now, Babe. (12:17 AM)

What are you doing up so late? (12:17 AM)

I don't really know. I woke up a few minutes ago. I slept through dinner. I thought Nanny was here, but she's not. I'M HOME ALONE! CALL ME! (12:18 AM)

My heart is pounding. My head is hurting. I feel like I'm going to throw up! Am I having a stroke? When is Kylan going to call me? It's been nearly five minutes since I texted him. Is he mad at me? *Ahhhhhhhhhh!*

Buzz, Buzz...Buzz, Buzz...Buzz, Buzz...

Oh, thank God! "Hello?" I ask in a slight panic as if not knowing it is Kylan on the other end.

"Babe! I've been trying to call you for the past five minutes, but your phone keeps going to voicemail. Are you ok?" Kylan asks with fear in his voice.

"Yes, I'm fine, I think. That's weird about my phone. I've been sitting here staring at it wondering why you hadn't called already." I let out a huge sigh of relief.

"So, you're home alone?"

"Yeah, and I'm puzzled as to why. Mom said Nanny would be coming over to stay because she didn't trust me." I roll my eyes. "You know, like I'm up to something."

"Are you up to something?" Kylan says snickering.

"Geez...no, I'm not! I'm just scared and trying to figure out where my family is. That's all."

My mom has been very particular about making sure someone is always home with me at night since the whole thing with Ashley happened. Now that Nanny and Chas live right down the road from us, Nanny just pops over and hangs out until my mom or dad get here. I've even stayed at their house a time or two when Nanny is really tired. So that's why I'm so confused as to why no one is home with me right now. Especially since Maria is staying at her house tonight. Which leads me to wonder...how long is Maria staying at her house? I'm already starting to miss her.

"Oh, Babe, don't worry. I'll talk to you until you fall asleep."

Ah, Kylan. He's such a sweetheart. I bet he thinks I'm crazy half the time. I truly think he is the love of my life. I'm definitely the luckiest girl in this world.

"Thanks. I appreciate that," I say knowing good and well that Kylan would like to be sound asleep himself right now.

"So, I talked to Peyton this evening." Kylan pauses. "Or should I say yesterday evening since it's technically Saturday."

"Oh yeah. What did that piece of crap have to say for himself?" I'm so angry with Peyton right now. For some reason, he thinks he's God's gift to women all of a sudden. I knew he was acting strangely at band camp the other day. But I would never in a million years thought he would hook up with Cass. Yuck!

I can hear Kylan taking a deep breath on the other end of the phone. "Well...he said he's sorry that things had to happen like they did. Can I tell you something he told me? You have to promise not to tell Maria."

"I promise."

"So I asked Peyton what in the hell possessed him to do that with Cass the other night. And you'll never believe what he told me."

"What?" I ask wondering if I even want to know his response.

"You promise you won't tell Maria?"

Oh, this has got to be good! "I already said I did. So, what is it?"

"Well, he said there was no way he was going to wait until marriage to be with Maria. He thought he was about to get her to do it with him the other night in the hammock at camp. You know, that hammock that belonged to Cass?"

"Um yes, Kylan, how could I forget!"

"Oh yeah, sorry Kimmy, It's only like after midnight. I haven't slept a wink unlike someone else I know who slept the entire evening away."

"Sorry. Ok, cut to the chase." I can tell that Kylan is very hesitant about what he is about to say.

"Ok, I hope you're sitting down, because I'm about to throw you for a loop." Kylan pauses. "Peyton and Cass have been having a secret affair since last fall."

I gasp! Then my heart sinks to my stomach. "Did you know about this?" I ask hoping Kylan will say no, but he doesn't say anything. "Did you?" I demand.

"I had some suspicions, but I didn't know for sure. I never worked up the nerve to ask him and quite frankly, it was none of my business to know. If he would have wanted me to know, he would have told me. So really, it was only a matter of time that they would get caught fooling around. It's just too bad it had to happen at band camp in front of the whole entire band. This is going to make for a miserable marching season with those three."

I'm speechless. I have no idea what to say. Talk about mixed emotions, I've got them all right now but mostly anger and sadness for Maria and also embarrassment. She must be completely humiliated right now.

"What made Peyton think that was ok to do?"

"Well, Babe, let me tell you something. Most guys are not like me."

"What do you mean by that?" I ask knowing good and well what he means by that, but I just want to hear him say it.

"Kimmy, I think you know what I'm talking about. We've both been tempted many times with it, but our strong will has kept our promise to each other. Peyton, on the other hand, doesn't have that strong will like us. He's weak if you know what I mean. He has given in to his teenage hormones and desires. Peyton knew that Maria wouldn't give it up to him, so he looked elsewhere. And it just so happened that his elsewhere would end up being trashy ole Cass. I would never in a million years even think about putting anything of mine inside of her. I've heard she's been with a whole slew of guys since she's been in high school. There's no telling what Cass has picked up from all those dudes over the years."

I sit there in complete shock! I look around my bedroom at what was once a familiar place to me but is now like a foreign country. This past year, Maria and I have shared everything together. We've been by each other's sides when we needed it most. But now, it's different. I know a secret that Maria doesn't, and I don't want to tell her. Last year, we promised each other to never keep secrets ever again, but I just cannot tell her this. Plus, she's probably thoroughly pissed off at me right now for telling my mom I didn't want her here anymore.

Suddenly, I hear a tapping at my bedroom door! My heart instantly starts racing one hundred miles an hour.

"Kylan," I say in a whisper. "Did you hear that?"

"Hear what?"

"Something just tapped on my door!" I put my hand on my chest as I am afraid my heart is about to explode. My poor heart has been under a tremendous amount of pressure here lately. I'm not sure how it is even surviving.

"Oh, Kimmy, I'm sure it was just your imagination." Maybe he's right. Maybe I'm just hallucinating from lack of sleep. Wait, no, that can't be. I just slept like five hours solid.

Tap, Tap, Tap, Tap

"KYLAN, I JUST HEARD IT AGAIN!"

"Go answer it!"

"NO! I've watched scary movies. I know how they end," I hiss.

Tap, Tap, Tap, Tap

"GO AWAY! I'M CALLING THE POLICE RIGHT NOW!" I scream to whatever is on the other side of my door. That's when I hear it. The same voice I've heard since the moment I was born.

"Kimberly Ruth Favre, open this door right now. It's Dad!"

Relief rushed over my entire body from my head all the way down to my feet like a cool December ocean wave.

"Dad, is that really you?" I say as I walk toward my door.

"Yes, it's me. Who else would it be."

I crack open my bedroom door just to make sure I'm not being tricked. Sure enough, it's my dad. I take two steps over to give him a huge bear hug.

"Do you know how happy I am to see you, Dad? I thought I was home alone, and you were an intruder."

Dad kissed me on the top of my head and hugged me even tighter. "Did you really think we would leave you home by yourself?"

I shrug my shoulders. "I don't know. I've not done anything bad to lose your trust, have I?"

Dad shakes his head, "No, you've not lost my trust, but maybe your mom's. You know how she is, Kimmy."

I agree with Dad. Mom tends to overreact sometimes when things happen. I guess she has every right to, though, especially after everything we've all been through.

"I looked outside a few minutes ago and didn't see any vehicles in the driveway, but I smelled the heavenly aroma of Nanny's homemade spaghetti."

Dad grins. "I left my truck at the shipyard and caught a ride home with Jason. I was in the middle of changing my oil when I realized I was short by one quart. I figured your Nanny was ready to leave, so I just told Jason we'd pick up a quart in the morning. What are you doing up so late? And most importantly, who are you talking to on the phone?"

So, I told Dad about how I slept all afternoon and woke up thinking that I was home alone. I got scared and called Kylan. KYLAN! Oh crap! I forgot I still had Kylan on the phone!

CHAPTER 22

Well, today's the big day! It's my first day of high school! I'm beyond excited and oh so nervous. The beginning of a new school year is always bittersweet for me. The bitter part of it is that my days spent doing absolutely nothing and lying around the beach are coming to an end. The sweet part of it this year is that I get to see my boyfriend every single day of the week! And he gets his driver's license in a few days! Mom said he can pick me up for school in the mornings and bring me home in the afternoons after band practice. Yippee! I finally get some freedom!

I had a long conversation with Maria the other day. It was hard not to tell her about the whole Peyton and Cass thing that Kylan had told me about. But I kept my promise and made sure my lips stayed sealed.

Maria and I agreed that spending a little time apart might do our friendship some good. She said she was enjoying being back with her family. And guess what? Alex ended up moving out of his bedroom last week during camp so he and Joni could get their own place. So, Maria was able to take over his room and make it her own. She wants me to come over and help her do some painting and spruce things up a bit. She had to buy some potent air fresheners from the store, because she said Alex is a stinky boy.

Maria seems to be over Peyton already. When we hung out the other day, she didn't cry one single time. She said he pressured her to do things she didn't want to do and often made her feel uncomfortable for not giving into him. I did not pry for details, but I suspect I know what she meant by all that. She did confirm that they never did it, if you know what I mean.

So, Maria's transportation plans dramatically changed when she and Peyton broke up. Her plan was to ride to and from school with him, but now that's out the window. So, we are being forced to ride the bus once again until Kylan gets his license. But that's ok, because Liz and her dad just moved into an apartment close to our neighborhood, so she'll be riding our same bus. At least I'll have someone to talk to when Maria gets moody with me.

"Oh, Kimmy, I'm so anxious about this first day of high school! What if I accidentally run into Peyton and HER?"

I turn my head to look out the bus window trying to imagine a day without drama. "Well, Sis, I guess you'll just have to put on your big girl panties and deal with it."

Maria scoffs at me. "That's not very nice! You have the perfect boyfriend who would do anything in this world for you. I have no one now!"

I take a deep breath and think about how to respond to her. I've noticed here lately that my brain seems to be processing things a little bit faster. I'm not sure if it's because I'm getting more mature, or if it's all this medication I'm on for my heart. But whatever is going on, I like it!

"Maria, you are a beautiful girl, and you know it! I'm sure you could have any guy you wanted with a snap of your fingers." Maria looks down at her lap like she's getting ready to cry. "Peyton was no good for you. He's a liar, cheater, and definitely not someone you want to spend the rest of your life with. Could you imagine having kids with someone like him? Yuck! He probably doesn't even know how to change a diaper."

Maria looks up with tears in her eyes and slightly giggles. "Kimmy, you always know what to say to make me feel better, even though I never want to hear it." She tilts her head to the side and looks me square in the eyes. "What do you know about Peyton that you're not telling me?"

Oh no! She knows! OMG, what do I say to her? Here we go! The palms of my hands instantly get so sweaty that I can't even hold onto my phone. I fumble around trying to stick it in my jeans pocket but end up dropping it on the floor of the bus when the bus driver slammed on the brakes to make a stop.

As I bend down to pick it up, I notice something strange on Maria's ankle. It looks like a homemade tattoo. Like she has carved a little triangle in the side of her leg and filled it with ink from a ball point pen. I study the mark for a few seconds until I feel her tapping on my shoulder.

"What 'cha looking at, Kimmy?" Maria asks with a growl in her voice.

I carefully formulate my words once again to make sure my point gets across. "Maria, why do you have a triangle tattoo on your leg?"

"What are you talking about? I don't see a triangle tattoo on my leg." She pauses and squints her eyes. "I see a symbol of hope for my body, mind, and spirit."

I just sit there staring at her. What on earth is she talking about? "I don't understand," I reply with my eyebrows raised so high I can feel my hairline. "Did you do that yourself?"

"Of course, I did! Doesn't it look great?" Maria pulls her leg up on the bus seat to show me her work of art. "First, I drew it out. Then, I took a razor blade I found in Dad's shed and carefully etched it into my leg making sure not to pull up any blood. Lastly, I had an old gel pen in my backpack that I broke and emptied onto my skin."

What did she just say to me? I have no words. I just shake my head. I cannot believe that Maria would do this. "Have your parents seen it?"

"Um, not really. I've been wearing socks around the house. I don't think they'll mind, though."

"Maria! You're crazy if you think your mom and dad won't get mad! They're going to kill you!" I say without thinking then realize what I just said, so I quickly put my hand over my mouth and apologize. "I'm sorry. I didn't mean it like that. I just meant that you're going to be in big trouble when they find out."

Maria rolls her eyes at me and goes back to looking at her phone. Just when I think she has forgotten about asking me what I know about Peyton she jerks her head around and nearly spits in my face when she says, "So, Kimmy, spill the beans!"

I freeze! My mouth goes numb. I cannot even open it! I feel like my stomach just did a flip inside itself. I think I'm going to throw up. What am I going to tell her? I promised Kylan I wouldn't tell Maria. Ok, I've got it! I'll say something else about her tattoo. That will distract her.

"So...does Alex know about your new tattoo?"

Maria looks at me with that look of death she is ever so famous for. Her eyes appear to be on fire! "Of course he knows, Alex is my new BFF now that he's moving out of the house! You didn't answer my question, Kimmy."

If I tell her, Kylan will be mad at me. If I don't tell her, she'll be mad at me. What's that old saying? I'm damned if I do and damned if I don't. Either way I'm screwed! I could lie to her. That's it, I'll tell a lie. No that's not it. I'm a terrible liar. She'll know I'm lying as soon as I open my mouth.

"Peyton has been messing around on you with Cass since last fall." There I said it.

Maria just stares at me and blinks her eyes a few times. Then she turns her entire body toward the aisle of the bus and lowers her head down all the way to her lap. I can feel her body trembling next to me. I have destroyed her. I have betrayed my best friend in the whole entire world. The one who knows all my secrets and would sacrifice her freedom just so I can have mine. My Maria.

Maria raises up and slowly turns toward me. "I'm not mad at you. I knew all of this already. I just needed to know that you weren't going to lie to me."

I look over at her stunned. "How did you know?" I ask.

Maria shakes her head. "I found Cass' driver's license in the back seat of Peyton's car back in the winter when I was looking for my phone. It was shoved up under the passenger side seat. I confronted him about it, and he said that he was just giving her a ride home after practice one day. A ride, yeah." She rolls her eyes. "Then, a few weeks later, I found the corner of a condom wrapper just sitting there in plain sight on his back seat. I was like, what the hell, Peyton? He denied it and came up with some stupid story about how he caught this random guy and girl in his car one night after a ballgame. I didn't buy it though."

"Maria, why did you stay with him. You could've easily broken up with him!"

"I wanted to give him the benefit of a doubt, but I always knew that something wasn't quite right." She takes a deep breath and slowly lets it out. "I loved him, Kimmy,

I really did. I just knew we would get married one day. I would watch you and Kylan and see how happy y'all were. Then I would look at me and Peyton and yearn for that happiness. So many times he tried to talk me into having sex with him. We would get so close to doing it. Then something would interrupt our moment. It was always something random. Kind of like God was putting all these obstacles in our way to try and prevent me from doing something I would regret. In the back of my mind, I thought if we did that together then our relationship would be perfect. I guess you could say I've been blinded by love."

I gently place my hand on Maria's shoulder. "I had no idea any of this was happening. Why didn't you tell me?"

Tears start welling up in Maria's eyes. "I was embarrassed. I knew that you and Kylan were content with waiting until marriage and you wouldn't understand."

"Oh Sis, but I do understand. I have wanted so many times to do it with Kylan and we've come very close too. But the difference with us is that Kylan is a good guy and understands me. He would never in a million years pressure me to do something I don't want to do. See, that's how we are different from you and Peyton. Peyton is a jerk who is only wanting one thing from you. And when he realized he wouldn't get it, he went elsewhere. You deserve better than that, Sis!"

Maria looks down at her phone and gets a funny look on her face. "Peyton just texted me. He says he wants to talk."

I shake my finger at her. "No, Maria. You have nothing to say to him. Don't give in to this. I'm not going to let him pull you around like a toy. Cass probably broke it off with him already, and he's trying to get you back but don't fall for it!"

"I know, I know. But why would he want to talk to me? I haven't heard from him since I slapped him across the face at camp. What would he want from me now?" Maria questions.

Just then, the bus comes to a stop and we both look up. "How did we get to school so fast?" I ask Maria in a pure state of shock.

Maria shrugs her shoulders. "I don't know."

I put my arm around Maria as we stand up to get off the bus. "Today is the first day of the rest of our lives, Sis. Let's put the past behind us and make it the best one ever!"

Maria laughs with sarcasm, "Might as well, what've I got to lose!"

CHAPTER 23

When you're a member of the Bay High School marching band, the Saturday after the first home football game is always reserved for the huge back to school beach party called Making Waves. I'm so excited to get to go this year! Kylan was telling me that last year they played beach volleyball, had a sandcastle competition, and even gave a prize to the one who could catch the most crabs. They give away door prizes too! Kylan said everybody will go home with something including a full tummy because they grill steaks and seafood. I'm not really sure where Mr. Mayberry gets all the money for this party, but I think businesses donate stuff, so the band doesn't have to pay for anything.

The theme for this year's party is the Olympics since we will be having the 2012 Olympic games coming up in the summer. We are supposed to dress like our favorite Olympic sport or athlete. I'm going to dress like a high diver. Since Mr. Mayberry said the girls have to wear one-piece swimsuits, Nanny found me a really cute one-piece sporty red, white, and blue suit that looks just like something the USA swim team would wear. I asked Kylan to dress like a diver too, but he refused. He said they wear these suits that look like tighty whities and he wouldn't be caught dead in something like that. Also, he said he didn't want to show off his sexy body in front of all the ladies that it was for my eyes only. Haha!

So, Maria seems like she has pretty much gotten over Peyton. She hasn't mentioned his name in a couple of weeks now. And she actually has been talking to this new kid at school named Hugo. I think he's part Hispanic part something else. He speaks fluent Spanish and is really good looking. He's a junior at our school and moved to Bay St. Louis from Texas. Maria says she doesn't like him like that, but I don't believe her. Hugo's not in band, so he can't come to the party tonight.

Now that Kylan has his driver's license, Mom lets me go everywhere with him. Can you believe that? Before she would let me ride with him, Mom made Kylan drive her around town. She pointed out all the roads and places that he wasn't allowed to take me. It was actually kind of strange. She even made him drive her over to the casino where she works and showed him how to get his car parked with a valet. I don't know why she did that, but Kylan just went with it.

The party tonight starts at six o'clock on the public beach where the pavilion is at. The city of BSL ropes off a large section of beach and reserves it for the band only. We have quite a few members and they want us to have our privacy. Plus, since the party is at night, they put tiki torches up everywhere so we can see. They also hire a lifeguard to monitor the ocean in case someone gets out there and drowns in a foot of water. Kylan said last year everyone was swimming. This time of the year our ocean water is super hot! And when I say hot, I mean like ninety degrees HOT! Even when the sun sets, the water temperature stays up.

Another reason why I'm so excited about the party tonight is because I haven't spent much time on the beach since we've been back at school. That's usually how it goes for me. I typically spend my entire summer on the beach and then weekends when school starts, but this summer was very different you know with my surgery and all. Maria and I have only gone to the beach once since band camp and it ended up raining on us, so it was a bust. The forecast for today is hot, humid, and zero chance of precipitation.

"When's he going to be here?" Maria asks as she's looking in the mirror putting on her makeup.

My mom agreed to let Kylan pick me and Maria up for the party tonight and Maria is planning on sleeping over. That's another reason why I'm so excited. Maria hasn't spent the night with me since she moved back home after band camp.

"In about twenty minutes. Why are you putting on makeup?"

Maria swings her long black hair around and nearly hits me in the face with it. "You never know who you might see out at the beach, Sis. I might meet my future husband tonight!" Then she spritzes some fruity body spray all over her like she's trying to put out a fire.

"Girl, you're going to attract every mosquito in Hancock County with all that perfume! You know how bad they are this time of year."

"Pish, I just want to smell good. You know I'm back on the market and on the prowl!" she says as she bats her hands at me like she's sinking her claws into fresh meat. I just roll my eyes and shake my head. I was right, she's definitely over Peyton now.

I've noticed since Kylan and I have been dating, I haven't been as concerned about getting fancied up to go places. I guess you could say I am comfortable with myself and my looks. I'm still super skinny. My hair is always a big ball of messy beach waves. Even when I straighten it with a flat iron, it is big and poofy by the end of the day due to all the humidity in the air around here. I do wear makeup every day, though. My eyelashes are so blonde it looks like I don't have any, so I make sure to put on a little waterproof mascara before leaving the house.

"He's here!" I squeal. "Let's go!"

"How do I look?" Maria asks as she twirls around in her gymnastics outfit. She found this cute leotard at the thrift store the other day and we bedazzled it up with rhinestones from Nanny's collection.

"Like a slice of cake," I reply with a wink. "A very sparkly slice of cake actually!"

Maria giggles, "Sometimes you're too much, Kimmy."

As I turn to walk out of my bedroom, I realize that Oscar isn't standing there to greet me. Well, that's strange. I make my way down the hallway toward the living room and see why he wasn't there.

"Hey Babe!" Kylan says waving to me with a big ole Oscar in his lap. "You better be careful leaving your front door unlocked. I just sneaked right in. Oscar didn't bark or anything."

I roll my eyes at him. "Really, Kylan? You think Oscar is going to bark at you? You're his favorite person in the whole world. I'm sure he could smell you coming up the driveway."

Kylan lifts Oscar off of him and places him on the couch. "Babe, you look amazing!" Kylan says as I can see little hearts floating all around his head. Not really, you know, but if Kylan were in a cartoon strip the hearts would for sure be there.

Before I can say anything, Kylan swoops me up in his arms and plants a huge kiss on my lips. Then he leans me back and overexaggerates his kisses on my neck and down my arm. He's such a hopeless romantic.

"Eww, gross! Y'all stop! That makes me so sick!" Maria sticks out her tongue with disgust.

"Oh, come on. I've witnessed quite a bit of disgustingness with you too Sis! Do I need to remind you of some of the times I've wanted to throw up in my mouth watching you and you know who?"

Maria grins, then shoves her hand in my face like a stop sign. "Nope, I'm good!

We get to the party about five minutes late because Kylan is such a careful driver when I'm in the car with him. He makes sure I buckle my seat belt before he puts his car in drive. So, I've told you a little about how much money Kylan's parents have, but I haven't told you about Kylan's vehicle. For his 16th birthday, Kylan's parents gave him a brand-new Land Rover. Can you believe that? He was actually expecting a used Mercedes that his parents were saving for him, but they surprised him with the SUV. They said it's something that is safe, and he can drive to college. I'm sure I'll never have anything as nice as that when I start driving. Grandpa Eugene promised me a car one day, but we'll have to see about that. He has money, but he's getting old and I'm not sure how much longer he'll be around.

We step out of the car and can hear the music blaring. It's still daylight on the beach, but the sun is slowly starting to set. The tiki torches are lit and blazing a fiery orange glow. I can already smell the steaks sizzling on the grill. Oh man, my mouth is watering!

Then I see it! I'm stunned! It's the lone osprey swooping down to catch its prey. I stop in my tracks and watch this beautiful bird suddenly disappear into the ocean. I look away at Kylan for a fraction of a second just to look back up and see it flying overhead with a fish dangling from its claws. Kylan looks over at me and smiles the sweetest smile I've ever seen.

"I saw it too Babe. It's going back to feed its baby." Kylan tilts his head to the side and gently kisses me on the cheek. "There's something about that bird that really intrigues you. I can tell." I shake my head agreeing with him but not sure how to explain it.

Before we can even make it down the seawall, I hear my name being shouted from across the beach. "Kimmy!" I look around, but I don't see anyone calling for me. There are already a lot of kids here. "Hey Kimmy!" they shout again. Then I realize that it's Liz yelling as she comes running up to me in her fencing outfit with her face fully covered.

"Hey Liz! You look absolutely ridiculous! Where did you get that hideous costume," I laugh at the thought of her trying to use the bathroom in that get up.

Liz smacks me on the shoulder. "It was my dad's when he was in college. He tried out for the US Olympic team. I had no idea until I told him about this party, and he produced this outfit. Crazy, huh?"

I just stand there staring at her. "Yeah, pretty crazy. How do you use the bathroom with all that on?"

"Very carefully!" Liz chuckles. "I'm going to take this mask off, though, it's pretty hot in here."

I start scanning the crowd for Peyton and Cass. They're nowhere to be found as far as I can see. I've got to keep Maria away from him tonight. He's been calling and texting her a lot here lately. As far as I know, she's shut him down every time. She told him to leave her alone and that she's moved on with her life. We'll see about that, but my job tonight is to be on patrol for anything suspicious with those two.

Since this whole break up ordeal with Maria and Peyton, Kylan and he have drifted apart as friends. Kylan said he feels like Peyton was never truthful with him about things and he doesn't want to hang out with someone he can't trust. Plus, Kylan despises Cass, therefore, any time she's near, Kylan goes the other direction. Since Peyton and Cass are always together, Kylan steers clear of the two of them.

It's kind of sad to think about, though. Kylan and Peyton have been such good friends for so long that Peyton had his own bedroom at Kylan's house. Then this whole breakup happened, and he lost his best friend. But since then, Kylan and Brad have become big buddies. I like that because Brad and Liz are officially dating now, and Liz is my second best friend next to Maria. Like I said before, she's a lot less moody than Maria, too.

I mingle around the crowd arm in arm with Kylan. I bet you're wondering what he ended up dressing as tonight. Well, he decided that if I was going to be a diver, I would need a coach. So, he's wearing black athletic pants and a Mississippi State pullover. He said that's the closest he could find to red, white, and blue. Sometimes I just have to shake my head...men!

CHAPTER 24

And the grand prize winner of the sixty-five inch TV is..." Mr. Mayberry paused for what seemed like at least five minutes. I'm sure it was only for about five seconds, but it felt like an eternity. "Kimmy Favre! Come on down! You're the grand prize winner!"

I stand there in shock! I cannot move. I look over at Kylan unsure of what to do. It's like my brain stopped working as soon as Mr. Mayberry said my name.

"Go Babe! He called your name!" Kylan gently pushes me toward the makeshift stage that is set up at the top of the concrete seawall.

I stare at the seawall thinking about how I'm going to gracefully climb down the steps holding a sixty-five inch TV. I can picture myself carrying this huge TV over top of my head when all of a sudden I trip and start tumbling down the two feet tall steps!

I blink my eyes to try and snap me out of this trance, but it doesn't work. Then I feel Kylan taking me by the hand and leading me up to the stage. I don't even realize how far we've walked when my eyes focus in on Mr. Mayberry and Mrs. Sheila standing there staring at me.

"Congratulations, Kimmy!" Mrs. Sheila says as she pulls me in for a hug. Hey, maybe she does like me after all.

I let go of Kylan's hand and reach for the TV as Mr. Mayberry leans down to my level. "Oh no, Honey, you don't need to pick it up. We'll deliver it to your house after the party. It's way too heavy for you to carry home."

I giggle and think about how dumb I was for thinking I could just pick that up and carry it around on my head. "Thank you for the prize!" I say with a beaming smile on my face.

As Kylan and I trek back to our friends, I see Cass out of the corner of my eye. "Don't look now, but there she is!" I whisper to Kylan.

"Who?" Kylan asks looking straight forward.

"Her!" I say with my teeth gritted. "I don't want to say her name. People can hear us."

Kylan's eyes widen. "Oh...*her!* Is *he* with her?"

I look in that direction trying my hardest not to make eye contact with Cass, but it's too late. She spots me and starts walking our way with Peyton trailing closely behind. "Oh God, Kylan. Here they come. What do we do?"

"Just act natural, Babe. Just pretend like nothing ever happened."

I wrinkle up my forehead knowing good and well that I'm not a very good actor. I can feel my eyebrows crossing in the middle of my face. Kylan always gets on to me for doing that. He says I'll have wrinkles when I get old, but I just can't help it. When I get angry or frustrated, my face instantly turns this way.

Cass prances up to us dressed as an Olympic tennis player, racquet and all. "Well, hello there friends!" she articulates with confidence in her voice. "What've y'all been up to here lately?"

I look past her to see Peyton with his head down staring at the sand. He knows he's in the doghouse with us and that he'll probably never get out. Just thinking about what he did with Cass disgusts me.

Kylan speaks up. "We've been pretty busy with school starting back and such. What about you?" He talks directly to Cass as Peyton glances up for a moment to nod at Kylan then puts his head back down.

"Oh, you know. Just hanging out with my hunny bunny and enjoying life," Cass replies. "I think Peyton's been a little lonely since you two stopped hanging out." She nudges him in the side. "Right sweetheart?"

Peyton looks up at Kylan in shock not knowing what to say to Cass' remark. But Kylan, oh my very intelligent Kylan, always knows exactly what to say. "Well, Cass, it's a shame that my dear friend Peyton is so lonely when he's with you. Maybe you should take that as a sign!" Kylan snaps back.

Cass is so thrown for a loop by Kylan's comment that she doesn't know how to reply back to him. I look over at

Peyton who is now looking up at Cass with a grin on his face. This poor guy is like a lost little puppy dog looking for his home. I actually kind of feel sorry for Peyton. I wouldn't necessarily say sorry for him but puzzled as to why he is so attached to her and not Maria. Oh yeah, I remember now.

As Cass stumbles for her words, she coughs then turns and does a fake sneeze. Ok, now that was weird!

"Um...I just wanted y'all to know there's going to be a beer bust tonight over at my uncle's beach house in Long Beach. You two are invited to come have some real fun not like this little kid party that the school is throwing. They'll be any kind of drink imaginable and best of all, no parents will be there! Just a few of my family members who will act as bouncers and lookouts in case the cops get called."

I look over at Kylan in pure amazement at what Cass has just said to us. Then she continues, "Oh, his house has like ten bedrooms, so if you and your princess want to spend the night and have some alone time," Cass winks, "you're more than welcome to one of the rooms. I'll even put a reserved sign on it for you, so nobody goes in and wrecks the bed before you get there."

I just stand there. There's no way in hell I would ever go to a party at Cass' uncle's house. Especially one that's going to have free flowing alcohol. I learned my lesson on that last year for the rest of my life.

Kylan clears his throat as I can tell he's as surprised as I am. "Thanks, Cass, for the invitation. That sounds like a lot of fun, doesn't it Kimmy." Kylan looks over at me as my facial expression still hasn't changed since they walked up. "I'll let you know if we decide to stop by. As for that bedroom, you can let someone else have it. We're waiting until marriage."

"Well, isn't that nice," Cass hisses. "Some of us just want to start enjoying our lives a little bit sooner than others, I guess. Anyway, if you decide to come out, just let me know and I'll make sure that security lets you in. Tootles!" Cass pivots around on her toes in the sand and walks off before we could even say anything back to her.

"Stop that face right now! You know good and well that we aren't going to Cass' stupid party. I have no desire to ever touch alcohol again in my life and I certainly don't want to go hang out with Tweedle Dee and Tweedle Dumb!" Kylan takes a deep breath and slowly releases it. "Peyton has pissed me off to no end and the way he's acting when he's around *her* is disturbing! I've got half a mind to call his dad and let him in on Peyton's little secret."

In the year that Kylan and I have been together, I've not once seen him get mad. Kylan's mom says it's not in his nature to get mad. His whole family is a bunch of calm clams.

I shake my head. "Oh, Kylan, please don't do that. Peyton knows all your deepest darkest secrets too. There's no telling what he would do to get back at you. It will all come out in the wash. At least that's what Nanny says."

As Kylan and I stand there in silence, I look around at the partygoers and notice a lot of people have already left.

Hopefully they're going home and not to Cass' beer bust. Nothing good can come from that!

"Hey Sis! Where've you been!" Maria squeals as she bounces up next to me. "Look who showed up!" Maria steps aside and pushes Hugo in front of her.

"Oh hi, Hugo! Good to see you. How'd you get in the band party?" I ask.

Maria instantly blushes and leans down to whisper. "I let him in," she giggles. "Nobody has noticed yet." Maria looks around to see if anyone is watching us.

"Well, y'all better be careful. You don't want to go and piss off Mrs. Sheila. You'll never hear the end of it, Maria." I glare hard at Maria hoping she gets the clue.

"Hey, did you hear about that big party over in Long Beach?" Maria asks.

Kylan and I look at each other then back at Maria. "Um, yeah, it's at Cass' uncle's house on the beach. We got a personal invite from the Bunkhouse Big Sis herself."

Maria lets out an overly emphasized sigh. "Really? Well, that's a bummer." Maria turns to Hugo. "Did you know Cass was hosting this party?"

Hugo shrugs his shoulders. "I'm sure it will be fine. I was really looking forward to going and showing you off."

Kylan and I swap glances. I look over to Maria. "Showing you off, huh?"

Maria buzzes, "Yes, meet my new beau, Hugo!" Pretty sure her face just turned ten sheets of red. "Well, you already knew him, but not as my man. So, it's official! We're a thing!"

Maria is such a beautiful person inside and out. She is a spitting image of her sister Ashley which makes her even more attractive to most guys who knew Ashley. Ashley was such an amazing soul. She'd do anything to help someone in need. Maria is similar to Ashley in that aspect, but she still has some room to grow. This new guy, Hugo, whoo-ee he's a hot one! Next to Kylan, he's the cutest guy I know right now. Obviously, Kylan is the most handsome guy in my school, but Hugo is a close second. Maria did well with this one.

"I have an idea!" I pipe up. "How about we all go back to my house and hang out for the night. I know it's not a wild and crazy party or anything, but we can make some popcorn, set up my new sixty-five inch TV, and watch a movie. What do ya say?"

Kylan puts his arm around me and kisses the side of my head. "I think that's a great idea! What about y'all?"

Maria looks up at Hugo. "Oh, I don't know. We were kinda looking at getting into something a little more exciting tonight. Weren't we?"

Hugo bends down and gently kisses Maria on the lips. Hugo is probably at least six feet tall if not taller. He towers over Maria. She looks like a little shrimp compared to him.

"I'll do whatever you want to do, Maria. As long as I get to hang out with you, I don't really care," Hugo says in a deep grown voice.

You know, Hugo's voice is really deep. He doesn't have any facial hair, but Maria told me that most Latinos don't have facial hair. Maybe he's just really mature for his age.

Maria steps closer to me. "How about this?" Maria pauses and looks up at Hugo for reassurance. "How about I just meet you over at your house around ten o'clock? Your mom won't be home yet and if your dad's there, I'm sure he'll be sound asleep. What do you think?"

Hugo seems like a pretty good guy who will look out for Maria. He drives a nice car and makes good grades, I think. At least that's what Maria told me. "That's fine with me. What do you think Kylan?"

Kylan leans down and slowly kisses me on the lips. He leans back slightly to where he's about an inch from my face and says, "I think that's fine with me." His breath tastes sweet on my lips. "I'll take every second of alone time I can get with you, Babe." Then he leans in and kisses me again. "I just can't wait to get you home," he says with a slight growl to his voice.

When Kylan talks to me like that, it makes my insides melt. I start feeling warm and tingly all over. If I weren't such a good girl, I'd get him in my bed tonight and let him take full advantage of me. But, I know better, or do I?

CHAPTER 25

I t's nearly ten-thirty, Kylan. Where is she?" Yes, I am starting to panic. I'm sure you can hear it in my voice.

"Oh Babe, don't worry about Maria. Hugo can take care of her. I know she's mean as a snake, but he seems like he can handle it. Just enjoy the last few minutes without her." Kylan rolls me over on the couch and slowly crawls on top of me.

As he moves my hair off my face he squints his eyes and looks down at me. "You're worried aren't you? I can see it in the lines on your face."

I nod my head. "Yes, how'd you know?"

"Well, it's obvious. You've been checking your phone every five minutes for the past thirty minutes. Then you let out a groan when you see how much time has passed."

"Oh, Kylan. You know me all too well."

Kylan lowers his entire body on top of mine and kisses the side of my neck. I jump when he touches a particular spot that's sensitive. That one little spot can set me on fire in a matter of seconds and he knows that.

We must've got wrapped up in each other because the next thing we knew, Maria and Hugo were standing over us giggling. Thank God we were still fully clothed!

I push Kylan off of me and jump up as fast as I can. "OMG! Hi guys! What's up?" I say as I can feel the heat of embarrassment sweep through my entire body. I try to flatten out my hair as I rake my fingers through the knots.

Maria and Hugo just stand there with crap eating grins across their faces. "Oh, nothing much!" Maria puts her arm in Hugo's and holds on tight. "We went by Cass' party for a few."

My smile instantly drops. "Why?" I ask.

"Hugo wanted to show me off, and I didn't mind being shown off to everybody. There were tons of people there. You guys should've gone with us. Her uncle's house is amazing, too! It's three stories tall and right on the beach. It has a pool in the front yard with this cool waterfall that lights up different colors. Oh, Kimmy, I hate you missed it."

I look at Maria not knowing what to say because I'm pretty sure she's lost her mind, again. "Well I don't. We enjoyed staying home and watching Mr. Mayberry set up this gigantic TV." I point to the TV I won at the party wondering how my parents will react to it when they get here. "And sometimes it's just nice to snuggle up at home and not worry about other people."

"What time are your parents getting home?" Maria slyly asks.

Puzzled I reply, "I don't know. Mom usually doesn't get home until sometime after midnight, and Dad is usually home by now. You should know this. You lived here for an entire year."

"Oh, I know. I was just checking to see if Hugo and I could get a few more minutes together. Right Hugo?" Maria looks up at him as he slowly leans down and kisses her lips. They're really moving along fast in their relationship. Maybe it's because Hugo is so much older. Well, he's a junior but he's already seventeen Maria said.

"I don't know and I don't care what y'all do. Just know that when I wake up in the morning, you better be somewhere in my house." I sternly look at Maria like I'm mad, but can't hold that expression for long because I'm really not. "I'm just kidding, you know," I laugh.

Maria looks at me confused then smiles. "Well, we're going to go sit in Hugo's car and listen to music until your mom gets home."

I feel someone shaking me by the shoulder but don't recognize the voice. I know I'm safe because I'm wrapped up in my very protective boyfriend. I lift Kylan's arm off of me and roll over to see my mom standing in front of us in the living room. "Honey, wake up and get in bed."

"Mom, your voice. What's wrong with it?"

Mom clears her throat a few times then says, "We had an issue at work tonight with a customer. He touched one of my waitresses, and I had to yell at him. Then things got ugly. But I'm fine. Mr. Hernandez was working late and caught everything on camera. He had to come down and take care of the customer. I got a little upset about it, but I promise you everything is fine now. My voice is just a little hoarse."

I stand up and reach out to give my mom a hug. Which is something I don't do often now that I think about it. It felt good to hug her. I could tell she was still hurting inside. Every time something happens at work she stresses over it for days. I hope this won't be one of those times. The last time she had an incident at work, I'm pretty sure Mom lost ten pounds worrying herself sick.

Mom turns to the new TV and points, "What's this?"

I perk up and announce, "I won this at the band party tonight! Mr. Mayberry brought it over and set it up. What do you think?"

"Oh, Kimmy, it's great! Dad and I were just talking about getting a new TV this year for Christmas. Now we won't have to!" Then mom wrinkles her brow. "Why didn't you clean up this house first? It's a disaster in here. I'm embarrassed that he had to see this mess!" Mom pauses and looks around the living room. "By the way, where's Maria and who's car is parked out there on the street?"

I look over at Kylan who is now sitting up on the couch with sleepy eyes and raise my eyebrows. "Well, that's Hugo's car and Maria's in there with him."

Mom tilts her head to the side just like Oscar does when he's trying to figure out what I'm saying. "Um, Kimmy, who's Hugo?"

I laugh. "Apparently, he's Maria's new boyfriend."

Mom widens her eyes and pauses as if she wants to say something but then stops. "Well, I was hoping she and Peyton would get back together. Y'all all got along so well. What a shame he had to go and be a bullheaded turd."

Kylan stands up and walks over to my mom. "Mrs. Nina, I think this is probably for the better. Hugo seems like a pretty good guy, and Peyton is not the same guy he was when he and Maria first started dating. He's changed and not in a good way."

I can tell my mom didn't want to hear what Kylan just said. She just shakes her head. "Ok, then. Kimmy go get Maria and tell her to bring this new boyfriend in the house so I can approve." She looks over at Kylan. "Are you staying or going? If you're staying, you'll have to sleep on the couch. If you're going, you need to text your mom and let her know you're coming home."

Kylan looks at me and winks. "If you don't mind, since it's so late, I guess I'll stay. I'll text my mom and let her know I'll be here for the night. I'm sure she won't care."

"All right, y'all go get Maria and her fella while I get Kylan's bed made," Mom says as she starts to take her hair down.

As Kylan and I head outside, we notice Hugo's car slowly rocking back and forth. I stop and look at Kylan and he looks back at me in terror.

"What the hell? Did we just catch them doing it?" Kylan sputters.

I shake my head back and forth so fast I make myself dizzy. "Oh God! No! She promised me!" I run over to the car in a panic to try and stop this from happening, but it's too late. The car stops rocking and the black tinted windows in the back seat begin to roll down.

Maria and Hugo are laughing so hard neither one of them can speak. I just stand there in disgust.

"Haha! Got you!" Maria yells in a hysterical fit.

I take a deep breath. "Maria! I'm going to kill you! You just about gave me a heart attack!"

Maria chuckles, "No worries, Sis! Hugo's not like that. He agrees about waiting until marriage. He has nine siblings and understands firsthand what happens when couples get a little too frisky."

I stand there and think to myself, nine siblings? Wow! His parents have been really busy! There's no way on this earth I'd have that many kids. I'm not even sure if I like kids let alone a whole herd of them.

"Well that's great," I say with sarcasm. "Um, Hugo. My mom wants to meet you. Can you come in for a few before you leave?"

Hugo looks over at Maria for reassurance then looks back at me and replies, "Sure, if I need to."

This Hugo guy seems pretty good for Maria. I guess you could say I like him. He is pretty passive which is good for Maria. She likes to boss people around and he appears to not mind it. Well, not right now at least. And best of all, he has a good sense of humor which is hard to find these days. Hugo is nothing like Peyton. Peyton was such a dodo bird. He would say some of the most stupid things you've ever heard.

Since my parents took Maria's bed out of my bedroom, she has to either sleep head to toes with me tonight or by herself in the guest room. I offered her the guest room, but she said it reminds her too much of Ashley. So, we decided we'd sleep in my room in my teenie bed. Mom made her a pallet on the floor in case we get uncomfortable.

"Did you ever imagine I'd be dating a Latino?"

As I lie here in bed, I'm pretty sure I can smell Maria's feet, but I don't care. It's Maria. She's my best friend in the whole world and probably the cleanest person I know. I'm sure her feet just got sweaty in her dance shoes she was wearing with her outfit tonight.

"Actually, Maria, I never thought either one of us would ever have a boyfriend. Look at us now. You're on your second and my first is sleeping in the living room of my parent's house and my parents don't mind. You know, Sis, we've really got it made, don't we?"

My bedroom is so dark right now that I can't even see my hand in front of my face. I raise up to see if Maria is already asleep. She raises up at the exact same time that I do.

"Kimmy, can I tell you something?" My heart drops for a fraction of a second until she speaks. "I don't like being back at home."

I wait for her to continue, but she doesn't. "Why is that?" I ask. Maria doesn't say anything. I think I know why, but I don't want to say it.

"Ashley is still in that house. She hasn't left yet," Maria mutters. "I feel like her soul is in limbo between Earth and the afterlife. Like she hasn't entered the gates of Heaven yet." Maria pauses. "Kimmy, I'm afraid she's in purgatory getting her soul cleansed from where she had premarital sex with Jason. I'm worried that purgatory is painful for her and that's why I can feel her in the house still."

My stomach churns at the thought of my beautiful Ashley being in pain. I just can't bear the thought of it. "Maria, a lot of people have premarital sex. Do you think all those people go through purgatory before they can get into heaven?"

Silence fills my bedroom for several minutes until Maria finally answers my question.

"We were in Mass a while back and the priest was talking about purgatory and the types of things that would get you there. I kind of zoned out for a minute because I was bored, but the last thing he said was that the Bible says that nothing unclean or impure can enter into Heaven. They all must go through purgatory before they can enter. I did some research, and purgatory is bad from what I've read. This has been so heavy on my mind that I can't even sleep at night."

I lie very still trying to process what Maria just told me. I don't know much about the Catholic church, only what Maria has taught me. Surprisingly, she's a very religious person and knows a lot about it. "Maria, I don't think this is something you need to worry about. It is all beyond your control, and one day we'll all get to see Ashley again in Heaven."

Maria quickly snaps back, "But what if she is still in purgatory when we die and we never get to be reunited with her? Kimmy, I'm worried for her soul."

At this point in our conversation, I decide that I have nothing more to add. Not because I don't want to talk to Maria, because I really do. But because I really don't understand what she is talking about, and I don't want to sound like an idiot. Plus, I'm starting to get really upset just thinking about Ashley and I don't feel like crying right now. So, I close my eyes tightly and try to think happy thoughts and my sweet boyfriend sleeping on the couch with my chocolate donut, Oscar.

CHAPTER 26

I love a nice Mississippi fall day! I know our seasons here are quite different from other places, but we do have a few subtle changes. The leaves on our trees start changing colors around November. Some of them fall to the ground, and some of them just hang around on the branches until the new spring leaves come in. There's also a slight crispness to the air. Probably not like you would experience up North, but when you head out in the mornings and the temperature is in the low sixties, you just get that cozy fall feel.

Although it's late October, I still wear flip-flops every day to school! I had a cold a couple of weeks ago. My mom made me go to the doctor, because she thought I was getting bronchitis. When the doctor entered the exam room, the first thing he said was, "If you were wearing some halfway decent shoes, you'd probably not even be sick right now." I don't really know what he was meaning by that, but since then my mom has made me put on tennis shoes before I leave the house for school. But what she doesn't know is that I keep my flip-flops in my backpack and change into them as soon as I get on the bus. She'd probably ground me for life if she ever found out! Anyway, I didn't have bronchitis. I just had a bad cold.

So, this weekend is the fall festival at Bay High School. The band is setting up several booths. We will have a food booth where we will be selling po boys. We also have a couple of games set up. I am working the Plates for Pennies game except it's not pennies, it's quarters. We will have all these old, mismatched plates, bowls, cups, and saucers strategically set up on boards. People will come up and toss quarters at the dinnerware, and if their quarter lands on a piece, they get to take it home. Most of the time the quarters bounce off and that's how we make money. Surprisingly, this game is the most popular at the whole fall festival!

"What game did you say you're working?" I ask Maria as she mopes around the living room.

"The stupid photo booth," she says with her head down focused on her phone.

"Don't worry, he'll call you soon," I reassure her. Maria's not heard from Hugo since last night when he dropped her off at home after their date to the homecoming dance. Something really strange happened there too. When they were checking for his name on the list to get in, it wasn't on there. Mrs. Vickie, our school nurse, said she recognized Hugo and they let him go in. The only thing we could figure was that since he was new to the school, his name wasn't on the list yet.

We had a pretty good time at the dance. It wasn't anything spectacular, but we all enjoyed ourselves. Kylan's shoulders were sore from carrying around his snare drum at the game, so we only danced to a couple of songs then hung out in the corner.

Maria and Hugo ended up leaving the dance early because Cass and Peyton had to make a grand entrance. Cass was running for homecoming queen all week so we had to suffer through that. She even gave a speech in front of the entire school on Thursday during the pep rally. I wanted to throw up! But what was really funny last night was at the ballgame when the homecoming queen was crowned. They announced the queen's name on the stadium's loudspeaker, and it wasn't Cass! The look on her face was priceless. I actually busted out laughing at the sight. I only stopped laughing because Mr. Mayberry turned around and gave me a dirty look. I guess since Cass is in band I should've been rooting for her, but she was the cause for my best friend's heart to be broken, so now she's my enemy. I'd never vote for her for anything!

Maria looks up from her phone with a grin. "No worries. He just texted. He said his phone died last night and he forgot to charge it."

"See, I told you!" I teased. "He's in love with you, Sis. I can see it in his eyes."

Maria smacks my shoulder and puts her hand on her hip. "Oh hush up. He's not told me that yet."

"Well I'm sure it's coming soon!" I laugh. "Is he coming to pick you up from here or are you riding with us? You know Nanny will need to know ahead of time so she can plan. You know how she is about things."

My Nanny is the most awesome grandma in this world! But there's something you should know about her. She doesn't like surprises! Isn't that interesting? She loves to surprise others, but she doesn't like to be on the receiving end. She told me the reason why one time and I'll never forget it. She said that when she was young, her older sister was hiding behind the shower curtain in her bathroom. Apparently, Nanny really had to use the bathroom. Before Nanny could even sit down on the toilet, her sister jumped out from behind the shower curtain and literally scared the pee out of her. Ever since then, Nanny has been terrified of surprises.

"Hugo's coming to get me in around fifteen minutes. He said he had to stop by Froogel's for something then he would be on his way." Maria walks over to look at my baby pictures hanging on my living room wall. She abruptly stops and turns around facing me with a somber expression. "Every time I look at these pictures, it reminds me of our last day with Ashley. She was so curious about them for some reason. We didn't know that reason at the time, but we do now." Maria wipes a tear from her cheek. "She would've been an amazing mom."

Knock, Knock, Knock

Deep in thought, Maria and I both almost jump out of our skin.

"EEK!" Maria screeches. "That's him! I get so excited just knowing he's on the other side of this door!"

I smile back at her knowing how truly happy she is right now. And to think it wasn't too long ago that I was concerned about her recent breakup. Pish! I should've known better!

"OMG! Look what Hugo brought me!" Maria holds up the most beautiful bouquet of flowers I've ever seen! "Aren't they gorgeous?"

I lean down to smell them and feel the coolness of the petals. I look up at Maria and nod. "Yep, Sis!"

About that time, Hugo bends down, kisses Maria on the cheek and whispers, "Gorgeous just like you," into Maria's ear, but he made sure to say it loud enough so I could hear it. Geez!

"Next!" I keep yelling to the kids in line so they can get a chance to flip their quarters. It's actually pretty hilarious to see how proud these kids are to win a piece of dinnerware. I mean, what do you think they do with these dishes? It probably just pisses their mothers off when they bring home some random pieces. I know my mom would be like, "Why did you bring this mismatched crap home, Kimmy? We have enough already without you having to add to it."

Then I look up and see Cass and Peyton standing in line. I sigh with aggravation. Do they really have to play my game? Well, it's not mine personally, but the game I am working? I roll my eyes as they keep inching closer. I decide it's time for my supper break, so I step over and tap Liz on the shoulder. She jumps as she was concentrating on dodging flying quarters that this little boy is flinging all over the place.

"Hey, what's up?" Liz asks with the look of frustration on her face as a coin goes whizzing between the two of us.

I smile really big at her and clench my teeth together. "I'm taking a break before those two clowns get up here."

About the time I get my last word out to Liz I hear, "Oh, hi Kimmy! Long time no see, friend!"

I turn and look out to the crowd trying to ignore them. It's really loud in here so maybe I can just turn around and act like I didn't hear them.

"Kimmy, I'm talking to you. I know you can hear me!" Cass shouts over the crowd.

Reluctantly, I focus my attention on her. She is wrapped around Peyton tighter than a burrito from the Taco Wagon. I wave, "Oh hey there!" I say. "I thought I heard someone saying my name, but the noise is just too much," I nervously laugh.

"Well, I was hoping you could help us win some dinnerware for our future house. You wouldn't mind helping little ole me out, would you?" Cass asks with a sugarcoated tone.

I stand there and just stare at the two of them trying to process what she just said to me. Your future home? What the hell is she talking about? Peyton is only sixteen and there's no way his parents are going to let him move in with her any time soon.

"I'm not cheating on this game for you," I gulp. "Anyway, I was fixing to take my supper break and go see Kylan."

Cass huffs, "Well, can't you at least just give me change for a five-dollar bill before you leave?"

I roll my eyes at her. "Sure. Give me your money." She is really starting to piss me off now. As soon as I hand her the change, she instantly starts flinging quarters at my head. "Hey! What's that for?"

Cass laughs with an evil grin on her face. "I guess you'll learn your lesson eventually. You know the saying, you scratch my back, and I'll scratch yours," she says still grinning at me like a possum eating out of the garbage can.

I shake my head, "Nope, can't say I've ever heard that one."

"Hmph," Cass puts her hand on her hip and straightens her back. "Oh yeah, I forgot that you're in special ed. Well, why don't you ask your friend Maria what it means. She can explain it to you."

As Cass turns around, she takes her entire handful of quarters and throws them square at my head. Luckily, I have catlike reflexes and am able to squat down and miss every single one of them.

"OMG! Are you ok, Kimmy?" Liz hunkers down to the floor with me.

I look at Liz as we both hear *CLING, CLING, CLING!* It sounds like a thousand slot machines hitting the jackpot all at one time. I pop back up and yell, "Winner, winner, chicken dinner!"

"Why did she do that to you?" Liz asks with her eyebrows crossed.

"Because I wouldn't cheat on this game for her. That's how she is you know. She's a snake!"

Then a sweet little girl comes up and asks, "Does that lady not want her dishes that she won?"

I shrug my shoulders and reply, "I don't know, but would you like to have them?"

The girl's eyes light up and she smiles back at me, "I would love to have them. I've already tried four times with her," she points to Liz, "but I haven't had any luck. My mom and I just got a brand new apartment and she would be so proud if I gave them to her."

I turn and look at Liz as the little girl walks away with an armful of dishes. Liz says, "Did that just melt your heart or what?"

"Yeah, that was a sweet child," I mutter to Liz still trying to figure out what Cass just said to me.

"She said what, then what?" Kylan shouts at me over the crowd.

I put my finger to my lips, "Shh, stop yelling! I don't want anyone to hear!"

Kylan looks at me bashfully, "Oh, I'm sorry, Babe. Cass is such a bitch! I don't know why Peyton puts up with that. Oh wait, yes I do, never mind." Kylan rolls his eyes. Then he explains to me what Cass meant by all that back scratching business. I feel like such an idiot that I had never heard that saying before.

Kylan kisses me on the forehead and nudges me back to my game. "Go have fun and watch out for flying quarters! I highly doubt you'll see them again tonight. That's how she rolls. Cass never comes back to give others a chance to get even with her. She always has to be ahead." Kylan winks at me and walks away.

Just as I get back to the front of the booth, I see Peyton walking up. Oh Lord, what does he want this time?

"Hey Kimmy, I'm really sorry about what happened earlier with Cass." Peyton suspiciously looks around like someone might be watching us. "Cass wanted me to come back and get the plates she won. She said she needed to go talk to a friend and wouldn't be able to stop back by here before she left."

I look Peyton dead in the eyes as if I could cut through to his soul. "You're so stupid! Those plates are long gone."

He looks back at me and thinks hard before he speaks. I really feel like he wants to tell me something but can't. Instead he just shrugs his shoulders and says, "Ok, I'll let her know." Then he turns and walks away.

CHAPTER 27

Do you think we'll get married one day?" Lying on my back, I gaze up at Kylan as he looks out to the ocean. I can tell he's got a lot on his mind just by seeing the lack of expression on his face. He's really been missing his friendship with Peyton. Kylan won't admit it, but I know it's true.

The past few months have been really hard on Kylan. He and Peyton did everything together. I'm pretty sure they were tighter than Maria and I have ever been. Kylan told me the other day that he likes hanging out with Maria and Hugo, but Hugo just isn't the same as Peyton.

Kylan leans down and gently kisses my forehead. "I'm sure we probably will," Kylan assures me. "You never know, though, one day some tall, dark, and handsome feller might come along and sweep you off your feet."

I giggle, "He already has!"

Kylan gives me a side eye and grins. "What? Are you cheating on me with another dude?" he sarcastically growls.

I raise up off the sand so hard I give myself an instant headache. "No, silly! I'm talking about you!"

Kylan slowly turns to me and moves my hair out of my eyes. "I know, Babe," he whispers. "I just love you so much. I'd never want anyone to steal you away from me." Kylan pauses and looks back to the ocean. "All that crap with Peyton and Maria has really had me thinking here lately."

"What about?" I ask.

Kylan shakes his head. "Oh, it's too much to talk about right now. We are supposed to be having a relaxing day on the beach. Talking about my worries is not what I call relaxing."

I hate it when Kylan does that to me. He'll say something, then decide it's not a good time to talk about it. I feel like maybe he doesn't want to hurt my feelings, but what he doesn't know is that he is hurting me more by not telling me stuff. I tried to explain that to him one time, but he just didn't get it, so I stopped. Men!

"I'm not going to let you get away with that this time. Tell me what you're thinking about!" I demand.

Kylan instantly blushes. As he takes a deep breath, I can see a vein popping out of the side of his head that I've never seen before. "Kimmy, I've never felt this way about anyone in my entire life. When I look at you, it's like time stops. I'm being one hundred percent serious about someone stealing you away when we go to college. I mean look at you! You're gorgeous!"

Puzzled, I ask, "Are you under some kind of spell, because I'm pretty sure I look at myself every day in the mirror. Obviously, we're not seeing the same thing."

"Oh, come on, Babe. You're beautiful and you know it!" Kylan pushes me back down to the sand and rolls his body on top of mine. "You could have any guy in our school, and you chose me."

I look deeply into his big brown eyes and think about what Kylan just said. Then I think about how I appear to others who don't know me. Maybe I do look pretty good after all. I do have a lot of guys who try to talk to me at school but stop as soon as they find out I'm with Kylan.

"You have nothing to worry about," I tell him.

Kylan leans down and slowly starts kissing my lips. I can feel him lower his body on to mine as his kisses become more passionate. Our bodies are humming together in their natural rhythm until I get the feeling that we're being watched. I hesitantly open my eyes.

"Ahhhhhhh! What are you doing here, Nanny?" I push Kylan off of me and immediately jump to my feet.

Nanny just stands there with her hands on her hips shaking her head back and forth. "Young lady, I believe I should be the one asking you that question. Does your mom know you're here on the beach making out with this hot stud of yours?" Nanny laughs. "Come on, love birds. Chas and I thought we were getting stood up by y'all. You were supposed to be at Cuz's fifteen minutes ago!"

I grab my phone to check the time only to realize that Kylan and I had seriously been making out for over thirty minutes right there in front of everybody at the public beach. Thank goodness it's the off season and we weren't surrounded by those crazy tourists.

We trudge up the steep steps of the sea wall and finally make it to the top. Gosh, I'm totally out of breath! They really need to do something about these steps. They're really going to get me one day!

As we get seated at Cuz's, I notice that it's really busy here for a Sunday afternoon. Maybe everyone is coming in for those to-die-for seafood nachos. I know that's what I'm ordering.

"So, Nanny, what did you want to talk to me and Kylan about that was so pressing we had to meet today?" I look between Nanny and Chas hoping to get some kind of indication about what's going on.

Nanny smiles, "We really didn't need to talk about anything. Chas and I just wanted to spend a little time with you guys. We feel like we never see you since we've moved over here to Waveland." Nanny sighs, "I think we saw you more when we lived in New Orleans."

"Well, Nanny, I'm a busy high schooler now!" I grin. "Actually, we have been really busy with band this fall, but since the season is almost over, you should be seeing me a lot more."

Nanny tilts her head to the side and winks. "Well, that's good to hear, Sweet Pea. Chas and I have missed all of y'all, including Maria and Peyton. Well, maybe I should just say we've missed Maria," Nanny snorts. "Yeah, I'm still pretty pissed with that Peyton. I can't believe what he did to my sweet baby Maria."

Kylan and I sit and just stare at Nanny and Chas knowing good and well that neither of us want to discuss this topic anymore. You know they say just as you're getting over something bad, someone will pour salt in the wound and relight the fire. I just shrug my shoulders.

As the bartender walks up to take our order, I notice a strange look on his face. "Well, hello there my friends!" he says. "Your friend Maria just left. I'm surprised you didn't run into her."

I look over at Kylan trying to rack my brain as to how and why Maria would be at Cuz's without us. She never comes here unless she is with me or my family.

"Yeah, she was with this nice young Hispanic gentleman, but he's a lot older than you kids," the bartender explains. "They came in acting like a couple or something. They were holding hands and kissing in the back booth." He shakes his head, "At first, I thought Maria was with her uncle, but when they started kissing, I was like, um, no way!"

I look at Kylan and he looks at me as we both bust out laughing at the same time. I am laughing so hard my side starts hurting and I have to jump off the barstool just to catch my breath.

The bartender gives us a look of disgust and flares his nostrils. "What's so funny?"

When I finally regain my composure, I respond, "That's Maria's boyfriend, Hugo! He's a junior in high school. He's seventeen but looks a lot older."

The bartender asks, "Are you sure, Kimmy?"

"Yes, I'm sure!" I snicker.

He rolls his eyes, "Whatever, I'm just trying to look out for my girls! Do you want the usual?"

I smile my biggest smile, "Of course!"

We had such a wonderful meal with Nanny and Chas. It was really good to catch up with them. Nanny was right, we haven't seen them at all since they moved here. So, she invited Kylan and I to stay over at their house next weekend for a sleepover. Well, Kylan and I will be sleeping in separate rooms, obviously, but still under the same roof. Nanny told me to ask Maria to stay too, but she's not so sure about Hugo until she gets to know him. I told Nanny that Maria will probably decline unless Hugo can stay. They are pretty much attached at the hip!

Kylan and I were surprised to see Dad at home when we got there. You remember how he used to take off every Sunday and take me and Maria to Cuz's for lunch? Well, since he's been slammed at the shipyard, our Sunday lunch dates have ended. I guess that's why Nanny mentioned making this a weekly thing for us.

Anyway, back to my dad. So he was at home sitting on the couch when Kylan and I walked into the living room. And you want to know what else he was doing? He was smoking a cigar! My dad never smokes cigars!

"Dad! Put that thing out! You're going to give us cancer!" I yell.

Dad looks at me with a possumish grin on his face. I snarl up my lip like I smelled something funky! "You're never going to believe what happened at work today, Honey," Dad hints ever so nonchalantly.

I look over to Kylan as he takes hold of my hand. I can tell that Kylan is nervous because his hand is so sweaty it can barely grip mine. Dad is acting kind of strange, though.

"What?" I snip back at him.

"Well, if you're going to act like that, then I'm not going to share it with you." Dad leans his head back on the couch and closes his eyes. As he takes a big puff off his cigar, he coughs and starts laughing at the same time. "Oh, what the hell, you'll get it out of me anyway. So, I might as well just get it over with now."

Kylan and I both stand there in awe at the way my dad is acting. He's so relaxed! Usually, my dad is in and out in a flash. He comes home, takes a shower, and bolts out the door before anyone can stop him. This is so uncharacteristic of him.

As Dad starts to speak, I hear a tone in his voice that I haven't heard in years. I can't quite put my finger on it, but I can sense he's happy for once.

Dad stands up as he blows out a cloud of smoke. "You are looking at the new manager of East Port Shipyard!"

"Oh wow, Dad! That's awesome!" I cheer.

"Best of all...it comes with a huge raise! We're never going to have to worry about money again!" Dad announces.

I start jumping up and down screaming. I run and give dad a big bear hug as I try not to collide with his lit cigar. "That's the best news I've heard in a long time! When do you start?"

"Today! I started today!"

"Why didn't you tell me about this? Did Mom know?" I ask puzzled.

"Oh Honey, of course your mother knew. We wanted to keep it a secret until my first day. I wanted to wait until your mother came home to tell you, but I was about to bust holding it in," Dad boasts.

My dad has always been my biggest fan. He would do anything in this world to make sure my mom and I are content. If that meant working overtime seven days a week, he'd do it just knowing that we were being taken care of.

"So, what does all this mean?" I ask dad once our excitement settled.

"Well, it won't be much different. I'll still be working my ass off over at the shipyard, but instead of taking orders, I'll be giving them!"

Kylan and I decide to celebrate my dad by going to the store to get him a cake. We picked out the biggest most delicious looking one we could find. By the time we got back, Mom was home from work, and we all hung out in the living room talking about how we were going to spend Dad's first big paycheck.

When Mom and Dad went to bed, Kylan and I decided to watch a movie on my giant TV. I learned today that sometimes it's the little things in life that make such a huge difference in the way we live.

CHAPTER 28

OMG! Who is calling me so late at night? I roll over to check my phone to see Peyton's name run across the top of it.

"Really, Peyton, it's too late for this mess. I know you're still in love with Maria, but she's completely over you," I say out loud knowing good and well he can't hear me, but I really don't want to answer my phone right now. I'm so tired and pretty sure I just fell asleep.

I raise up and check the time, twelve forty-five AM. Geez. Just as I am settling back with my covers pulled up to my chin, I hear it again.

Buzz, Buzz...Buzz, Buzz...Buzz, Buzz...

Nope! I'm not doing it! Last time I answered a call from Peyton, he was sobbing like a little girl. I'm not dealing with him right now. I need my beauty rest!

I look over at my phone again. Sure enough, it's Peyton. I press the button on the side of my phone to silence all the buzzing. There, now I can finally get some sleep.

Knock, Knock, Knock...Knock, Knock, Knock

You've got to be kidding me! "Yes, I'm in here Mom! Kylan's on the couch."
Nobody responds.

Knock, Knock, Knock...Knock, Knock, Knock

Ok, now this is strange. Why wouldn't my mom peek her head in and say good night to me? I throw my covers off and decide I need to see who is knocking on my door. I know it's not an intruder, because Kylan is sleeping on my couch in the living room. He is the lightest sleeper I've ever seen. One time, I sneezed in my bedroom in the middle of the night with the door shut and next thing I knew he was checking to see if I was getting sick. How on earth did he even hear me sneeze?

"Kylan, what's up?" I look at him with my head tilted to the side in a confused manner.

Kylan takes a deep breath and releases it. "Peyton has called my phone three times now, but I just can't stand the thought of talking to him. What should I do?"

"What do you mean he's called you three times? He's called me twice in the last few minutes and I just keep silencing his call."

Kylan and I both stand there in the middle of my hallway staring at each other in complete silence. Finally, I have a thought. "Maybe he and Cass broke up and he's drunk or something."

Kylan shakes his head. "Nah, I don't think he'd be drinking, but it is possible that they broke up. Maybe you're right. He's probably calling to try and get back with Maria."

At that exact moment, both of our phones start vibrating! I look down at mine. "Liz is calling me. That's strange. Should I answer it?"

Kylan looks at his phone, "Peyton, again."

I go ahead and answer my phone as Kylan just stands there staring at his.

"Hello?"

"Kimmy! What the hell?" Liz says in a disturbed whisper.

"What do you mean?" I ask.

"Peyton has been blowing up my phone. When I finally answered it, he asked for you. When I told him you weren't with me he said for me to get a hold of you ASAP! He sounded quite panicked!" Liz continued, "Is something going on with you and him that I should know about?" she asked.

I look over at Kylan with a scowl on my face. "Really Liz, I can't believe you would ask me that. He's probably the most disgusting human being I can even think of right now."

Liz giggles, "Well, that's what I thought too, but I was just wanting to make sure we're both on the same page."

I roll my eyes as Kylan puts his arm around my shoulder and kisses my cheek. "So, I guess I should give Peyton a call back. Maybe his car broke down or something. He keeps calling Kylan too. I'm sure he's just being overly dramatic as usual. I'll let you know if anything shakes out of this."

"Good deal! Talk to you later." Liz hangs up the phone first and my screen goes blank.

I look up at Kylan. "So, who's going to be the lucky one to call him back."

Kylan stands back and holds out his hands. "There's only one way to decide. Rock, Paper, Scissors," he declares.

After three rounds of Rock, Paper, Scissors, Kylan wins two out of three times. "I guess it's my turn, again, this time. I just don't know how much sobbing and carrying on I can handle right now. Let's make a deal. If it gets too intense, I'll say my mom's coming, and I have to go."

"Sounds like a plan, Babe!"

I look down at my phone, and what do you know? Peyton's calling me. "Hello?" I press the button on my phone to put him on speaker so Kylan can listen in on the conversation.

After a long pause, Peyton finally speaks. "Kimmy, are you safe?"

"Peyton, yes, I'm safe at home with my parents and Kylan. What's up?" I ask in an annoyed tone.

"Can anyone hear me?" Peyton asks. Now, I can hear a slight panic in his voice.

"Um, yeah, Kylan is right here, and I have you on speaker phone."

"Kylan! I've been trying to call you too! Why won't y'all answer me? Anyways, this is an emergency!" Then Peyton whispers the words that I never, ever wanted to hear. "Maria is in danger!"

My heart immediately stops beating. My mouth instantly goes dry just hearing the tone of Peyton's voice. I cannot speak. This is serious! I can tell by the way he's talking.

Kylan grabs my phone out of my hand as I burst into tears. "Peyton, what is going on with Maria? Why do you think she's in danger?" Kylan calmly asks.

"I can't talk. I gotta go. Cass is coming. Call Maria now if you ever want to speak to her again!" Then my phone screen goes blank.

Kylan lowers me to the floor of my hallway and wraps his arms tightly around me. I can feel his heart beating rapidly on my arm. I'm pretty sure our hearts are beating equally as fast.

"Breathe, Babe. Come on, this is a time when we both have to remain calm and figure out what to do."

Kylan starts taking deep breaths which in turn helps me to regulate my breathing. When I am able to speak, all I can say is, "Call her!"

Kylan scrolls through my phone to find Maria's phone number. When he presses "Send" it goes straight to her voicemail. "What do we do? Should I go get my mom up?"

Kylan shakes his head. "No, let's just sit here for a minute. Are you ok, Babe?"

I look over at Kylan who is now pulling up my text messenger in my phone to send Maria a text. "I'm not ok. Text Peyton too. Maybe he will respond."

We patiently wait for a response that seems to never come. Then the messenger bubble appears.

> Hey, what is going on with Maria? (1:02 AM)

> Hiya Kimmy! Nothing is going on with Maria. Why would you ask such a question like that? (1:05 AM)

I look over at Kylan and he looks at me. I know that we are thinking the exact same thing! "Hiya? Who the hell says hiya?" Kylan narrows his eyes so small that all I can see is the black of his pupils.

"Oh my God, Kylan! Cass has Peyton's phone! He would never text those words to me!" I shriek.

Kylan picks up his phone off the floor and proceeds to call Peyton. "Now he's not answering me."

"I'll keep calling Maria on my phone and you keep calling Peyton on yours. Don't stop until someone answers," I tell Kylan in a frantic state.

We sit here on the floor of my hallway for the next fifteen minutes calling each of them. Nothing.

"Kylan, something is wrong! I can feel it!"

Then finally, Maria picks up! "Hey Kimmy! You ok?" Maria asks in her normal calm sounding tone.

"Uh, yeah, everything is good here," I hesitate. "What about you?"

"Oh, you know, Hugo and I are just driving out to the country to look at the stars. You know, he's so romantic!" she gushes.

"Maria, you're driving out to the country at this time of the night just to look at stars? Where do your parents think you're at right now."

Maria let's out a nervous laugh. "Well, yes, we are driving out to the country to have some alone time together. And to answer your other question, I'm supposed to be at your house."

I guessed it! Maria is lying to her parents again and sneaking around with Hugo just like she did with Peyton. "Maria, I cannot be dishonest with my parents. If my mom asks me, I have to tell her the truth."

"Oh, I know, I know. Don't lie to your mom. Let me take the blame. Just please let me have some fun while it lasts."

I can sense something different about Maria right now. "MARIA! Have you and Hugo been, you know?"

Maria quickly responds, "No, Kimmy! Why would you think that?"

So, then I ask the ever-pressing question of our friendship, "Are you planning on doing that with Hugo tonight?"

Maria doesn't respond. "Oh, Kimmy. Don't worry yourself over me now. I'm big enough to handle anything that comes my way."

I look at Kylan as tears fill my eyes. I don't have the words to respond to Maria right now. This is it! This is the night that she totally and completely lets me down as a friend. But I have to remember what Liz told me back at camp about not being able to control others.

"Ok, Maria," I say with a sigh. "Call me if you need me."

Then she hangs up.

I look over at Kylan who is pinching the skin between his eyes. I can tell he's really tired and wanting to go to sleep now that we've gotten in touch with Maria. "Something still isn't right, Kylan. I don't know what it is, but it's not right. I can feel it all over my body and deep down in my bones."

"Babe, I don't know what else to tell you. She said she was fine. You have to believe her as hard as it may be. She'll get caught one of these days and then her social life with Hugo will be done and over with. As soon as that happens, she'll be asking to move back in over here and all that crap."

I give Kylan a frown and gently bang my head against the wall. I say gently, because I really don't want to cause myself a headache this late in the night or should I say this early in the morning.

"So there's really nothing that we can do?" I ask Kylan with uncertainty.

He brushes the hair out of my eyes and swoops in with a slow sensuous kiss. "No, Babe. Maria's got to learn these lessons for herself."

I lie in bed with my eyes wide open. No amount of allergy medicine could make me fall asleep right now. I'm awake with that strange pit feeling in my stomach. It's a feeling that I used to get a lot before I had my heart surgery. Anxiety is what it's called. My thoughts are racing about Maria. Then I start thinking about Ashley and how she should still be here with us with a babbling baby on her hip.

Then I go back to thinking about Maria again and how much living she still has in her. I just can't stand the thought of her giving herself to Hugo. I know he's Latino and all, but why would you give it up so easily to someone you just met a couple of months ago.

Just when I think that my thoughts have slowed enough to fall asleep, it happens. My phone begins to vibrate on my bedside table. Not this again!

CHAPTER 29

You know those times when you're about ninety-nine percent certain that something bad is about to happen and you just don't want to advance to that moment? Well, this is one of those times. I can hear my phone buzzing beside my bed and I just don't have the strength to roll over and look at it. I know that whoever is calling me at this hour in the night doesn't have anything good to tell me. And if they did have good news, it could definitely wait until the morning.

Finally, my phone stops and I just continue to lie here in a nearly comatose state. I first heard that word, comatose, on one of our visits to Grandpa Eugene's home. He was describing this guy who lived next door to him and said, I quote, "Marvin lives in his bed. He's been comatose ever since they brought him in."

I had no idea what that meant so I asked if comatose meant you lived in your bed. Well, long story short, Grandpa Eugene explained it to me. He also told me that Marvin's wife got mad at him, shot him in the head, and that's how Marvin ended up comatose. Yeah, that's a really sad story. Poor Marvin. I think he died a while back from being so comatose, or something.

For now, I'm just going to lie here and ponder on life for a few.

Knock, Knock, Knock...Knock, Knock, Knock...Knock, Knock, Knock...Knock, Knock, Knock

My eyes fly open, and I catapult myself out of bed to see that I have nearly slept the morning away! It's seven fifty-seven!

"Coming!" I shout with a pounding heart.

As I open my bedroom door, Kylan rushes into my room nearly smacking me in the face.

"OMG! What is wrong with you?" I ask in disgust.

He turns toward me and eases my door shut while holding his finger to his lips. "Your parents are in the living room. They cannot hear what I'm about to tell you." Kylan takes a step closer to me and puts both his hands on my shoulders. "You promise me you won't scream?"

I nod my head feeling my heart starting to beat faster. "Yes, I promise," I croak out.

Kylan takes a deep breath. "Maria is in serious trouble," he blurts.

"Of course she is! She was supposed to stay the night over here last night and she ended up staying out all night with Hugo, right?"

Kylan looks at me with what seems like tears welling up in his eyes and shakes his head. "No, that's not what I'm talking about, Kimmy. It's Hugo. He's not who he says he is."

I wrinkle my forehead so hard I can feel my eyebrows crossing. "What do you mean? I don't understand."

Kylan sighs. "Peyton was right last night with what he was telling us. I texted Ken and gave him Hugo's name. Ken did a little research and found out that Hugo is twenty-three years old and a convicted felon who possibly has connections to R.L."

I slam my hand to my mouth and bite the inside of my fingers trying my best not to scream. Then it hit me! I can't breathe! I can't see! I can't stand up! All my strength is gone. My legs turn into spaghetti, and I collapse onto my floor.

But I never hit the floor, because Kylan swoops me up in his arms and holds on to me. I hear him talking, but I'm not really sure I'm understanding what he is saying. As he is speaking, I can feel him forcing my legs to walk over to my bed.

He puts his hand to my forehead. "Babe, you're cold as ice! Here, get under your covers and warm up." He pulls my covers up to my chin and ever so gently tucks me in.

What seems like an eternity passing was probably just around five minutes. After about one hundred slow breaths and Kylan putting a wet washcloth on my head, I am finally able to comprehend what is going on. Something was triggered inside of me when he said the name, R.L. We all vowed to never speak that name out loud for the rest of our lives. When Kylan said it, I knew this had to be serious.

"Ok, Babe. Let's talk," Kylan calmly speaks. "Ken wasn't able to find much on Hugo, but he was convicted on a felony drug offense several years ago. He was arrested one night with R.L. However, as we have learned, R.L. got off scot-free and Hugo and a few others served jail time over it."

I lie there in awe. Not really knowing how to respond, so I just don't.

"Did you call Maria back last night? I'm just curious where she stayed," Kylan hesitates like he's about to say something else but doesn't.

All I do is nod my head. I'm still trying to process all this. Just then, I remember my phone buzzing in the night and refusing to answer it. The wave of panic returns.

"My phone!" I yell. "Get my phone!"

Kylan nearly falls off my bed as he hurriedly grabs my phone and puts it in my hands.

"Oh God, Kylan! I ignored my phone last night and fell asleep. Peyton called me back. I just couldn't answer it. I knew it would be bad news, and I didn't have it in me to receive it. After hearing Maria's voice, I was at ease knowing she was alive and well although she was about to make the biggest mistake of her life. So, I just left it at that."

"Babe, call him back now! I don't care what time it is and if he stayed up all night. CALL HIM!"

I raise up and lift the cover off of me. Kylan climbs up next to me and props me up with my pillows. I push on Peyton's name to call him back, but he doesn't answer.

"It's ok, Babe. We'll call again in a few. He's probably asleep."

Just like with Maria last night, we take turns calling Peyton to see who he picks up for first. He doesn't answer. After about thirty minutes, we give up.

"So, he's going to see about a thousand missed calls on his phone when he looks at it. Maybe he'll have enough sense to call us back." In case you didn't know this, Peyton is not the brightest crayon in the box. He's probably book smarter than I am, but not common sense. He's actually quite dense!

In the meantime, I decide to text Maria.

> Where are you? Are you coming home? (8:45 AM)

> I'm sitting in the driveway right now in Hugo's car. We accidentally fell asleep out here last night and just woke up. Do you think it's safe to come inside? (8:47 AM)

I breathe a huge sigh of relief. "She's outside in the driveway. They fell asleep. Maria is ok. Now we have to get her in the house without Mom and Dad knowing."

Kylan grins at me then looks over at my bedroom window and points. "Well, I'm pretty strong. I can try and pull her up."

I giggle, "It's worth a try. At least it won't be the first time this window has been used for sneaking out, or should I say sneaking in?"

I text Maria the plan and it works! Hugo is able to boost her up enough for Kylan to snag her arm and hoist her into my bedroom. How on earth my parents never saw all that going on will truly remain a mystery.

Once we get her on solid ground, I stand back and examine Maria. "You look exhausted! Actually, you look like hell, Sis! What happened to you?"

Maria closes her eyes and smiles. "Just the most romantic night of my life!"

I have no words for my best friend right now. My face turns ten shades of red as I look over at Kylan. Who immediately looks away.

"And before you even ask, no, we didn't do it last night! Guys can be romantic without having sex! Right Kylan?" Maria looks over at Kylan as I'm sure he wants to crawl under my bed and die right now.

"You know what, ladies. I'm gonna let y'all have your little girl talk while I see my way out of here." Kylan turns, looks at me over his shoulder, and winks. "Kimmy, I'll be in the living room having coffee with your parents, if they're still here."

Maria pipes up, "Oh, they're still here. Both of their vehicles are still in the driveway. Trust me, I know!"

As soon as Kylan leaves the room, Maria proceeds to tell me all about her "amazing" night with Hugo. I sit here and listen to Maria as I try to figure out how I'm going to tell her who her prince charming really is.

As she just keeps going on and on with some of the most intimate details I've ever heard in my life, all I can think of is nasty old R.L. and how he was once friends with Hugo. What the crap? How did this happen?

"Maria! Stop talking!" I interrupt. "Hugo is not who you think he is!"

Maria busts out into laughter. "Oh Kimmy, stop being so naive. I know exactly who he is. He's twenty-three years old, and he is the absolute love of my life! I didn't have sex with him last night because I'm on my period and that's just disgusting."

I just stand there and stare at Maria feeling like I'm looking at a stranger in front of me. Who has she turned into? Her period? OMG! I just cannot believe what she is saying to me right now.

"And for the record," Maria states. "Even if I wasn't on my period right now, I'm not dumb enough to spread my legs without being on birth control. Hugo is taking me over to the clinic in a few days to get me on some. His sister is a nurse there and she can get me in without my parents' consent."

Once again, I have no words. I just stand there in complete shock! Then I realize that I still have the upper hand in this conversation.

"Hugo is friends," I pause, "or used to be friends with R.L." There, I said it. Now what, Maria! What are you gonna say about that?

Maria makes a weird face like she just bit into a sour lemon. "Why did you say his name? I thought we all vowed to never utter it out loud. WHY, KIMMY, WHY?"

"I'm just trying to look out for you. Peyton was in a panic trying to get a hold of me and Kylan last night. When we finally got him on the phone, he was with Cass and saying stuff like we better call you if we ever wanted to talk to you again. Now, what's that all about?"

Maria looks at me with her famous look of death. "Well, if Peyton is involved in this, you know it's fake. He and Cass were probably drunk or high. He's just not the same person he used to be."

"It sounds like Hugo isn't who you think he is either, Sis." I raise my eyebrows up at Maria as I can see her face starting to calm down.

"Oh, Kimmy." Maria puts her hands over her eyes as if she doesn't want me to see her. "I just don't know who to believe these days. I've been betrayed by so many people." Then she suddenly stops and looks up at me. I hate it when she does this to me. It makes me so nervous. "Who told you that Hugo and you know who were friends?"

"K...K...Ken," I stutter out knowing I should've kept my mouth shut. "Kylan got in touch with him last night after our little ordeal with Peyton. Ken did some research and looked up his record. Hugo is a convicted felon, Maria. You're hanging out with a convict."

Maria snarls, "That's not true. Ken has got to be lying. Hugo would have told me this. Don't you think?"

I shrug my shoulders. "I don't think Ken is lying. What benefit would he get from that?"

Maria begins sobbing. I try to comfort her, but she just pushes me away. This is when I know I should just back off like Liz told me. "What am I going to do, Kimmy? I'm in love with Hugo. My parents are going to die when they find out. They just might kill him!"

As Maria continues to cry. I just sit and stare at her not knowing what to do next. How did she get herself into this mess? And how has Hugo not been caught yet? Then I remember back to how the bartender at Cuz's was acting yesterday and asking about Hugo. I didn't really think it was odd at the time, but now it all makes sense.

CHAPTER 30

I always feel anxious on Sunday nights before I have to go to school the next day, especially when I've been off school for a whole week for fall break. I'm not really sure why. I'm actually one of those weirdos who loves school. I love it mostly now because I get to see Kylan every day. I also really enjoy my classes. I have always liked to learn new things and make myself a better person.

But the anxiety that I'm feeling tonight is a little different from my typical Sunday evening stress. We've had a drama free fall break, because Hugo had to go back to Texas to visit family. So, Maria and I were able to spend some girl time together. I just can't stop thinking about Maria and everything that has happened to her here lately. I'm not really sure how she has coped with it. I think she's been doing things she shouldn't, but I have to remember that it's truly none of my business.

Did you break up with him? (5:32 PM)

I'm out with him right now! I'm not sure I can do it. I just love him so much! What should I do? (5:36 PM)

Maria, you have to break up with him. What he is doing is illegal. A 23 year old can't date a 14 year old. And that's gross too! (5:37 PM)

I've been sitting here staring at my phone for nearly thirty minutes now waiting for Maria to respond back to my text. She doesn't. Oh well, I've done my job. There's nothing else I can do.

"So why are we having a family dinner tonight?" I ask Mom with serious suspicion.

My mom looks me up and down like something is wrong with me. "Sweetheart, this will probably be the last Sunday night that your dad is off work for a long time. Plus, I just wanted to invite Nanny and Chas over because we've all been busy since they moved in. I feel like we've kind of neglected them. They moved here to be closer to us and spend more time with us, but we're all just slammed right now."

I shrug my shoulders at my mom and look past her noticing Dad cutting up vegetables. He never does that! "Ok, whatever," I say.

I turn around to go grab my phone out of my room but suddenly feel Mom's hand on my shoulder. "Kimmy, come over here with me for a minute," she whispers.

Mom walks me into the living room, turns me toward her, and gets so close to my face I can feel her breath. "What's going on with Maria?" she asks as she is looking at me dead in the eyes.

I freeze and my voice instantly leaves my body. I shake my head as I can feel my heart beating in my throat. "Um...um...um..." I can't speak. I don't know what is going on. This is my mom asking me a simple question and I can't get any words to come out of my mouth.

"It's ok, Sweetheart. I know your anxiety has been in full force here lately. When you're able to talk, I'm here to listen to you. All I have to say is..." Mom strays off and looks toward the kitchen. "Please don't follow Maria's lead. I know what she's doing. We live in a small town, and everybody is talking about it."

My eyes are probably bulging out of my head right now as I look at my mom. "What are you talking about, Mom?"

"Oh, Kimmy. Please don't play dumb. You know what I'm talking about."

I can always tell when my mom is serious about something because she uses my first name. Typically, she will call me, Sweetheart, Honey, or Sweet Pea. I stand there and just stare at my mom thinking about everything Maria's been doing and what she said about getting on birth control. Then it hit me, Catholics don't believe in birth control. So, why would Maria go against her religion for Hugo. I distinctly remember her telling me that Hugo is Catholic too, so shouldn't his sister be as well? I'm just so confused right now that I don't know which way is up.

"Mom, I just don't want to talk about Maria right now. She and I have not been getting along very well here lately. I think she's obsessed with Hugo or something." I look away hoping that will suffice.

Mom shakes her head. "Well, when you want to talk, I'll be here. Just please promise me that you won't act as foolish as she is right now."

I look at my mom and see the seriousness in her eyes. "Mom, you don't have to worry about me. I learned my lesson last year. Kylan and I are in love, and he respects my choices."

Mom leans in for a gentle hug and squeezes my shoulders. "I know he does, Honey. Kylan is a good kid. You need to be respectful to him as well."

I nod my head knowing what she is meaning by that statement. Sometimes I'm not real nice to Kylan. Actually, a lot of times I've not been very nice to him. I'm kind of surprised he hasn't broken up with me yet. If he did, OMG, I don't know what I would do. Ok, so maybe I need to clean up my act a little bit with Kylan.

"Speaking of Kylan, can he come over for dinner?" I ask Mom knowing that this is supposed to be a family dinner, but my parents consider Kylan as part of our family.

My mom hesitates to say anything. When she finally speaks, what comes out of her mouth scares me to death. "Kimmy, our family needs to discuss a few things tonight that are strictly family topics. You can share that later with Kylan." My mom wipes her brow with the back of her hand like she's been sweating, but it's not hot in here. "Besides, it's a school night and you guys have a busy week ahead of you."

Busy week? Does Mom know something I don't? I have absolutely nothing planned for this week. Why would she say that? I slump my shoulders and slowly walk toward the kitchen to see what Dad is doing.

"Hey Dad," I mutter. "What are you doing?" I slink down into one of the chairs at the kitchen table.

Dad looks at me over his shoulder as he is stirring something on the stove. "Oh, hey there! I was deep in thought." Dad gives me a strange look. "Why the long face?"

I stick my bottom lip out and overexaggerate my expression. "Mom won't let Kylan come over for dinner."

Dad mimics my look then his face becomes expressionless. "It's probably best that he's not here, Honey. We have a lot to talk about."

What the crap are they talking about? Is somebody dying or something?

"Dad, tell me what's going on?" I demand.

My dad seems different. There's something not exactly right about him at this moment. Typically, he's a pretty even keel dude, but here lately he's just not been himself.

"You'll find out soon enough, then you'll be wishing you didn't know." Dad slowly turns around and goes back to stirring what he's cooking on the stove.

It's always an awkward situation when we're all sitting around my kitchen table. I take the head of the table. I'm not sure why, that's just how it's always been. My mom sits next to me with Dad next to her. Nanny is on the other side of me and Chas next to her. Of course, Oscar, is sitting under the table at our feet just waiting for a crumb to fall to the floor so he can clean it up. We joke about how we never have to clean the kitchen because we have Oscar to do the job.

I nervously wait on what the big news is that we're going to talk about. Everything seems completely normal right now. The adults are all talking and I'm just over here trying to enjoy my dinner, but I have a strange sick feeling in my stomach. Like something's just not right.

Just as I start to take a sip of my water, my phone starts vibrating in my pocket. I get it out and set it on the table. It's Kylan.

"Mom, can I be excused to answer my phone? It's Kylan."

When I speak, everyone at the table stops talking and looks at me like they just saw a ghost. I look at each of them individually not knowing what to expect next. I halfway feel like I could be verbally attacked for asking to take a call. You know like when you're swimming in the ocean, and you feel like there might be a group of sharks swarming around you. Yeah, that's the feeling I'm getting right now.

Mom takes a deep breath and sighs loudly. "Yes, Honey, but please make it quick. We all need to talk."

I snarl up my nose at her not really wanting to hear what they have to tell me. I'm sure it's something stupid now or they would've told me already.

I hurriedly run to my bedroom to answer Kylan's call, but unfortunately, I don't make it, and he hangs up. Before I can even call him back, my phone starts ringing. It's Kylan again.

"Hello?"

"Babe, I'm on my way to your house. We have trouble!" I can hear the panic in Kylan's voice.

"No, No, this is not a good time. Nanny and Chas are over here eating dinner with me, Mom, and Dad. They have something important to tell me and didn't want anyone who's not family to be over here. I'm sorry."

Kylan's voice suddenly changes. "KIMMY, DID YOU NOT HEAR ME? WE HAVE TROUBLE! MARIA IS IN SERIOUS TROUBLE!"

"What? No, I didn't hear you say that! What's going on with Maria?" I ask in fear that she might be hurt.

"Hey, let me call you back. Peyton's calling me. Never mind, I'll see you in a minute." Then he hangs up the phone without me able to get in a word.

Oh no! What am I going to do? Mom said specifically that Kylan cannot come over for dinner. What should I do?

It didn't take long for me to have to make a decision, because Nanny peeked her head in my door to see what was going on.

"Nanny, we have a problem."

Nanny's face drops. "What is it, Honey?"

I stand there and stare at Nanny trying to figure out what the problem is, but I can't. "Nanny, I don't know what it is. Oh gosh, Nanny, I'm so confused."

Nanny takes me in her arms and lays my head on her shoulder. "Kimmy, it's ok, you can tell me anything and I promise I won't get mad."

I shake my head into Nanny's shoulder and feel the wetness from my tears on my eyelids. "But Nanny, I can't tell you, because I don't know."

Nanny raises my head up. "But dear you have to know something, because you are obviously upset."

I look at Nanny with all seriousness. "Kylan is on his way over here. All he said is that Maria is in trouble. And Mom told me earlier that she didn't want Kylan coming over for dinner tonight. That it was a family thing. What am I going to do when he shows up here in like five minutes?"

Nanny looks at me square in the eyes. "Kimmy, you're missing something. Kylan said Maria is in trouble! Don't worry about Kylan showing up. That's the least of your concerns right now. Your mom will understand. You need to be worrying about what's going on with Maria. Have you called her?"

"OMG! No." I look down at my phone trying to push the buttons as fast as I can. But when I call Maria's phone, it goes straight to voicemail.

"Nanny, I have to tell you something." I know Nanny can hear the fear in my voice because she takes my hand and walks me over to my bed. As we both sit down, I hear a knock at the front door.

"Honey, go ahead. I'm sure it's just Kylan," Nanny reassures me. Then I told Nanny everything that's been going on with Maria. I told her how old Hugo was and how he had been arrested and convicted of a felony drug charge. I told her how Maria is supposed to break up with Hugo tonight, but in my last text message with her, it sounded like Maria was backing down on that.

Nanny just sits there staring at my wall. "Kimmy, why do you keep doing this to me. It's like a pimple that's festering. You know one of those that you keep picking at hoping to make it better, but in reality, you're just making it worse. Then all of a sudden, it pops open and all that infection flies all over the place."

I look at Nanny is disgust. "Really, Nanny? Did you have to put it that way?"

Nanny smirks, "Well, my child, if I don't put in it terms that you understand, then there's no point in even saying it."

As soon as Nanny stops speaking, I hear my mom scream my name from across the house. The tone of her scream isn't like any other I've heard before. This tone is full of alarm and terror. So, I jump up off my bed and run into the living room. It seems to take forever just to get from my bedroom door to where my mom is at. When I finally make it, I stop in my tracks.

"Officer Jane? What are you doing here?" I ask.

Chapter 31

"Kimberly, tell me everything you know." I hear the young police officer say as I look around the concrete block walls of the room. It's the same room that Kylan and I had to go to when we told our version of the night Ashley passed away. The memories start rushing back in and I am struggling to even sit upright. Kylan is beside me again holding my hand as tight as he can. All I can think about is Maria and if I've lost my best friend in the whole entire world.

With tears streaming down my face, I finally screech out a few words. Kylan has to translate them to the officer, because they are unintelligible to him. I look over to the door where my parents are sitting outside in metal chairs that look like they came from an old prison.

The police officer repeats over and over what Kylan says as he shakes his head back and forth. I can tell this is bad, really bad. I'm too scared to ask what has happened or why we're here. I'm afraid I don't want to know.

Kylan squeezes my hand even tighter as he knows I'm struggling to stay alert. "Mr. Officer?"

The officer looks up from his notepad and makes eye contact with Kylan. "You can call me Brian," the officer says as he puts the cap back on his ink pen. The tiny little click of the lid snapping in place jolts me back to reality. "Yes, Kylan, did you want to ask me something?"

Kylan hesitates for a moment, then asks, "How is Maria?"

The officer shifts from one side to the other. I can tell something is terribly wrong. When he finally responds, my heart sinks down to my toes. "I'm so sorry," the officer says. "I cannot disclose any details to you right now. You will have to reach out to the Hernandez family. They can give you the information you're looking for. As for now, this is a highly confidential case that involves several minors. I ask that you don't share any of the information you gave me with anyone else. If you two think of anything to add, please let me know ASAP. As for now, you're free to go." The officer puts his hand out to shake Kylan's hand, "Please take care of this young lady. The next few days are going to be tough."

I look at the officer with a puzzled expression. "What is going on Mr. Brian? Why can't you tell us anything about Maria?" I take a deep breath. "DON'T YOU UNDERSTAND? SHE IS MY BEST FRIEND! IF SOMETHING HAD HAPPENED TO YOUR BEST FRIEND, WOULDN'T YOU WANT TO KNOW?" I shout at the officer.

Both of my parents come running into the questioning room and wrap their arms around me. "Kimmy, please lower your voice," my mom calmly states.

"Mom, I'm just so confused right now. Is Maria ok? Did something happen? Why won't anyone tell me?"

My mom turns me toward her, and I hear the news that I was fearfully dreading. "Sweet Pea," Mom says as the tears start to stream down her face. "Maria is not well." Mom looks over to my dad. "Jimmy, please tell her, I can't this time."

I can feel the pain rush through my entire body. My feet go numb as I can feel my heart completely stop beating. I lean back into Kylan as he embraces me so tight I can barely breathe. I start screaming in pain and sadness before my dad even speaks.

"Kimmy," my dad strays off, drops his head, and begins crying.

I yell at the top of my lungs, "WILL SOMEONE JUST TELL ME WHAT IS GOING ON HERE?"

"Babe, come out here and sit down. Let's gets some fresh air." I hear Kylan say from behind me as he wraps his arm around my shoulder and kisses the top of my head.

The four of us walk out of the questioning room and down the hallway. I'm still not sure what is going on, but I'm fixing to find out. Once again, I am in one of those moments that I don't really want to happen. I am about the get some news that is going to change the rest of my life.

We finally get outside and my parents lead us over to a park bench. I sit between Mom and Kylan on the bench and Dad squats down in front of me.

"Honey, it's not good," he shakes his head. I take a deep breath and grab onto my mom and Kylan bracing myself for the bad news. "Maria was set up this evening. Her boyfriend took her up to the state park where some girl named Cassidy and her friends were waiting for them. When Maria got out of his car, these people attacked Maria and beat the hell out of her. Maria is over at Memorial Hospital in Gulfport in the intensive care unit. As of right now, that's all we know."

Kylan and my mom are both rubbing my back at the same time. I lean down to put my face in my hands not sure if I'm going to be able to survive this. Then my dad says something that I've never heard come out of his mouth my entire life. "Kimmy, we need to say a prayer for Maria. I've been told that people can be healed when others pray for them."

Suddenly, I have an overwhelming feeling of calmness take over my body. I'm not sad anymore, and I'm not scared. My dad wants to pray with me. This is the most amazing thing I have ever had happen to me! My dad places his hands on my knees and leans in so close that our foreheads touch. He then recites The Lord's Prayer by memory. I was right, this was the moment that will change the rest of my life.

"That was beautiful, Dad," I proclaim. "I didn't know you knew The Lord's Prayer."

My dad blushes, "Well, Sweetheart, I didn't know you did either." My dad smiles at me with his flushed cheeks. "When I was a little boy, Nanny used to take me to church downtown New Orleans every Sunday. You know those beautiful cathedral churches that you always admire when we're down there? That's where we went. I never wanted to go, but she pretty much made me. Nanny would tell me that if I sat still the whole entire church service, then she would take me over to the ice cream shop on the corner and buy me anything I wanted. Even though I struggled, Nanny would always keep up her end of the deal. When we would get home, Chas would have lunch ready for us. I would never be hungry since I ate a huge ice cream cone on the way home. Chas would ask why I wouldn't touch my food, and Nanny and I would just laugh. I think he eventually caught on to our little secret, but he never said a word about it."

I look at my dad's worn face. His creases are deep even though he's not very old. Mom has always told me to wear sunscreen unless I want my face to end up leathery like Dad's. But when I look at him this time, something is different. He has a sparkle in his eyes that I've never seen before. It's not a sadness. It's more like a glimmer of hope mixed with a little joy.

"How about we head on over to Gulfport and see what we can find out about Maria," Mom says with slight exhaustion in her voice.

I look down at my phone to check the time. "Mom, it's almost nine-thirty! Can I stay home from school tomorrow?"

My mom gives me a side hug around my shoulders and says, "Of course, Honey. I think we'll all be staying home tomorrow." Mom leans forward and looks over to Kylan. "Why don't you call your mom and let her know what's going on. You can stay in our guestroom tonight. I'll let both of you sleep in tomorrow morning. Right now, we need to be with the Hernandez family."

The ride over to Gulfport was pretty solemn. Even though it only takes about twenty minutes to get there, it seemed like twenty hours. I sat with my face glued to the window with so many unanswered questions running through my brain. When I looked over to Kylan, his eyes were closed, and his mouth was wide open. Most girls would have been repulsed by this, but not me. I'm just lucky that he's mine. So many girls at school have crushes on him and would love to be his girlfriend, but he chose me over all of them.

When we walk into the waiting room at Memorial, I immediately see the entire Hernandez family. It hurts me so much to see they are having to go through this with Maria when they just buried Ashley a little over a year ago.

Mr. Hernandez stands up and walks over to us. "Oh, Nina and Jimmy! We're so glad you came. We didn't expect you all to show up since you were having your family dinner tonight. How did everyone take it?"

Mom puts her finger to her lips like she's telling him to be quiet. "We had just gotten started with dinner when we received the news about Maria. Our family discussion can definitely wait."

How does Mr. Hernandez know what's going on with our family and I don't? As if my life wasn't confusing enough, now I have something else to try and figure out.

"Speaking of dinner," Dad says. "Can we run out and get you all some food? I'm sure you're starving."

Mr. Hernandez shakes his head. "Nah, but thanks, Jimmy. We took the kids down to the hospital cafeteria before it closed. Surprisingly, the food was pretty good."

I look around the room to scope us out a seat. This place is packed! Then, I see a strangely familiar face sitting in the back corner of the waiting room. "Kylan, is that Peyton over there?"

Kylan squinches up his eyes. "Um, yeah, I think it is. Why is he way back there?"

I shrug my shoulders. "Who knows, but let's go talk to him. I don't think he sees us."

"Hey man! What's up?" Kylan asks Peyton as he raises the bill of his hat.

Peyton looks up at us with bloodshot eyes and a flushed face. "I'm surprised y'all are talking to me," Peyton whispers. "Can you believe this? I'm so hurt in more ways than one right now."

"Peyton, you are still my best friend even though I don't agree with the things you've been doing here lately with Cass. We'll always be best friends until the day we die." Kylan sits next to Peyton in the empty seat. "Man, none of this is your fault."

Peyton quickly snaps back, "You wanna bet? All of this is my fault. If I hadn't been dumb and messed around with Cass, none of this would've happened. It's all my fault!"

In the year and a half that I've known Peyton, I've never seen him look like this. He truly looks like he just lost his best friend. "Where is Cass?" I ask.

Peyton rolls his eyes. "I'm done with her. She broke up with me a few weeks ago."

I snarl up my nose like I smelled something foul. "Then why are you still hanging out with her like you two are together?"

"That's a good question, Kimmy. Cass is a very powerful person who can make people do whatever she says. Somehow, I fell under her spell and couldn't break it. She has used and abused me over the last month. But after all this with Maria, I'm never speaking to Cass again." Peyton looks down at the floor. "I'm still in love with Maria and I want to be right there beside her as she recovers from all this. The guilt is eating me up inside!"

When he looks back up, I notice something that I didn't see a second ago. Peyton has a black eye! "Dude," I say as I point to his eye. "What happened?"

"Didn't I just say that I've been used and abused? I wasn't kidding about that."

Kylan stands up and reaches his hand out to Peyton. "Come over here and join us."

Peyton lets out a long sigh. "I can't. Maria's family hates me. That's why I'm all the way over here."

"Peyton, get over it. They don't hate you. You have done nothing wrong."

Peyton puts his hand over his eyes as tears begin to fall off his cheeks. "But Kylan, you really don't understand." Peyton takes a deep breath then let's it out. "I was the one who called the police. I was there."

CHAPTER 32

If she can make it through the next forty-eight hours without finding anymore brain bleeds, then her chances of surviving this will greatly increase. But these next couple of days will be critical for Miss Maria," the doctor says in a monotone voice.

Mr. Hernandez drops to his knees like he's pleading to God to save his daughter. "Oh, doctor, when can we see our precious child?"

"It's going to be a while, sir. Maria will not be allowed to have any visitors until we get her stabilized. Her life is in danger, and we can't take any chances. But if you'll give me a few minutes, I will go check with the surgeon to see if you and your wife can come back and spend a moment with Maria before she is taken to surgery." The doctor looks around at the Hernandez children who are climbing all over the hospital chairs like little monkeys.

Mr. Hernandez stands up to hug the doctor. "Oh that would be wonderful. Our friends here," he points to my parents, "can watch the children. We just really want to see our precious daughter."

Mr. and Mrs. Hernandez were in the back with Maria for about thirty minutes. In the meantime, while my mom, Kylan, Alex, and I were watching the little kids, Dad was having a discussion with Peyton. We'll probably never know what they were talking about, but Peyton seemed to perk up after their talk.

When the Hernandezes walk out of the double doors. I could tell it wasn't good. I run up to Mr. Hernandez. "So?" I ask him.

He grabs a hold of me and his wife and wraps his arms around both of us. "Oh, Kimmy, my dear. I just don't know what to say." He trails off slightly as if he doesn't want me to know something. "I could lie and tell you she's going to be fine, or I could tell you what we saw back there. The doctor is right, all we can do is wait and see."

Peyton walks up with his head drooped. "Sir, can we talk?"

As Peyton and Mr. Hernandez walk to another part of the waiting room, I grab Mrs. Hernandez's hand and walk her back to the children. I know this is not a time of joy or happiness, but I had to giggle a little just seeing the Hernandez children wallering on Dad and Kylan. Mom, however, has the youngest Hernandez cradled like a baby trying to rock her to sleep.

Mom stands up and hands over the child to Mrs. Hernandez. "I sure do miss these days, Lucia." Mrs.

Hernandez looks over at me and grins. "Well, Dear, it won't be long before you have little grandbabies running all over the place," she says in her thick Spanish accent.

We all sat around the waiting room anticipating the latest news. I look down at my phone to see it's nearly three o'clock in the morning. I'm pretty sure I've fallen asleep several times already on Kylan's shoulder. Alex decided hours ago to take the Hernandez's children home and get them in bed. I promised him I would call as soon as we heard something, but no one ever came out to talk to us. Every time a doctor or nurse would walk out from behind the double doors, I would gasp, but soon they would walk over to another family and share their news.

Then suddenly, I look up to see a doctor we hadn't seen before walk out. He was old and white headed. He walked straight over to where we were sitting. Oh no, this is it. I can tell by the look on his face.

"Is this the family of Maria Hernandez?" the old doctor asks.

Mr. Hernandez is quick to speak. "Yes, doctor. Yes, it is."

The doctor takes in a deep breath. "Well, Maria's surgery is over. We were able to repair three of the four brain bleeds. Maria did very well. We are hoping the fourth very small bleed takes care of itself. If not, we will go back in and repair it as well."

We all breathe a huge sigh of relief. I'm sure it could be heard over the entire waiting room.

The doctor continues, "Maria is now able to have visitors if you all would like to go back two at a time. Please remember that Maria is sedated, and she will not respond to you when you speak to her. She can hear you but is unable to talk or open her eyes. She will be this way for a few days until we determine she is out of the woods. That's when we will give her the medicine to wake her up. Also, make sure you mask up and put on the gowns. We don't want Maria catching a sickness right now with her trying to heal since it's flu season and all."

I nod my head acknowledging the doctor's orders. Then I raise my hand to get the doctor's attention. "Will I be able to go back and see Maria?" I ask the doctor with hesitation.

"How old are you, Miss?

"I'm fourteen," I reply.

"Here at Memorial, we require all visitors to be at least fifteen." The doctor looks over at my parents. "But I'll make an exception if one of your parents go back with you."

I nod my head to the doctor and mutter out, "Thank you."

Mr. and Mrs. Hernandez were the first to go back. As they were back there, I called Alex to check in. He sure was glad to hear from us. I could hear the babies screaming in the background. He said he had to call Joni to come in for backup, because he couldn't handle the herd of kiddos on his own.

After Maria's mom and dad went back, my parents went back together. They didn't stay nearly as long as Maria's parents did. When I saw them walking toward me, I knew it was my turn. I was thankful that the doctor approved me visiting Maria, but I sure was scared. The feeling of dread took over my entire body. It was a feeling that I've felt too many times in the past two years. All of a sudden, I felt like I was going to throw up, but I knew it was just my nerves.

Kylan took hold of my hand and patted it with his. "Babe, it's your turn."

I look over at him and try to remember the last time I saw Maria. Although it was just yesterday morning, it feels like forever ago. "I'm scared, Kylan. I'm scared of what I'm going to see when I go back there. I wish you could go with me."

"Just remember, Babe, Maria would be right by your side if you were in that hospital bed right now."

And Kylan's exactly right. Even though Maria and I haven't been as close here lately, we are still best friends. I have to be strong for her and do this.

"Ok, Sweet Pea," Dad says. "Are you ready to go back and see her?"

It takes all my might to stand up. I feel Kylan's hands placed gently around my waist helping to raise me up. I grab a hold of my dad's hand to steady myself. I lean against

Dad's side and get my balance. "Yes, Dad. I'm ready," I whisper with uncertainty.

Dad and I walk slowly down the hallway of the surgery wing of the hospital. The smell of fresh blood and a hint of urine wafts through the air. The hallway is dimly lit, and I can barely make out the room numbers on the doors. I try not to, but I peek in each room that has an open door just to prepare myself for what I'm about to see. When we get to Maria's door, I stop. "Dad, is this it?"

Dad looks down at me and smiles. "You can do this, Kimberly Ruth Favre. You're the strongest person that I know. Maria would be extremely disappointed if you didn't visit with her."

Dad pushes open the door and my first view of Maria is breathtaking and not in a good way. I was profoundly shocked with all the tubes and machines they had hooked up to her. The machines were beeping like a horn player trying to keep up with a metronome. I walked over to the side of her bed. She is lifted so far up in the air, I am completely eye level with her. Her head is all bandaged up with white gauze and her face is so swollen, she is unrecognizable.

"Maria, it's me, Kimmy." Maria doesn't move. "Sis, I'm here for you. We've been waiting all night just to get to see you. I'm glad you made it through the surgery and you're going to be ok."

I look over at Dad who is standing at the foot of her bed. He gives me a reassuring nod.

"Sis, when you get out of here, we are going to go to Cuz's and eat as much food as we want and spend the entire day on the beach soaking up the sun."

She still doesn't respond. This is so strange. Maria always has so much to say. For me to tell her something and her not talk back to me is troubling.

"Hey Dad, can I touch her?" I ask my dad not really knowing if I'm allowed.

"I think it would be ok if you touched her toes. You don't want to spread any germs to her, remember?"

I walk down to the foot of the bed where my dad is standing. I slowly lift the covers off of Maria's feet. She has these air pump things on that keep inflating and deflating. I just stand there and stare at them as it happens over and over. When I finally work up the nerve, I put my hand on Maria's toes.

"Maria, I'm tickling your toes. Can you feel it?" I look up at her face as she is still expressionless. Then suddenly, she wiggles her big toe! "Oh, Maria! You can feel it!" I continue tickling her toes until her movement stops. "Ok, Sis, I guess Dad and I will head on out. I can't wait until you wake up! I have so much to tell you!"

"You guys need to head on home, now," Mr. Hernandez insists. "We'll let you know if anything changes."

My mom leans down to give Mrs. Hernandez a gentle squeeze and Dad shakes Mr. Hernandez's hand. I grab a hold of Kylan's arm as we walk toward the outside doors. As we're walking out, I realize that Peyton was not in the waiting room when Dad and I got back.

"What happened to Peyton?" I ask Kylan.

"Well, after he got done talking to Maria's dad, he waved goodbye to me and walked out the door. It was the strangest thing. He didn't stop or speak or anything. I texted him to see if everything was ok. He said it was and that he was going home to get some rest. Apparently, Maria's dad told him to leave and that he could come back tomorrow."

I tilt my head to the side. "Do you think he's still mad at Peyton?"

Kylan shrugs his shoulders. "I'm not sure. I don't even know what they talked about while you and your dad were visiting with Maria. I guess I'll find out later. It appears that we're friends again. Hopefully he'll really stay away from Cass this time."

"Speaking of Cass, did she get arrested?"

"I'm sure she did. My phone stopped blowing up a little around midnight. I guess everybody figured that I wasn't answering and just gave up on getting in touch with me."

I grab my phone from my pocket and check it. "Yeah, mine too. Liz and Abbey were obviously taking turns calling me. Gosh, I kind of feel bad for not picking up now. I'll call them back as soon as we wake up in the morning. I'm beyond exhausted!"

The four of us somehow manage to walk out of the hospital and find my dad's truck. It's pitch-black outside, but I can see a slight glow of orange on the horizon.

Once we were home, I got Kylan set up in the guestroom and went straight to bed. I didn't even brush my teeth or wash my face. My mom said she was too awake to go to bed and she was going to cook an early breakfast. I told her to save the leftovers for us for later.

As I lie awake in bed, the image of Maria in the hospital bed haunts me. How do I know that was even her there? She didn't look like the same person. What if I was tickling the toes of some stranger? I giggle at the thought, but I know that was her. I could feel our connection as soon as I stepped in the room.

I toss and turn several times and contemplate getting in bed with Kylan. My parents would absolutely kill me and probably never let him stay over again. Oh well, I've done worst things, right?

CHAPTER 33

B abe, get up! It's ten-thirty! We need to talk!"

I open my eyes to see Kylan standing over me. I rub the sleep out of them and focus on his interesting looking outfit. "What are you wearing?" I ask.

Obviously embarrassed, he answers, "Um, I think these belong to your grandpa. This is all I could find to sleep in."

I laugh. "Are you sure that's not Nanny's pajamas? I mean, she does have a pair of flowery pjs just like that."

Kylan smacks his forehead and let's out a slow sigh. "Maybe you're right. Hopefully Nanny won't mind then. I honestly thought they were your grandpa's." Kylan swiftly moves over to sit on my bed. "Anyways, we need to talk. I have found out a few things about what happened last night."

I raise up in the bed and listen intently to Kylan tell me what Peyton had shared with him this morning. "All this was supposed to go down Saturday night, but Hugo backed out. Cass paid Hugo a large amount of money Sunday morning and Hugo had no choice but to take Maria to the state park and..." Kylan pauses, "...well you know what happened from there."

I look at Kylan in shock. "So, you're telling me that Cass literally set Hugo up with Maria so she could try and kill her?"

"Well, something like that. Peyton said that for some strange reason, Cass hated Maria. He never could figure out why. He even asked her a few times and she would just say that Maria's too much competition for her. Peyton overheard Cass talking to someone the other night and that's when he was frantically trying to get a hold of us. You know how much Peyton still loves Maria. He was devastated to hear that Cass wanted to hurt her."

I try and process what Kylan is telling me. I'm still half asleep and feeling a little groggy. "So, I guess my biggest question is, why was Peyton there when Maria got beat up?"

"I asked him the same thing. So apparently, Cass had told Peyton that they were meeting up with some friends at the park to party a little, I'm guessing drink alcohol, and hang out. Peyton really didn't think much about it because they've done that before. But he said the red flag for him was when he saw Hugo's car pull into the parking lot. Then, well, you know the rest." I sit and stare at my bedroom door not really knowing what to even think right now. Kylan continues, "So, when the police got there, Peyton was giving Maria mouth to mouth. He just knew she was dead, but he remembered our CPR training in middle school and if you give someone oxygen and pump their heart, they have a better chance of surviving."

That's when it hit me, "Oh my God, Kylan! Peyton really did save Maria's life!"

Kylan nods his head back and forth, "He most certainly did."

"How are we going to get Cass back for doing this to Maria?"

"Babe, I don't think we have to. I talked to Ken this morning, and he said that Cass, Hugo, and several of Hugo's Latino friends were arrested at Cass' house early this morning and were locked up in jail with no bond. He thinks they'll all be charged with attempted murder, kidnapping, and several other things. Ken said her days of freedom are over," Kylan pauses. "Oh, they're also probably going to charge Hugo with statutory rape since Maria was a minor and he's twenty-three."

My heart sinks, "But Maria insisted that they never had sex and weren't going to until she got on birth control." It makes me so sad to even think about Maria doing that. In a way, I'm glad she was waiting on the birth control.

Kylan frowns, "Well, I don't think Hugo could talk his way out of that one. Even if they never had sex, no one would ever believe him."

I really don't understand what Kylan means by that, but I just go with it. Kylan is such a smart guy and I typically don't question what he says. As long as the people who hurt Maria are punished for their crimes, I don't really care what happens.

"Do you think it would be ok if Peyton came over here in a few and rides with us to the hospital?" Kylan asks. "He's wanting to make amends to everyone he hurt and try to get back with Maria."

"I'm not really sure how I feel about that. I'm still very upset with how he treated Maria, but since he did save her life and all, I guess that's ok. Are you planning on driving over there or are we riding with my parents?"

Kylan grins at me. "Well, I was hoping your parents would let me drive us over there. I think your mom is still in bed. Your dad's truck was gone when I got up."

"It's up to Mom then, and she loves you. So, I'd say if you do a little sweet talking, she'll cave in." I give Kylan a wink and he kisses me on the forehead.

Sure enough, she caved! It might've helped that Kylan was whipping up some breakfast when she walked into the kitchen. He filled us up on bacon, eggs, and pancakes. He's such a sweetheart! He made enough for all of us to get our tummies full, even Peyton. I'm not sure if I can even move after that huge breakfast!

Riding over to Gulfport felt almost normal. We turned up the music in Kylan's car, Peyton sat in the back seat and sang at the top of his lungs while I sat shotgun to Kylan rolling my eyes and shaking my head. At one point,

I had to put my fingers in my ears to block out the terrible sound!

But it all changed when we turned down the road to the hospital. Kylan completely turned off the radio and the feeling of dread crept over my body. I worry of what news we might receive when we get there along with the awkwardness of sitting in the waiting room with Maria's parents without mine being there to deflect any weirdness. I love her parents, but now that Peyton is back in the picture, it just doesn't feel the same.

Kylan and I walk hand in hand through the waiting room doors. Peyton trails behind us. As soon as we cross the threshold, I see Mr. Hernandez stand up and start walking our way. He's wearing the same outfit as he was when we left here earlier this morning. I look around and notice that Mrs. Hernandez isn't with him.

"Hi Kimmy, Kylan," Mr. Hernandez pauses and squints his eyes, "and Peyton." Ok, now that's the strangeness I was just talking about with adults. Maybe he's just really tired, or maybe he's not at all excited about seeing Peyton here trying to get back with his daughter.

"Mr. Hernandez," I reply. "Do you have any updates on Maria?"

He bends down to my level. "Yes, child, we do." Mr. Hernandez reaches for both my hands and puts them in his. "We have some fantastic news!" His eyes light up. "Maria is doing much better than expected! The doctor's feel like she's going to make a complete recovery!" I can hear the excitement in his voice. "She is not awake yet, but since her progress over the past few hours has been trending upward greater than expected, the doctors are planning on bringing Maria out of the coma this evening. I was hoping you would be here when it happened."

I stand there in front of Mr. Hernandez emotionless. I don't really know how to respond. Is this a truly happy moment? Or is this a moment that he's trying to make happy not really knowing what to expect? And why would he want me here if there's a possibility that Maria might not wake up? At least that's what my mom was saying.

Kylan pipes up since he can tell my brain is moving a little slow right now. "That's great news, Sir! We will stay as long as you need us here. Right Kimmy?"

I shake my head to indicate I agree with Kylan. "Of course, yes, yes, we will do whatever you need us to do."

"Good. I knew I could count on you all, even Peyton." Mr. Hernandez smacks Peyton rather hard on the shoulder and chuckles. "Until then, how about we all just relax. Lucia is back there with Maria right now. She wanted to have a few moments alone with our precious daughter before they start taking her off the sedation."

"How long have we been here now?" I ask Kylan.

"It's been about four hours, Babe. Are you getting tired?" Kylan puts his hand around my shoulder and kisses the top of my head.

I sigh. "Yeah, somewhat. I'm just ready to see her." Before I could get another sentence out, Mr. Hernandez comes busting out of the double doors and runs over to us.

"Guys! She's awake! It's a miracle! And we owe it all to Peyton!" Mr. Hernandez grabs up Peyton and slings him around in a hug just like you would see in the movies.

I look over at Kylan with utter confusion. Then I whisper, "I guess they are good now?"

Kylan shrugs his shoulders. "Sure does look like it."

Once Mr. Hernandez puts Peyton down, he walks over and sits beside me. "They are getting her all cleaned up and ready for visitors." He wipes his forehead like he'd been working out. "But please keep in mind that Maria might not be the same person you remember. She cannot talk right now and her responses are very slow, but she is alive!" he cheers.

The time finally came for us to go back. We walked into Maria's new hospital room and the first thing I notice is that her window is facing the ocean. As the sun is setting, I can see the palm trees swaying outside and the waves gently rolling into shore.

I walk over to her being very hesitant about my actions. "It's ok, Kimmy. You can touch her," Mr. Hernandez reassures. I look up and down Maria's arms and see bruises in between all the IV tubes running down her arm.

Mr. Hernandez grabs a chair, places it by Maria's bedside, and insists I have a seat in it. I look up at Maria as my stomach starts to churn. Maria blinks her eyes and moves them in my direction.

"Sis, you're going to be ok." I lean closer to her bed and angle my face towards here. "How do you feel?" I ask her not really knowing what to expect. Maria blinks her eyes. Then I see a slight movement on her forehead as her frown lines begin to show. "Oh, I know, Sis. I know you're in pain. I'm so sorry." I raise my hand up to touch hers but pull it back afraid that I'll hurt her.

I look over to Mr. Hernandez. "Does she know how she got here?"

Mr. Hernandez replies, "All we've told her is that she was in a terrible accident and Peyton saved her life. Once she starts feeling a little better and is able to talk, we will ask her what she remembers. Until then, we're not going to worry about it."

A smile spread across my face as I look over at Peyton. "It's your turn." I motion to Peyton with my hand waving him over.

Peyton slowly gets up while looking over to Mr. Hernandez for approval. Mr. Hernandez nods his head, and Peyton proceeds to take small, measured steps towards Maria's bed. I stand up and offer Peyton the chair. He sits down and just gazes up at Maria. We all stare at Peyton wondering what he's going to do next.

"Maria," Peyton says as he stands up and leans over her body. "I don't care who is in this room and hears me say this. I don't care if I embarrass you right now. Maria," Peyton pauses and takes a deep breath, "I love you more than anything in this world. I want to be your boyfriend and soulmate until the day I die. I will honor and respect your thoughts and decisions in every aspect of life. It doesn't bother me if you want to save yourself until marriage. I'll do whatever I have to do to be with you and take care of you through all your healing." Peyton looks back to me and Kylan with tears in his eyes. "These past few months have been hell for me. Just seeing you with another guy has been a nightmare. I'm so sorry for everything I put you through. Will you please forgive me?"

Silence fills the hospital room like a thick fog. I look over to Mrs. Hernandez who is sobbing into her sweater as Mr. Hernandez offers her a tissue. I can feel the hot tears streaming down my face and I nuzzle up into Kylan.

"I know you can't answer me right now, and I definitely don't deserve to be with you, but I'm pleading with you to take me back." Peyton stretches his arms across Maria's body ever so gently. Maria's eyes close as I watch a tiny tear trickle down her cheek. We all stand around watching this moment unfold in front of us. Peyton raises up and moves his face next to Maria's. "I love you, Maria," he whispers. "Please give me some kind of sign that you want me here, if not, I will go, and you'll never have to see or hear from me again."

Peyton raises up from Maria's bed. Just when we thought Maria was done with Peyton the most amazing thing in this world happened. She grabs ahold of his shirt and pulls him back down to her bed. I'm sure our loud cheering could be heard a mile away.

Mr. Hernandez walks over to Peyton and puts his arm around his back. "Son, that's her sign. She wants you to be here. Please stay." Mr. Hernandez looks over at his wife and smiles. "Lucia and I forgive you. Your slate has been wiped clean with us now. We invite you in as one of our family."

CHAPTER 34

After two weeks of being in the hospital, Maria finally got to come home! Kylan, Peyton, and I went to the hospital every single day she was there. Maria's parents even allowed Peyton to stay with her overnight on the weekends. She's still not completely well, but she's on the road to recovery. Maria has all these drainage tubes coming out of her head that will be there for a while to drain the fluid off. She's starting to say a few words, but her speech has been damaged. Her doctors are optimistic and keep telling her that her brain will heal itself and she'll be back to normal in no time. I'm a little worried about her, though.

It will be a very long time before Maria will be able to go back to school. My mom says she probably won't go back until next school year. She will be getting all these therapies at home to help her walk and talk again like she used to. School just isn't the same without her.

This evening, we are having a party at the Hernandez's house to celebrate Maria's homecoming. It won't be a big party, but several of our friends from school are coming. Alex and Joni plan on being there along with Jason. It seems like an eternity since I've seen Jason! Maria is starting to eat regular foods, and she has requested homemade tamales. Maria's mother makes the best tamales around! I've tried them at Mexican restaurants and they're terrible compared to Mrs. Hernandez's.

Oh, I totally forgot about some very important information concerning Maria's accident. Well, that's what we are calling it for now. Maria doesn't remember anything about what happened, which is good. Peyton has shared bits and pieces with her. She remembers everything that happened right before she got hit in the head. She remembers being in love with Hugo and them planning a night at the park with friends. Surprisingly, Maria remembers seeing Peyton there at the park that night, but that's pretty much all she can recall.

Maria has actually woken up several times and asked for Hugo. Peyton has to remind her why Hugo isn't here. Hopefully one day she'll wake up and remember that she's truly in love with Peyton and Hugo is an awful person who is locked up in jail. Since Maria can't talk much, we have been asking her yes and no questions. She responds the best that she can.

Do you want to hear the kicker about this whole deal with Maria? So, you already know that Cass hired Hugo to date Maria but listen to this! Ken did some of his handy dandy researching. Since Ken is going to college to be a criminal investigator one day, he has access to all sorts of databases. Yeah, I know that he probably wasn't supposed to use the data for personal reasons, but he has been able to help the Hancock County Sheriff's department with this case.

So anyway, Ken did some digging and discovered that Cass and R.L. are first cousins! Yeah, you heard me right! Cass' mom and R.L.'s mom are sisters. So that's why Cass hired Hugo to go out with Maria. She was trying to kill Maria to get back at the Hernandez family for locking up her cousin. Talk about a corrupt family!

We all suspect that Cass was only dating Peyton to get information about Maria and try and break her down mentally. When Cass figured out that Peyton was still in love with Maria and wouldn't divulge any secrets about her, Cass had to come up with another plan. Somehow, she must've known that a smoking hot Latino guy would seal the deal for her. I do have to give Cass credit for that part. Maria fell for him hook, line, and sinker. Do you remember that big party Maria and Hugo went to at Cass' uncle's house in Long Beach? Well, that house belongs to R.L.'s dad! Whew, it makes my head spin just thinking about it. I'm just so glad that Kylan and I didn't fall in Cass' trap like Maria did or there's no telling what would've happened to us.

"Hey Babe! Let's take a quick walk on the beach before we meet your family at Cuz's." Kylan grabs my hand and kisses the top of it. My stomach fills with butterflies.

We're meeting up with Nanny, Chas, and my parents to have Sunday brunch. Since things with Maria have settled down some, they want to finally talk to us about what's been going on with them. I am so worried that someone is sick. Mom has been acting kind of strange here lately and dad is keeping his distance from everyone. Kylan and I have been so wrapped up with helping out Maria's family that we have barely even seen them.

It's such a beautiful, warm November day. It's hard to believe that just two weeks ago to the day everything happened with Maria. I shake my head as I look around the nearly deserted beach. There are tons of oyster shells washing up on the shore. In the distance I hear children laughing and splashing in the surf. I shiver thinking about how cold they must be right now even though the high for here today is supposed to be seventy-five degrees, the ocean water is still freezing cold.

Kylan plops down on the sand and pats his hand for me to join him. "I really wasn't wanting to get all sandy today before we go eat, but I guess a little sand never hurt anyone." I ease down and try my best to stay clean, but it's really no use. Mississippi sand sticks to everything! In my opinion, if you don't like the sand, then stay away from the beach.

"Do you remember the first time we came out here?" Kylan looks at me and asks.

I have to rack my brain since we've been out here so many times together. "Um, I think I do. Why?"

"No reason in particular. I just remember that day was when I knew I loved you even though we'd just met a few hours earlier. Neither one of us had a single care in the world that day." Kylan leans over and kisses me on the cheek. I can feel my face starting to flush as he starts kissing around my ear to my neck.

I breathe in deeply as the crisp salty air nearly takes my breath away. "Oh, I don't remember what it was like back then. We had no idea that Ashley was gone or that Peyton would betray Maria like he did and everything in between." Then I look up to the sky. "Yuck! Go away you lonely ole osprey! You're bad luck!" I yell to the bird. "Every time I see you, something bad happens!"

Kylan snickers. "Oh Kimmy, leave that poor bird alone. What did it do to hurt you?"

"It did nothing! Not a single thing! It's not pretty, it doesn't do anything special, and obviously no other birds like it since it's always flying alone!" I rant.

Kylan smacks his forehead with the palm of his hand. "Geez, Babe! Stop being so dramatic!"

"Me? Dramatic? No way!" We start laughing until I'm nearly in tears. That's when we hear Nanny calling for us.

"You ready for this?" Kylan asks.

I shake my head. "No," I sternly reply. "Let's just get it over with."

You know the saying about there being an elephant in the room? Well, that's how our entire meal at Cuz's went. We all knew something was about to happen, but only my parents knew what it was. Chas would crack a joke and Mom would nervously laugh. Obviously, he had no idea what my parents were about to tell us and was trying to lighten the mood as usual. I think Nanny knew but showed no expression whatsoever.

Since my emotions have been in overdrive with Maria's accident, it really doesn't take much for me to cry. I felt that what my parents were about to tell us would send me over the edge to a very dark place, and I was worried. My palms were sweaty, and I was already feeling hot all over from my nerves.

When it was time, my mom stood up beside our table. She motioned for my dad to join her. The four of us sat with our eyes glued on them. Kylan put his arm around me to help calm my nerves, but it wasn't working. I put my hand on his leg to brace myself just in case I fainted.

Mom clears her throat and looks solemnly at us. "Jimmy and I have something we want to share. We wanted to tell you a couple of weeks ago, but you know, it just wasn't the right time. But we can't hold it in any longer for obvious reasons. Sooner or later, everyone will know." Mom looks down at the floor like she's about to cry. She grabs Dad around the waist and looks up at him. Then dad does something that I don't see very often. He leans down and kisses my mom on the lips. They're not a very affectionate couple and rarely do things like that in front of me. I'm not sure why, they just don't.

Then my dad speaks in nearly a whisper. "Well, y'all are never going to believe this," Dad says as he shakes his head.

That's when Mom's expression changed so drastically that it made cold chills run down my spine. A smile as big as Texas spread across her face and she opened her mouth to speak, "Well," then she pulled on the back of her shirt to make it tight around her stomach and I saw what she was about to tell us. "We're having a baby!"

The four of us just sit there looking at each other as both my parents are smiling with tears in their eyes. Is this real? Did I really just hear what my mom said? I know I have a slow processor, but I'm pretty sure my hearing is up to par.

Suddenly, cheers erupted from our table so loud that the bartender came running to the back where we were seated thinking we saw a mouse or something. When I realize that I'm not dreaming, I jump out of my seat and run over to her. "Mom! That's so exciting!" I squeal. "But how is this possible? I thought you couldn't have any more babies?"

Mom pulls me into her and kisses me on top of my head. "Sweet Pea, sometimes God works in mysterious ways."

I stand there and look at my mom and my dad and think about how fortunate I am to have such wonderful parents as them. Then I look back at Kylan who is still sitting all by himself at the table. "Come on, get in on this hug," I tell him.

We all gather around Mom and embrace her in the gentlest hug possible knowing that she is growing a tiny little human inside of her. She looks over at me and says, "I was so worried you would be mad at me. I know you enjoy being an only child and getting all the attention."

I giggle, "You have no idea how long I wished for this. I finally gave up a long time ago. Never in a million years would I have guessed that I'd be a teenager when I finally became a big sister."

Mom and Dad look at each other and laugh, "Neither did we!"

Acknowledgements

I must always thank my editor-in-chief first. My mother, Patsy, has graciously worked to clean up my mistakes and suggest changes to be made. Thankfully, there weren't as many in this book!

Thank you to my mother-in-law, Jane, for once again being part of the editing process. Your positive feedback always keeps me going!

I want to say a special thank you to my dear friend, Dena, for helping with editing. I truly appreciate your support!

Thank you to my husband, Ken, for all your love and guidance over the last year. You were patient enough to wait until this book was completely finished to read it. So many times, I had to bite my tongue to keep from ruining the ending for you. Here's to more crazy adventures together!